P9-BHY-803

AN UNCERTAIN MEMORY

AN UNCERTAIN MEMORY

Laura Basse

WILLIAM MORROW AND COMPANY, INC.

New York   *1982*

Library of Congress Cataloging in Publication Data

Basse, Laura.
  An uncertain memory.

  I. Title.
PS3552.A823U5   813'.54   81-16798
ISBN 0-688-00749-X   AACR2

Printed in the United States of America

First Edition

1 2 3 4 5 6 7 8 9 10

❧ Preface

I DID NOT KNOW how to mourn for Pete. Unsettled, needing to do something, I drove through the harassing blur
of New York traffic trying to find, beyond the gray factory
streets surrounding the Queensborough Bridge, the
old-fashioned set that had been my home, the neighborhood in which we had grown up, during the time when
everything was forever.

A ray of sun periscoped my middle-aged slack jaw,
inches beyond the windshield. Disembodied, my face
wavered, dissolved into the dark-haired little girl I had
been, peering out of a photograph, perplexed at the attention paid me, my socks drooping above high shoes,
the straight white cotton dress hanging unevenly about
my knees.

(For a second plucky Orphan Annie nestled against
me before turning back to Sandy and Daddy Warbucks
for inevitable rescue.)

Pete, in knickers, played ringaleevio and kicked the
can. I threw balls against the stoop, marked the sidewalk
for potsie, jumped rope, a double-Dutch expert.

On hot summer nights, we responded to the tinkling bell of the white Bungalow Bar truck, crowding around the back door where the refrigerated ice-cream pops were stacked in mists of rapid condensation.

I licked the chocolate covering to the vanilla ice cream beneath, until the pop was narrow enough to fit whole in my mouth, a cold richness savored and swallowed, ending as the taste of the stick emerged. And then—slowly—removing the stick—looking up first, wishing—finally looking down to see if the words Bungalow Bar were printed on the stick, to discover whether I was a winner.

Disappointed, I studied the blank stick. Pete, already restless, took it and broke it, uttering his sound of disgust.

He went home, and I went home, each knowing one did not win by chance. Reward was for those who proved they could do what they were told to do.

AN UNCERTAIN
MEMORY

✤ Before: 1

BECAUSE PETE WAS the only child, he and his parents were comfortable in the downstairs flat. But the upstairs flat Laura's family rented from Pete's was a little small for them. If she and her two brothers had been the same sex, it would have been all right. Her mother could have put them all in the same bedroom. As it was, she gave Laura the back bedroom and used daybeds in the front room for Georgie and Les.

The first thing Laura saw every morning was the pussy-willow tree in the backyard. She liked to see the little green sprouts appear in late winter, followed by yellowish haze in early spring. She wanted to ask Pete if he noticed the changes too, but for some reason she always felt embarrassed about asking. So she did not really know.

Her dresser, next to the window, had dust on it that sparkled in the sun of the morning. She studied the little dust balls' orbital movement under the dresser, until she surrendered her bed, in sudden, nervous need to go to the bathroom.

In the vacant kitchen, the yellow linoleum showed patchy areas of heavy wax where Laura had washed carelessly last Friday. Bread crumbs lay around the glass of spoons and forks in the center of the table. Laura moved through the kitchen into the bathroom, guilty for the spatters of dirt on the baseboards and the smelly, wet rag under the sink. Relieved, she moved into the small hallway outside the bathroom, which led, past Pete's side door, to the cellar.

She held her breath a moment, peering down into the grayish light. The furnace creaked, and Laura jumped back for a second. Then she went down the stairs, watching carefully for any sudden movement. In their part of the cellar her father's worktable was covered with metallic, dusty tools, immobile in the morning.

She went to the laundry bag next to the washtub, looking for a blouse suitable for school. She wanted to wear the strawberry-print blouse with the fluffy collar, but the sheer fabric let her bra show through. The knots she worked into the straps to make her breasts look higher made her worry. Someone might notice. She hated to choose the heavy white cotton blouse because the wrinkles had long since dried in, but there was nothing else.

"Laura. Are you down there?"

"Yes, Daddy."

"Put a shovel of coal in the stove and come up here. I need a shirt for work."

A heaviness encased Laura, slowing her movements as she found the little shovel for the coal. Her mother must have a headache again, and she would have to iron her father's shirt as well as her blouse. If she had to take care of Les, she would not be able to go to school on time. Laura looked at the dull red glow in the furnace and did not recognize its reflection in her stomach.

12

"Damn it, Laura. Can't you iron any better than that? Do the collar over for God's sake." Laura's father moved with solid steps, taking up all the room in the kitchen. The ironing board blocked his way to the stove; he kept bumping against the end of the board. When the shirt fell on the floor, Laura grabbed it up, frightened. There was dust on the end of it. She awkwardly rubbed it, streaking the button panel. Her father looked at her in disgust.

She kept moving the iron over the points of the collar, but each time the collar creased and turned. A small yellow tinge emerged, snakelike, wisping into the arc of the collar. She stopped and silently handed her father his shirt. He went into the bedroom without comment. She started to sprinkle her blouse, dispirited yet anxious to get out of the house.

Her mother walked very slowly into the kitchen, holding a wet rag around her forehead. She smiled faintly at Laura and sat down at the kitchen table, her elbows picking up the bread crumbs. Her mother's fine golden-brown hair glistened in the weak morning light.

"Who'll take care of Les, Ma? You don't feel well today?"

"I'll manage, Laura. Don't worry about it. As long as you got Dad's shirt done. That's the main thing. Did you put some coal in the stove?"

"Yeah."

"Did you check the damper?"

"I forgot. I'll do it before I leave."

"Do you want something to eat, Laura? Eat something."

"It's OK I'm not hungry. Do you want something, Ma? I'll make you some tea."

"That's a good idea, but don't throw out the tea ball like you did last time. Leave it. I'll take care of it."

She gave the tea to her mother who sat looking at it a long time. Laura sensed the effort to pick up the cup was too much for her, and she felt guilty she had not offered to stay home.

"Go get dressed, Laura," her mother said, wearily. "Don't stare at me."

Laura could hear Georgie yelling at Les not to pull up the shade in their front bedroom as she went to get dressed. George, eighteen and twice Les's age, was usually patient, but this morning Georgie sounded irritable with their little brother. That pleased Laura. Les always annoyed her.

Laura put on the heavy, masculine serge skirt her grandmother had cut for her, tucking in the blouse. Her abdomen swelled slightly beneath her skirt, noticeable because she was thin, without fleshiness. Standing on tiptoe to catch her image in the small mirror above the bureau, she thought she looked massive, so she removed the blouse from the skirt band and smoothed down the wrinkled edges with her hands.

She put a scarf under the collar, but it did not look right. Then she put the scarf over the collar, but it still did not look right. Finally, she crumpled the scarf into her drawer. She put on her plaid socks to add color to her costume and tied the plaid strings of her saddle shoes with a small feeling of triumph.

When she took the bobby pins out of her hair, the curls ended in tight, ugly wisps. She pressed the wisps down, watching with disgust as they popped up again. She touched her bottom lip tenderly. A scar had formed there one cold week when the skin had cracked and festered. It troubled her to display an ugliness so conspicuous. It did not really seem possible Pete thought she always looked nice. She felt he was the kindest boy in the world to say so, even when it couldn't be true.

14

Georgie and Les were eating cornflakes when she came out of her room. Mutt and Jeff. Small, wiry Les and tall, broad-shouldered Georgie, the smooth cheek and the shaved cheek crunching in unison. Laura touched her own cheek. At least she didn't have pimples.

Her mother was pouring coffee for her father, the headache rag and teabag waiting wetly on the sink. Her father looked at Laura suspiciously.

"Is she wearing a brassiere?" he asked her mother.

"Of course! What's the matter with you?"

Laura moved away from them in confused embarrassment, and getting her books, held them tightly against her chest. Then she put them down again on the covered washtub, remembering she was supposed to have a red pencil for math today. She slipped the pencil from her purse into her math book so she would be sure where it was when the time came.

"Oh, let me have the red pencil," Les said excitedly. "Laura, give me the red pencil. Laura, give me."

"No, I can't."

"Oh, for heaven's sake, Laura," her mother said. "Give him the pencil. He's only a baby."

"I need it for geometry. Honestly, Ma."

"I want it," Les yelled. "Ma, make her give it to me."

"Give him the pencil," Laura's father said.

Les laughed.

Laura handed him the pencil. Pete would loan her another. He would make the day at school all right.

"After I check the damper, can I go? Pete is waiting for me already, I'm sure."

"Well, don't come home late. Your mother will need you to go to the store," her father said. "Be a good girl."

Laura smiled at them. She was going to school after all.

Pete was recopying his history essay when she came out of the house. He had his papers spread out on the bottom step, held down by two chunks of granite he'd found somewhere. He held his notebook awkwardly in front of his knees, bending over to see what he had to copy, then standing up again to write the sentences.

Pete had never just waited for Laura. Even when he was a chubby eight year old he never just waited. He played with the leaves and sticks lying in the gutter, amassing all the bits and pieces of vegetation he could see, carefully removing papers and bottle caps until he had formed a dam that pleased him.

The dam blocked the sewer so that the first rainfall after that resulted in a stagnant, nasty pool of water right in front of the house. Laura's mother came downstairs, groaning slightly at the pressures of a bunion which caused her heavy black right shoe to bulge out the side. She told Pete to stay away from the sewer. He would get himself all dirty anyway if he kept doing that. She made Laura get the old broom with the stiff hairs jutting up every which way.

Laura had to sweep all the leaves and sticks away from the sewer and wrap them all up as quickly as possible in the old newspapers her mother gave her. Then Pete carried the soggy papers to the garbage can because the water made the package too heavy for Laura to handle alone.

Pete started waiting for Laura because of the big dog. He was a Great Dane who belonged to the Falcaros. Whenever he saw Laura, he whined and strained at his leash. Once he broke free and bounced up on her, licking her face with enormous tongue sweeps, lapping and drenching the ends of her braids. She screamed, dropping her school books, breaking her pencil box so the pencils and erasers and ruler rolled forever away into undiscovered corners of the Falcaros' front garden.

Pete ran up, yelled at the dog to get away, laughed at Laura for being such a baby, and went on to school. After

16

that Laura was afraid to walk alone so Laura's mother went downstairs and asked Mrs. Basse if Pete would mind just walking with Laura down the block until they were past the Falcaro house.

When they first walked together, Laura clutched the sleeve of Pete's plaid lumber jacket until they had passed the place of terror. Once Pete took Laura's hand in his. She liked the feel of it. She could hold him more tightly. He could not move as fast, because Pete always ran ahead once they were beyond the dog's yard. Laura could hear the immies jingling in his pocket when he started to run. She watched his books sway back and forth in his hand as he moved, laughing at him if one of the books slipped, even as she stooped to pick it up for him.

"Why do you suppose our hands move back and forth like that when we walk?" she asked him.

"Because we were fish once."

"We were?"

"Sure. First we were fish, and then we got on the dirt and lived like frogs or something, and then we stood up and were people."

"You don't think God made us?"

"Of course God made us."

"So how come he made us fish?"

"I guess it took him a while to get it all straight."

"I didn't know God could make a mistake."

"It wasn't a mistake. He was just figuring it all out. Sometimes that takes a while."

"Gosh, I wonder how long it took."

"Seven days, dummy." His blue eyes were briefly contemptuous.

"Yes." His eyes looked at her more softly. She was ashamed and did not realize it.

When they were in eighth grade, Pete stopped running on ahead, so they walked almost all the way to

17

school together. Their public school was beyond the elevated subway, two blocks over from the five-and-ten, from the big Loew's movie their parents went to almost every Friday night, and the bakery, with the dentist's office above.

Pete liked to stop under the el. He enjoyed hearing the roar of the incoming train. They would look up at the darkness the train created when it stopped at the station, waiting for the creaking sound the train made to increase slowly to louder, to very loud, to shriekingly loud, until the sound again roared as the train moved out of the station, permitting flashes of light to emerge between the cars of the train, darkness, light, roaring, until the train was gone, on toward New York City, its sound ebbing to rhythmic click, clacks, and then a very special silence after all the noise and movement.

The moving train sent down a shower of dust and black specks. Pete did not mind it, but Laura did. So usually they separated then. Laura walked on while Pete waited for one more train.

When they went to high school, they walked the other way, away from the train. Pete grew taller than Laura, his shoulders broadening. He dressed neatly, his brown tightly curled hair glistening slightly from the dab of Vaseline he used when he combed his hair. His eyes were a blue Laura found rare, unusual. His high cheekbones and tendency to squint sometimes obscured his eyes. Laura felt a faint sadness then.

His mouth was thin. When he was serious, his face was a series of geometric patterns, like the diagrams they were studying in math.

Laura carried her math book with her every day, together with texts of modern biology, *America: Its Glorious History,* English literature, a softcovered, smaller Regents review book, a cardboard black-and white-covered notebook—as required by Mrs. Garland, their deaf music teacher—a pencil box holding a rubber eraser, a protractor, pencils, and a ruler, all tightly strapped together, with a loose-leaf book forming the base of the educational pyramid. Laura held the heavy stack of books in the crook of her arm, cradling it against her chest as she walked.

Pete carried his books down, against his thigh, holding them with one white-knuckled hand. Pete's fountain pen was clipped to his shirt pocket. Laura kept hers in a soft cloth bag she held, together with Wrigley's Spearmint Gum, a Max Factor compact of dusty-rose beige powder she had never used, and a lipstick she put on in school.

There were wooden frame houses on either side of their narrow street. Alleys formed from the spaces between the houses. Each house had a front garden and a stoop. Snowballs grew behind the hedges. The hedges were budding green in the spring morning, but the snowballs yet remained stark and dry, unpromising.

Hilda lived two blocks from them, also in a two-family house. The trolley, which might have taken them to high school, ran in front of Hilda's house, but they never took it. No one ever suggested they should. Instead Hilda walked with Pete and Laura.

Cutting across the tracks to an adjacent street, they could walk behind a spice factory to the movie, smaller than the Loew's, near the school. This was the movie they could go to. They took time to look at the pictures of the current movie. They paid most attention, however, to the pictures of the coming attractions. That movie was always more exciting, with a more satisfying star, a more interesting story. Next week, *Dark Victory* was coming.

The girls in particular could hardly wait. They loved the Juliet cap Bette Davis wore in the ads for the picture.

They had even tried to find one at the dry-goods store but Mr. Levinson said he did not know what they were talking about. Laura thought the cap would have looked just right on Hilda.

Hilda was very pretty. Her clothes were neatly pressed, her feet small. Occasionally, the lace of her slip would show, and the lace was always delicate and unfrayed. There was a daintiness about Hilda that Laura enjoyed, a gracefulness to the way her fingers moved as she gestured.

Laura was accustomed to people complimenting Hilda on the way she looked. Sometimes, a person would add, "And you look nice too, Laura." When that occurred, something would jump in Laura's throat and clog it. Once she wanted to slap the person who told her she looked nice too. The mood passed because Pete said Laura always looked nice. He thought it was her hair. He thought her hair was so pretty she wouldn't ever have to wear a hat.

"It's too heavy and too straight," Laura said, pushing her fingers into her hair in an attempt to make it wavier.

"The color is nice," Pete said, inspecting her head closely. "It's almost black but it's got lights hidden in it."

"If they're hidden, how can you see them?"

"Because I have X-ray eyes. I can see right through the color to the lights and from there right through the bone to all the busy brain cells and nerves, connecting and sending out impulses all over you, all the time."

"Impulses?"

"Yes, ma'am. Like let's not go to school at all today. Let's go eat a hot dog and have a soda and go to a movie in the city."

"Pete!"

"Don't worry. I'll pay."

"With Regents coming up? How could we do something like that! And if my mother and father found out, they'd kill me. I'd never do anything like that."

"Laura, you're a nice girl, but you're such a drip."

Laura worried about that comment. Even now, walking with Pete and Hilda, she brooded about being a drip. She could not figure out a way to stop being one.

"Look," Hilda pointed, "Bobby's ahead of us. You know if Bobby's ahead of us, we *must* be late!"

They laughed, running to catch up with Bobby who never got to school before the first bell. Bobby was fat. His rear end jiggled against his Glen plaid slacks; his pen in his back pocket popped up and down as he walked. It made Laura uncomfortable to see it. She was relieved to move on ahead of him with Hilda, while Pete lingered behind to walk with Bobby.

"My grandmother had a terrible fight with my Uncle Joey," Hilda whispered as they continued on their way. "It seems he is going out with a Catholic girl and Grandma is ready to kill him. Then my mother started in on Joey, and my father started in on my mother, and before you knew it the whole family was screaming at each other. I thought Mr. Jacks would come up and throw us all out," Hilda giggled. "It was ridiculous. Then Joey said my father shouldn't upset my mother like that, and my father said, '*I* upset her!' and began fighting with Joey. So Grandma was mad because my father was fighting with Joey and she left in a huff."

"Who's Joey seeing anyway?"

Hilda was quiet for a moment. "Well, Rosie."

The girls walked on silently. Laura absently picked a long green bud from one of the hedges and rolled it luxuriously between her fingers, feeling the moistness of the node. Rosie was not a nice girl. She had a little boy and no one knew how she had him because he had no father. Hilda's mother was going to have a baby in June and Laura's mother did not think that was too good, not with Hilda already fifteen and her sister in fourth grade. So there was nothing for the girls to say because they did not know how to talk about these things.

As usual, though, Hilda brought up another subject. Her mother was planning to buy new linoleum that Hilda just simply hated. Hilda described the stripes and circles of the pattern all the way to school. It sounded awful, Laura agreed.

There was not much sidewalk space in front of their domed yellow-brown-brick high school, causing students to crowd onto the long, broad steps leading to the auditorium-like doors entering the school. Darcy threaded her way through the crowd. Darcy had a slight limp. Her pink and taupe plaid jacket and matching skirt coordinated with her blouse and bow; the cut of her jacket obscured her jutting, dislocated hipbone. She murmured hello to the girls, starting to move immediately into school, as she usually did. Darcy, although in all their classes, did not like to talk very much.

Pete stopped her. He smiled over at Laura, singling her out with his smile while he spoke to Darcy. He moved nearer to Laura, bending forward with a controlled eagerness that made her feel wary and odd. Automatically moving a step back, she bent her head and listened to him kid Darcy about the bow bouncing as she walked "like Hilda's curls." Hilda laughed good-naturedly, and told him the curl on his forehead wasn't much better. Laura looked up quickly at the curl being roughly smothered by Pete in that moment.

The gesture momentarily broke Pete's poise. He moved his shoulder slightly, touched his tie, and putting one hand in his pocket, reconstructed a nonchalant stance.

He somehow drew them around him—Laura, Hilda,

Darcy, and Bobby—so they formed a group. The other kids moved respectfully about them, not breaking into their public privacy. Laura liked to be part of Pete's group. They were all going to be inducted into Arista, the honor society, at the end of the third term. Even Bobby. Laura was as surprised Bobby was part of the smart kids as she would not be surprised if Pete was elected president of Arista. When he led the debating society to a five-hundred-dollar award for the school and an article in the Elmhurst *Clarion*, everyone knew he'd be elected.

Darcy had a straight-A average. She never got below a 92 on any Regents. She helped Laura all she could when they studied for the algebra Regents, but still Laura only made an 83. Hilda told Laura not to worry about it. It had been a tough exam. She'd only been able to make a 91, even though algebra was her best subject. But Laura still felt ashamed and somewhat grateful to Pete for treating her as part of the smart kids' group.

On this clear May morning, Laura hated to break it up, but she worried, "We shouldn't be late for Stedman's class."

"We know," Hilda and Pete chorused.

"Oh, why do we have to have her the very first thing in the morning!" Darcy groaned.

Darcy hated Stedman.

Early in the term, she had thrown a note to Laura during Miss Stedman's class. Miss Stedman told Darcy she had seen that and to pick up the note and read it to the class immediately. "No," Darcy quavered. Laura had been thunderstruck. Darcy had talked back!

Laura had wanted to pick up the note and tell Miss Stedman that maybe it was personal, but she did not have the nerve. She never could have lived through having to tell her mother and father she had butted in.

Darcy was sent to the principal's office. It seemed to take her a long time to limp across the room to the door. It made Laura feel bad. "Now, we've lost enough time with that nonsense," Miss Stedman announced. "Robert, state the prepositional phrase in the third sentence." Of course, Bobby did not know it, and the class laughed, the tension broken by this more routine nonresponse.

"Couldn't you just die?" Hilda asked Laura as soon as the period was over. "Why didn't Darcy just read the note? I don't think it was such a good idea to get sent down like that. Now she'll be in trouble all year. Everyone will know she's a troublemaker, and it will really be hard on her."

"Maybe it was personal."

"Well, a classroom isn't a place for personal notes, is it? So she has to be wrong, any way you look at it."

Hilda was right—Darcy had to be wrong.

A bathroom was a place to be personal, maybe a bedroom: closed off, personal . . . private . . . like Laura's parents' room. It was exactly like hers, but Laura felt some tension in their room, something crowded and dark.

There was a chiffarobe in one corner, always with a thick layer of dust on it. Only when the sun streamed through the window did the dust motes shine transparent. Her mother and father had a large bed, but when Laura's mother had a headache, she did not lie on it. She lay instead in the front room, with the wet towel over her eyes, her hands clutching her mouth.

When Laura got home, her mother was there, in the front room.

"How was school?" her mother asked her, without opening her eyes.

"Just fine, Ma. Pete gave me another red pencil."

"That's good. Listen, Laura, go over to Mr. Cohen

and buy a pound of chopped meat. Tell him to give you a bone for stewing and put it in the book."

"Do I have to, Ma? Can't Georgie go? I hate to tell him to put it in the book. I—"

"Don't be foolish. Do as I tell you. Who knows when Georgie will be back? He's so busy with his friends, butting into everyone's business, he doesn't have time for his own family. Go. Be a good girl. Don't make me more trouble. And it wouldn't hurt if you took Les for a little walk with you either."

Her mother sat up, holding her head with her hands, the wet towel falling crazily. She looked at Laura, her face soft and naked without her glasses.

"I'd go myself," she sighed, "but I can't. You'll just have to go. Be a good girl."

Laura went.

Pete decided their graduation party would be a costume party. Pete's mother and father liked Pete to give parties. They bought bottles of soda and put them in the washtub with great chunks of ice. They put out dishes of popcorn and peanuts. They even thought to put out a dish for the peanut shells. Pete's mother and father owned a delicatessen. Laura believed when you were rich like that, you knew to put out extra dishes.

Pete took care of the Victrola himself. He had all the Tommy Dorsey records and could identify the song being played before anyone else.

Bobby was definitely Hilda's favorite lindy partner. His increased height made him look stocky instead of fat as he had before graduation. Laura could understand why Hilda liked him, but as far as she was concerned, no one could hold a candle to Pete. His tall fluidity increasingly fascinated her.

Hilda chose to go to the party as a can-can dancer.

25

She bought six ruffled skirts; stiff and scratchy, they cut her hand as she sewed them into a fluff of color.

She helped Laura become an adagio dancer. Laura could wear Georgie's old sweatshirt and Hilda's old black, straight skirt. They cut a slit along the side.

They went to the five-and-ten and studied all the boxes of mascara, until they decided on Max Factor because that's what the stars used. The mascara burned Laura's eyes and ran each time she tried to outline her lashes. Eventually, her eyes were blotchy and black. She thought it made her look quite dramatic.

Bobby met them at Hilda's house where the girls had dressed together. He enthusiastically told Hilda she looked swell. He had a green eyeshade on and carried a large baton. "It will be a pleasure directing you," he told Hilda, putting his arm around her waist and pulling her closer.

They walked back silently. The two-family house in which Pete and Laura lived appeared flat against the deepening gray sky. The unseasonable January breeze was humid. A wetness encased them, condensing into separate beads on their mouths, their foreheads. Perspiration made the back of Hilda's clinging blouse darker, the strained threads around her waist taut and cutting.

The windows in Laura's upstairs living room were dark, although Laura knew her father and mother were home, listening to the radio in the darkness.

The windows in Pete's downstairs living room were bright, illuminating Les's figure sitting on the stoop. He watched them come toward the house, suddenly darting away as they drew near.

They could hear music before they went in. It seemed as though all the kids who had been in their senior class were at the party. Darcy stood at the window, drinking ginger ale, looking away from the rest of them. She had not worn a costume, and for a moment Laura felt foolish in hers.

Darcy had long blond hair, which Hilda and Laura had long since decided made Darcy beautiful from the waist up. They could not decide if she never smiled because of her limp or because her mother never smiled either. Hilda felt it ran in the family. They did not know Darcy's father too well. He was a traveling salesman, not around much.

Pete's parents were not home. They could go anywhere, anytime, because they owned a car. Pete's mother was a lady. She wore high heels every time she went out. She even wore white gloves when she came to their classes during open-school week. When she was home, she wore an apron over her dress rather than the housedress Laura's mother routinely had on.

Laura's mother liked flowered prints. Her regular housedress had brown and green daisies over it. Laura used to look for daisies in those colors. Now that she was grown up, though, she knew she could never find them.

Once Laura's mother said Pete's parents could afford to do anything they wanted. Their delicatessen was a gold mine. She hated to give them the rent for their upstairs flat sometimes, because Pete's parents couldn't need the money as much as Laura's. "But what can you do?" her mother sighed, "That's the way it always is."

Georgie said the Basses were definitely the bourgeoisie. Laura could tell from the tone of his voice that was not a good thing to be. It made her want to defend Pete, to protect him from being something not acceptable.

There was no need to protect him at the party, however. Pete was having a great time. He took out a Camel and lit up, smoking as though he did it every day. He asked Bobby if he wanted some rye and ginger. Pete drank a glass of it, sitting on the couch, humming along with the radio blaring out about love at last. Laura sat on the floor, relaxed against Pete's knees. She followed the amber spray of fine bubbles in Darcy's glass. She had the impression the effervescence did not disappear into Darcy's throat but arose infinitely, surrounding Darcy in a thin, eggshell-light veil. Laura moved, impelled by an unrecognizable need to reach out to Darcy, to separate the veil which separated Darcy from the rest of them.

Pete touched Laura's shoulder, drawing her back against his knees.

"OK everyone," Bobby announced. "It's charade time. Up and at 'em!"

"Not again . . ."

"What else you wanna' play—post office?"

"Yeah! Yeah!"

"Well, you're going to get hard ones all right."

Pete laughed out loud. Laura did not know why.

She had to act out the United States Marines in Honor of the Four Who Enlisted. Darcy got to act out New York University where Pete was going for six months until he was old enough to enlist. Hilda was delighted to do Brenda Cobina. Everyone applauded when Bobby said she also belonged with the young debs.

Pete gave Laura a warm, oily drink. It tasted like medicine but she did not want to be a wet blanket, or worse, a drip again, which she would be if she told Pete she did not like it. In a while, everyone seemed to be drinking. The living-room rug was rolled back with loud shouts of *heave ho!* Bobby and Hilda danced to the Dorsey records he put on, without turning off the radio.

Laura sat against Pete's legs, listening to the sounds in the room.

She smiled as she saw Darcy sitting with a group, talking animatedly. Hilda swirled, a red streak. Someone laughed, spilled her drink, and started to cry. Bobby walked over to her, shaking her shoulder. His mouth moved noiselessly.

A passing fire engine subsided into a fading scream. The Victrola sounds elongated, grew dense, ceilinged the party with sound. Pete's wet mouth suddenly was on Laura's. Saliva dribbled, tasting like alcohol against her clenched teeth. His hand rasped against her neck.

Pete spoke to the group at large. Laura could not hear him. The noise began pushing her out, away. She went into the bathroom where it was quiet. The black and white squares of the tile floor jumped at her. She squinted toward them. So many squares: 1, 2, 3, 4, 20, 67. She slid against the toilet: 90, 91, 96. She closed her eyes and smiled; her stomach lurched; shocked, she quickly opened her eyes, still counting the tiles. She touched the cool of 105, 106 and fell asleep.

A shadow woke her. Pete was standing above her, a colossus. He looked at her, unsmiling, steadily. She had never seen him so deadly serious. She closed her eyes again. Her mouth was filled with fermenting yeast. She moved her tongue over her lips, trying to remove the rancidity.

Pete sat down and pulled her against him. He put his face in her hair; he moved his hand slowly down to her breast. Laura tightened, pushing herself closer to him in an effort to block his hand. She pressed her mouth closed, afraid of her smell. He positioned her, flat against the tile, cradling her head, and lay down on her. She could not breathe through her nose and was afraid to breathe through her offending mouth. She suffocated.

He rubbed against her slowly, moving his hips, looking at her in that new, deadly serious way. She looked beyond him at the light, feeling her panties, skirt, bunching, crumpling, luxuriantly substantial under his swollen pants, pressing, rubbing her. She tentatively lifted toward him, closing her eyes against the light, to retreat into the undistracting darkness where she enjoyed the feelings beginning to radiate through her.

Pete moved his hand from under her head and stroked her neck, her breast, pinching suddenly, then pushing at her breast; inward, inward through her clothes, twisting his feet around her ankles, breathing hard on her face, in her hair, struggling with her, frenetically, propelling them toward higher, hotter sensations, faster, better, covered by darkness, deep velvet flashes, pulsating unfamiliarity.

She opened her eyes. Pete, flushed, gasping a little, smiled broadly at her. The deadly seriousness was gone. He rolled over on his side and cuddled her against him. She pressed against his chest. Pulling her crumpled skirt back down to her knees, she relaxed and dozed.

Hilda woke her up, giggling at her. "Hey, it's time to go home. Pete's folks will be back any minute." Laura wondered why Hilda was in her room, talking about Pete.

She remembered where she was. She got up, pushing her hair back, not looking at Hilda. Her throat started to convulse, forcing her down again. She fought the feeling, holding herself rigid. She looked down at the tiles and experienced a sudden, buoyant ease as her throat settled in its normal place. Pete was not in the bathroom anymore.

Later, in her bed, Laura lay curled on her side, in as small a space as possible. She looked at the top of the pussy-willow tree that grew outside her window. Its roots started so deep in the earth she could not conceive its depth, but its trunk grew straight up, past Pete's window below, to her own. She fell asleep looking at the tree they could both see, without acknowledging they saw different aspects of it.

✽ *After: 1*

I ALWAYS BELIEVED, when I was a kid, the first thing I saw when I awakened was the pussy-willow tree outside my window. The memory of the greening buds, of the halo of soft yellow fuzz, is vivid. I found the image exotic and inexplicably strengthening. But after Pete, I doubt the memory.

Still, I have a fondness for the early-blooming sprigs and I look for them in May. I used to cut some and put them in a vase on the kitchen table, but I do not do that anymore.

It's too bad, really. They looked so pretty then. Pete would come home from work. The table would be all set. The kitchen floor was a deep blue and Pete's eyes were a bright blue and, at least in my memory, the shine of both was intensely, deeply satisfying. That is probably not the way it was. It is a faulty memory, I am sure; but I have trouble correcting all the memories because there were so many and I never had any reason to suspect that what I was living was not really happening.

We did sit down at the table in the kitchen with the

blue floor. I know we did that. We always ate together. Sometimes, just Pete and I would sit alone, drinking coffee and eating hard seeded rolls with butter. Pete liked to put a heavy slab of butter on his roll but he never spread it out. Just ate the clots smashed in between the roll. I was more orderly, I guess. I spread my butter thin, neatly over the whole of the inside.

Most of the time we ate with the kids. It was nice. I think it was nice. I can remember them mostly, now, in their school years. Manny is about ten. His polo shirt always has some stains on it. He never seems to stay in one place too long. Sol doesn't either because he loves to follow his older brother around. Sol's hair is lighter than Manny's, with Pete's tight-curled look. Larry, the youngest, is more independent. Sometimes he follows them around; sometimes he sits by himself, coloring in pictures Pete draws for him. He is probably allergic to all the crayons he handles because two vivid red spots appear on his fat cheeks. Maybe I should have stopped him. I did not, though. He enjoyed grubbing away with all those thick crayons of his.

However, they were all basically healthy, so commotion at dinner was probably to be expected with three growing boys. Larry inevitably spilled his milk. There would be a lot of sopping napkins for a while. Manny enjoyed his clarinet lessons then. He liked to detail how Mr. Grayson thought Manny did hear the music. Sol thought he should win the spelling bee, and he practiced by spelling out everything Manny said. Pete said that would drive him crazy unless Sol stopped immediately. I thought Pete was kidding. Perhaps it should have occurred to me he was serious, but our dinners together seemed so natural I could not conceive how anyone would not feel the same.

When Larry grew up, he said the trouble was Pete

kept missing it. I am not sure what he meant by *it*, but I think he meant the feeling of a family. And in a sense Sol gave Pete what he wanted, too. He does not speak to him anymore. Not ever. Not even a courtesy Father's Day card. Manny sends Pete a card, but he does not play the clarinet any longer. I do not know if that has anything to do with what happened to us though.

I might have told the kids about it immediately, I suppose. They were not really kids then anyway. Larry and Sol were in their teens, and Manny was already away at college. But I did not tell them what happened to Pete and me for a long time.

At first, everyone assumed it was a middle-age crisis, and I let them think that. Pete is so handsome, it would make sense he would want to try other beds. He was always so physical anyway. Every Sunday morning he would put on his white shorts and T-shirt and go out to play tennis. He would come back all red-faced and sweating, but beaming. He was a terrific net player.

I would still be in my old housecoat, just finishing the crossword puzzle. I loved the silence of a Sunday morning; lazy, I would never have dressed. But usually, after Pete got back, I did. Then we would take the kids to a museum. Pete would drive, and if he did not want to join us in an initials game, I always thought it was because he was driving. Sometimes, though, he would play with us, and those were the best games.

Pete did not like us to eat out, so on the way back, I would start planning supper. I guess that was the end of Sunday for me. Then Monday morning they would all go away, while I would read the book-review section before making the beds.

I did that for so many years—read the book-review section on Monday morning and then got our house in order. And always had the table set when Pete came

34

home. I looked forward to, I waited for, Pete to come home. Sometimes, if I had nothing to do for an hour or so before he came home, I would sit on the steps waiting for him. It always seemed, though, he was late, and it became too cool, or a bee bothered me, or Larry could not find a pen, and I would go inside. So Pete never knew how much time I spent waiting on the steps.

I wish now I had some measurement of that time. Some neat way to file it in an orderly manner the way you should do recipes, all immediately accessible when necessary. But my recipes are scattered throughout old cookbooks—yellowing pages ripped from newspapers, little cards in unknown handwriting given to me somewhere, somehow, by someone. Some cards have spots of grease on them or old jelly smears. One is torn so I have no way of knowing anymore how long the pie should bake.

My time with Pete is like that—memories of nights out lying scattered, ripped, smeared in the recesses of memory—until the frigid night we went to the theater, as we had done so often before. That cold night terminated my carelessness about time. Before that is the streak of our twenty-five years; after that, seconds are definitive, groupings congealing in dead, stale air.

Pete said he was thinking about how it would be if we went our separate ways.

I thought about it for a while and I said, "I can't see any particular reason for that." I felt frightened when I finally managed to ask, "Can you?"

"No, not really," he said. "We just seem to have such separate lives, I thought it only logical."

He did not look at me as he spoke. He sat forward in the car, with unnatural concentration, as though the road were dimming and difficult to follow. I stared at his profile. The rapid movement of shadows and clarity from the sporadic lights of the highway made it difficult to see him clearly.

I said to my memory of him rather than my immediate view of him, "What's separate about our lives? We've known each other since we were kids. I know your mother and your father. And your friends and—"

"OK, OK." He was irritable, his face very dim now in shadows.

"We have the same children," I persisted. "We went to the same high school. I know where you work. I know what you like to eat and don't like to eat. . . ."

"Forget it," he said.

Even now, I cannot believe it; but I did.

Pete began to lose weight. His face was drawn; his eyes seemed to glitter rather than shine. I bought some multivitamins for him. He threw them out. I made an appointment with the doctor for him. He canceled it.

"I'm not your child, damn it!"

"I never thought you were, but you sure as hell are acting like one."

"I can't sleep with the light on, that's all. Do you have to read so long every night?"

"I'll wake you up to remind you you can't sleep with the light on."

Nonetheless, thereafter I read downstairs. When I went to bed, I crept around in the dark, not wanting to disturb him, listening to the insistent rhythm of his night groans.

One day, I found skimpy panties in our hamper. I held up the flimsy immodest bit of flowered cloth.

"Now who left that here?" I asked Pete. "I don't remember any woman up here in our bathroom, do you?"

"Don't be ridiculous," he said. "It's mine."

I involuntarily giggled. "Yours! These are shorts?"

"They're the new style. Don't be such a stick-in-the-mud."

I did not want to be a stick-in-the-mud, so I did not say anything more until Pete bought a pair of red and yellow striped slacks. I found I was slightly embarrassed. I did not want to go out with him when he wore them.

"Why not?" he demanded, not unreasonably I thought.

"I don't know. They just seem so—" I could not find the right word. "—inappropriate," I decided. "I mean, graying hair, flared pants."

Pete's hair was gray by then. He was only about forty, but his hair had changed. All the tight curls had pressed out into straight, white strands. His reduced weight accentuated the lines carved around his high cheekbones, around his eyes. Only the color of his eyes remained unchanged, that special blue I had always found so pleasurable.

He did not have a middle-aged paunch or roll of fat around his waist, but his appearance was no longer youthful. He was distinguished looking and still very handsome, but not young.

I was not, either, of course. My waist had thickened over the years, and there was a crepey look to my thighs that still surprised me. I hated the lines that went so definitely from the side of my nose to my mouth, but I did not cake them in with makeup the way some women did, and I never even tried on a bikini. So I could not understand why Pete should put on slacks with colors so loud I doubted our teenage sons would wear them—slacks that, in any case, were meant for kids, not adults.

Pete flung off the sock he was changing, throwing it with vicious anger against the bureau.

"Where is that written? Goddamn it, you've got all kinds of rules in your head. You may wear this. You may not wear that. It stinks. I'll wear whatever I damn please. I'll decide—not you—and not anyone else."

"You're right. OK? I just don't understand why you want to wear them. They're loud. I mean, Pete, they're vulgar. Can't you not wear them just because I don't like them?"

"No."

"No? My feelings are not a good enough reason for you?"

"No."

"What is a good enough reason?"

We looked at each other in a suddenly very serious silence. His gaze was steady; his slight forward movement of eagerness solidified in a steel line cutting diagonally toward me with a faintly threatening suggestion. I stepped back.

"Someday, I'll tell you," he said, averting his eyes.

"Tell me now."

"There's nothing to tell you. I don't know why I said that."

"Yes, you do. Tell me."

He started to cry.

One second, he was angry—tight-lipped with contained fury at me—the next, crumpled, strange—unknown. He sat down abruptly on the bed and covered his face. He made gasping, hawking noises. His chest and back heaved as his cries became convulsive sobs, loud, agonizing.

Then he bolted. I heard all the sounds of his departure—precisely locating him running down the stairs, opening the kitchen door, slamming it closed, grinding the ignition, backing out too noisily, awkwardly

38

grating the car against the driveway wall. I heard the right turn to the end of the street and the left turn that took him beyond my hearing.

I heard him and I saw him, but he was not in the bedroom with me. I was standing immobile in front of our bed, looking at the empty windows and then at the empty door—just standing there, not moving anything but my eyes, because if I dared to move from the spot I was on, the walls would fall down and smash our bed. The stairs would crumple. My children would lie broken under the debris of their own books and records and clothing.

The silence was enormous. My breathing hissed in it. I inhaled hoarse, ugly gulps of empty, silent air; I exhaled snores, grotesque in the silence.

I stood in the silence, marring it with my loathsome noises. For all I know, I am still, really, standing there; but the outside part of me went downstairs to make some coffee because it was morning, and in the morning I make coffee.

I think Sol had some trouble finding a turtleneck sweater he wanted, and I think I helped him find it, but I am not sure because he was a silhouette on a reversed negative. He had no substance. Only the coffee cup was three-dimensional and the part of me standing upstairs in the empty bedroom.

I said into nothingness, "You do not know what his teeth look like. You lived with him all these years and you cannot describe his teeth."

I could not. I could only feel Pete. His back and chest were expanses against which I had leaned—comfortable, supported. I could put my arms around Pete's waist and lean my head on his chest, and Pete's head could lean down to the top of mine, and we could merge.

Our dimensions were perfectly counterbalanced, forming a symmetry of rightness—all space in the world
properly filled.

Pete had heavy, yellow callouses on the soles of his
feet. His hands were large and his fingers big squares of
jutting flesh. His voice was musical, a tenor-bass; when
he laughed, his eyes crinkled.

I loved all of him. All I could describe and all I could
feel.

But he had cried and had gone away, and I did not
know why he had done either.

✎ *Before: 2*

LAURA VERY BADLY WANTED to know if what she and Pete did could make her pregnant, but she could not find a way to find out. When they had gone to high school, Darcy told her if a boy ever put a finger through the circle of his thumb and finger, she should walk away quickly. Once Laura asked her mother what *rape* meant, and her mother said, "Well . . ." Laura looked up the word in a dictionary and found it meant forcible carnal knowledge. She did not know what carnal meant. In a book she read, a man felt the cold slab of someone's breast, and Laura felt the same odd, constricting, pulsation she felt with Pete. She knew it all connected with babies in some way. Because she had to be careful, she only thought about it when she was alone.

As she did of the time when she was about thirteen and her mother unexpectedly called her into the bathroom. Her mother's face was so tense Laura thought she was having another headache.

"Do you want a cold towel, Ma?"

"No. Listen to me a minute. Just listen. In a little

while, every month, you're going to bleed. I don't want you to worry about it. It's just the bad blood that has to come out. When it happens, you won't feel so good, but it will pass. You'll have to put this on." Her mother jerked her dress up so Laura could glimpse a sanitary napkin. Her mother just as quickly pulled her dress down and said, "All right? Understand?"

Amazed and embarrassed, Laura mumbled, "Sure."

"Oh, don't take a bath, of course, till all the blood is out."

Laura wanted to ask her mother how her body knew how to stop at bad blood and not permit good blood to start coming out. She wanted to know whether she should wear a sanitary napkin all the time, just in case the bad blood decided to come out.

She studied the graceful women of the Modess ads. In their beautiful gowns, they said *Because....* Because babies had to drink their mothers' blood until they grew their own? Why should babies have only bad blood? It did not seem fair.

Bursting with knowledge, Laura, hypocritically casual, asked Hilda, "Do you think Bette Davis acts when she has her period?"

"Of course not." Hilda was as scornful of Laura as her good nature would permit her to be. "You're all crampy then, and blue, and very weak. You can't act when you feel like that."

"Do we have to stay in bed?" Laura tried to remember when her mother remained in her room.

"No," her authority replied, "just take it real easy."

Maybe, Laura thought, that was when her mother said she had headaches. Too personal a thought, Laura relegated it to the times when she wondered, daydreamed, alone, in bed. She wanted then to sort out the confused image she retained of her mother's wrinkly leg flesh, of golden curls of pubic hair wisping beyond the white, white napkin. The intimacy of that knowledge saturated Laura's senses. Her father, Georgie, and Les would never know what Laura and her mother knew. It was their secret, an isolated rarity of special communication. She was sorry Pete, too, had to be excluded.

Laura's first period began in late spring. She stared at the drops of blood on her panties. It seemed like any other blood to her. She found her mother ironing in the basement and told her. Laura was astonished to see her mother smile at her. The next day, her father kissed her cheek and said, "So my little girl is a young lady." Laura could not understand why her mother had betrayed their secret to her father. She felt ashamed enough of her lack of femininity: she was neither crampy nor weak. She could not find any blouse, any skirt that looked even passable on her that day. She remained home, wearing her mother's old green housecoat, miserable with her inadequacy as a woman.

Laura became reluctant to tell her mother when she menstruated. Her mother always sighed, a sad murmer of despair, which further convinced Laura, despite her mother's initial smile and her father's still inexplicable gesture of affection, that a period should be a problem, something worrisome, trouble. When Darcy referred to it as the curse, Laura was certain that was exactly what it should be.

She was paradoxically relieved, then, to discover that in time her periods did become days of discomfort and anxiety. She experienced an agony of embarrassment when she went to buy a box of sanitary napkins. She hung around outside the drugstore until there were no customers before she entered. Sometimes, if there was only a male clerk, she raced out, feeling like a thwarted thief.

She found the napkin chafed her thighs and left little cotton clumps on her vaginal hair. She smelled. She had trouble discarding the soiled napkins without anyone seeing. Then, in a P.E. class, the teacher said a girl could take a bath when she had her period, although that might be stewing in her own juice. It was wiser to take a shower.

It took Laura another few months to disobey her mother's injunction against a bath. But when the chafing, and the cotton clumps, and the smell disappeared, and everything else seemed to be all right, Laura decided her mother was wrong.

She longed to write for the little booklet which promised to help mothers tell their daughters about this personal thing, but she could not find a way to do it without having her mother know. It seemed shameful to read about a period.

Although Laura realized she was dirty-minded, she again broached the subject with Hilda. Hilda felt it was OK to tell another girl when you had your period, so your friends could know you did not feel very strong, but as to why it happened—well, it was just part of being a woman, like growing breasts.

Laura, visualizing a crushed-up baby gulping in her blood someday, asked Hilda if she thought that's why babies made those little lip movements all the time. Hilda assured her that had to be it.

Laura remained anxious that her mother would know she was taking a shower while menstruating. She avoided letting her mother see her face. She had no doubt if her mother saw her face, she would know.

Now she was also afraid, if her mother saw her face, she would know Pete pressed and rubbed against her. She knew her mother would not like it. There was something wrong with it, and it had something to do with babies, just as the bad blood coming out every month did.

The house seemed unusually crowded that June of 1940, because her father stayed home more and more frequently. His arms hurt him. Laura's mother rubbed them with hot towels but it did not seem to help. At night he groaned, the bedsprings squeaking as he turned, trying to find a position where his arms would not bother him.

Then, about the time the bramble roses bloomed in wanton profusion, the house became unusually empty. Her father went to the hospital where he drank thick eggnogs and searched, without success, for a way to stop his arms from hurting.

Laura's mother went to visit him every day, carrying a large cloth bag, moving hurriedly, anxiously. Laura went to visit whenever her mother took Les to their aunt's. She tried to get there just before visiting hours were over.

The trip to the hospital was long. First, she took the el to Long Island Plaza. Then she walked down the long bridge steps to catch a ferry to the island. She saw the hospital from the ferry, growing larger as the ferry moved nearer to the docking slip.

Her father's hospital was gray and dome-like. The white gowns rustled as the patients moved, sick faces yellow against the pillows.

Laura sensed a starkness she could not define, a lack of color, of adornment, that frightened her. She glimpsed metallic waves through the windows, miniscule, moving restlessly with directionless energy. The hospital halls were cavernous, echoing her footsteps, heavy-sounding, flat, as though the rooms were emptied of anyone living.

If her father was asleep, Laura sat and watched him until he awoke, looking at the dark gray bristles on his cheeks, the tight V-line of his mouth, memorizing him without confronting the necessity. Only once did she permit cognizance of the situation.

She felt an electric shock of fear. If her father died, she would not have to be there. She would be freed to stay in the sun, away from the terrible gray shadows of the peopled emptiness of the hospital.

She never knew what to say to her father. He always said to her, "Don't come so late, Laura. I don't like to think you won't be home before it gets dark. You should be here earlier so you can get home while it's still light. It's not a good idea for you to be out when it's dark. You have to be careful. You're a big girl now."

"OK, Daddy. Don't worry about it. I'll be OK. How do you feel today?"

"Ah, who knows? They gave me another treatment this afternoon so I guess it won't be long now. One of the treatments will work, I'm sure."

Their conversation petered out. They were not accustomed to talking to each other. Mostly, Laura had done what her father had told her to. Actions had been the required response, not words. The trouble was there was not enough for her to do during her visits. If she straightened out his night table, he told her to leave it alone. It annoyed him to have her move his drinking glass with the bendable straw, or to align his pipe and ashtray with the comb.

It was alien for them to touch after the hello kiss. So Laura sat, too stiffly, on the chair, wishing the moments away and wondering why she could not know exactly what he was feeling and thinking, and why she was she and no one else, and what her back looked like to him as she walked away.

She looked forward to leaving the hospital, to walking rapidly from the station, to seeing Pete. Pete was

46

working for his father during the summer, so Laura usually went directly to the delicatessen. When she saw Pete, she forgot the hospital.

Sometimes the spicy, garlic-pickle smell nauseated her. She drank a glass of Dr. Pepper slowly, trying to ease her nausea. Sometimes the spicy, garlic-pickle smell made her ravenous. Then she ate a frankfurter with hot sauerkraut, savoring the mustardy zest, tang of salt, meat, and soft bun.

Pete never charged her. She waited while he washed the glasses, forcing them against a whirling brush in hot, sudsy water until they shone. He lined them upside down to dry on a stainless steel counter, his movements quick, efficient. He spoke quietly to his father before removing the long white apron he wore.

Then he and Laura strolled home through the soft night. Pete's arm on her shoulder was warm in the heat. Moths fluttered endlessly around the streetlights. People sat on their stoops watching the summer night.

Laura and Pete did not talk very much that summer. They walked, and they kissed in a shadowy alley before they reached the house—soft kisses, like the night; easy, like summer.

When Laura's father died, Laura's mother screamed and cried. Laura had never heard her mother make so much noise. She did not recognize her mother's contorted face nor her odd sounds. She held her mother's hand tightly during the funeral. She saw Georgie's shoulders heaving, and once he had to run out to vomit. Les kept looking for him until he came back.

Laura was aware that Pete, Hilda, Darcy, and Bobby were sitting near her. She could hear Hilda crying. It surprised her to realize Pete's father had left the store to come to the funeral.

Everything was artificial.

Especially her father's corpse with red spots worked onto his yellow, incredibly still cheeks. Laura thought of her father in browns—baggy brown suits and brown dirt under his nails. He put tips of brown pencils to his tongue before he moved his hands in preparation for jotting down numbers on a list—an odd, circling motion above the paper so that he seemed to write as a result of the downward force of acceleration. She watched him do that at night, after supper, when he blew hot soup on his spoon before swallowing.

He had been a salesman, carrying a heavy brown suitcase, filled with dark, metallic-brown saws and uniquely shaped nails. The figures had to match the saws and nails. Laura's father muttered as he worked on the list; he did not answer when her mother asked him if he wanted some tea. It seemed to be difficult to match the lists and the tools.

Laura wondered if the dead keep worrying about their unresolved problems. She wondered if her father knew they were all there, looking at his unnatural face. She cried in fear because he might not know.

After the funeral, her mother stopped making any noise. She sat. Her shoulders moved toward her chest. She kept her hands clasped loosely on her unmoving lap. She did not answer anyone who spoke to her, although she occasionally muttered to herself in some unarticulated mental conversation. Laura found her mother's withdrawn, uninterested eyes unbearable.

Georgie told Laura he and she would have to earn some money because the insurance would only last a few months. He took a job in a drugstore, moving heavy cartons and arranging little bottles, getting on the store's bike and delivering the bottles with yellow slips wound around the necks. Laura saw him sometimes, leaning vigorously over his bicycle, his old plaid lumber jacket

48

too tight around his broadening, tense shoulders. He periodically flicked dandruff from his shoulder, clenching the bike with one hand, never losing momentum.

She prepared supper carefully for him, bustling unnecessarily about the kitchen, trying unconsciously to break the still atmosphere, to roil the leaden quality of the house with the ping of dishes, the sound of water, the scraping of chairs against the table—always too few for the room, desolate in its sparseness. The chairs a constant, chronic reminder of their grief.

They mourned around the table, speaking to each other in monosyllables, in low voices. Their silent mother stood against the sink, watching them eat. Her blank face, Georgie's mechanical chewing, Les's constant, fidgety movements, thickened Laura's throat. She could not eat.

Les started to take his sandwich to the front room, where he listened to the radio as he pulled off bits of crust, eating his sandwich in fingered globules of dough. Georgie mumbled, "OK," to Laura when he finished eating and left immediately. As Laura cleared the table, her mother sat down, sometimes touching the porcelain top with one finger, a tentative gesture. Quiet, she sat, barely shaking her head in negative response when Laura asked her if she wanted to eat something. Laura put a cup of tea on the table for her mother. Her mother's almost golden hair dissolved over the steaming cup.

She startled them one night, speaking hoarsely from her spot by the sink. Les should not eat in the front room. Les laughed, leaving his sandwich on the table, not eating at all that night. Later, she told Georgie not to come home so late. He had to go to work in the morning and he needed his sleep. She told Laura to buy a chicken and some soup greens. It wasn't good for them to eat canned soup all the time.

Georgie smiled when he talked to Laura. He felt Ma

was OK now. If Laura could find a job, it would help a lot. He ruffled Les's hair as he passed him. Laura heard Georgie whistling when he shaved—a nice, noisy sound. Georgie kissed his mother when he went out. She looked up from her hands, but she did not smile back.

The next morning, Laura put on a pair of orangy silk stockings in preparation for an interview at the state employment agency to which Georgie had told her to go. She sat in the subway train, unreal, acting a role she had just been given without yet learning the lines.

She was hired by the executive office of a chain of stores to do inventory control. She checked off the merchandise sold in branches all over the country. The names of the cities on the slips were exciting to her—Dallas, St. Louis. She tried to imagine them, to imagine the person who lived there, who bought the sweater # 1682D on August 20, 1941. It kept her from looking at the clock and watching time crawl.

The working days were long, longer than any time she could remember, with a dullness she had never known before. The girls she ate with, the crisply dressed man who managed the office, remained strangers. The number five became magical, the fairy's wand that freed her to return to her own time, her time with Pete. Five o'clock, five working days, fifteen dollars for her mother's unresisting hands.

As the summer waned, she and Pete took longer walks. They followed the trolley tracks, past the spice factory that emitted exotic odors—odors that transformed China to Cathay, Marco Polo's horse to a steed, racing toward the horizon as Marco Polo's cape billowed against the sky, a pungent sensuous context.

They walked to the ledged wall around the public library, where they sat before turning back, their entwined fingers playing in and out of each other's hands.

Around the ledge English ivy grew, richly green in the August twilight, a glossy accent against the tanned stones of the library. Old trees hid the trolley tracks. Pete and Laura sat in a private garden.

"My mother scared the hell out of me," Pete said. "My father forgot to take his medicine, I guess, so he started to black out. My mother was yelling, 'My buddy! My buddy! What will I do without my buddy!' all over the place. Then when he took the insulin and drank some orange juice and felt better—all of a sudden she said to him maybe I could get an exemption from the army because he was sick. Christ, here I am counting the days until I can go and she wants to see if I can get an exemption."

He separated his hand from Laura's, bending down to untie and retie his shoelace. He pulled his socks up higher and ran his hand along the crease of his slacks. He tucked his shirt in, finally brushing his hand against his hair.

"What are you doing?" Laura asked. "Getting ready to stand at attention?"

Pete grinned, shamefaced. "I guess I was."

"You still have four months to go—"

"Four months," he sighed. "I don't know how I'll have the patience to wait it out. Maybe I just ought to lie about my age. By the time they find out, I'll be of age anyway. Maybe that's what I'll do."

"Do you think your mother would let you?"

"Not a chance." He put his arm around Laura, absently stroking the underside of her cheek. "I'll just have to make the best of it. There's no other way."

"Doesn't it help to know you'll get in a semester's work before you go?"

"I don't really care about it. It's not as though I'll probably ever use it."

"Pete!" Laura was horrified. "You're coming back. I mean you're not going away forever. There will be a coming-back time. Won't there?"

"For you, Laura. I'll come back for you. Yes."

Laura touched a finger to her tongue and traced Pete's eyebrows with the moist fingertip. "I read something funny, Pete. I read the thing that separates man and animal is the knowledge of death. The apple in the Garden of Eden isn't supposed to be that Eve found out about sex but that she found out about death. Do you think that's true?"

"I think sex is more important. It's better. God knows I like to think about sex, but I sure as hell don't even want to think about death." He took her finger in his mouth, licking it. Laura stood up, away from him.

"I keep seeing him there, Pete, in the coffin. Like a doll. I didn't know a dead person looked like a doll, did you?"

Pete moved next to her, holding her shoulders against a tree. She felt the hard bark against her back. "Try not to think about it," Pete said, "He was too sick. It must be terrible—terrible—to be so sick. Not to be able to move. Not to get out. To be trapped in one place." Pete closed his eyes, breathing in the darkness of no escape. Laura did not see.

"It's just that I can't seem to get that doll's face out of my mind—and I cry so much. I don't know I'm going to and I do. I can't understand it. And now my mother wants to move. She wants to live near her sister. Why should she do that?"

"It doesn't matter, baby. Wherever you are, I'll come for you. I won't ever let you be without me."

She hid her face against his chest. He smelled sweaty. He stroked her hair and held her. Laura felt wonderful.

✦ *After: 2*

THE FIRST THING PETE SAID to me when he came home was, "I'm sorry," and I said, "OK," and we left it there. Our neighbors came over that night. We played bridge and drank coffee and ate cake and worried about the increasing use of pot by our kids and whether it was fair for college students to be excluded from the draft for Vietnam and whether we should join the committee fighting the new tax assessment. It was a normal social evening, except I had this subdued feeling one gets when someone has just died—someone who is not in your immediate family so everyone does not stop and grieve. Everything goes on in its normal way, but underneath there's mourning, and it is hard to feel anything is real.

My body kept fragmenting, because part of me was still upstairs immobile, and part was crying for an unknown death, and part was talking. It made me very tired. I wanted so badly to go to bed and hold myself against Pete in the darkness—to be.

But when our friends left, Pete did not want to go to

sleep, so I went upstairs alone, skirting around the motionless image standing there. Just before I fell asleep, I heard Pete crying again; when I woke up, he was still downstairs.

I found him sitting in the living room, staring at the rug. The ashtray was overflowing with cigarette butts and wads of Kleenex. Next to his foot there were cups of coffee with congealed milk. I picked one up automatically. Then I put it down again because I could not think of what to do with it.

I sat down opposite him and looked at him looking at the rug.

I said, finally, "I guess we'll have to talk."

"There's nothing to talk about."

"Something has happened to you."

"Nothing has happened to me."

"Something is bothering you."

"Nothing is bothering me."

I started to laugh, and he looked at me, and at the ashtray and Kleenex, and he laughed too. Then he pulled his lip a little and sighed.

"I don't want to hurt you."

"It looks like you can't help it—one way or another."

"I know. I'm sorry. I'm so sorry." He seemed to think about the degree of his sorrow.

"So what are you sorry about?"

"You won't like it."

"Probably an understatement."

He smiled. His chin moved up, toward me. Maybe he saw me then. I am not sure.

"I don't want to be married anymore."

"Any particular reason?"

"No."

"There has to be a reason."

"There isn't. It has nothing to do with you. I love you,

and if I wanted to be married, I'd stay married to you. But—"

"But?"

"I just don't want to be a husband and father anymore."

"Do you have a girl friend?" I said, the sophisticate.

"No."

"Are you in trouble with gangsters?"

"No! Where'd you get such a crazy idea?"

"From the craziness I just heard from you."

"What's crazy about not wanting to play a role that makes no sense. Don't you understand what I'm telling you? I don't want to play that role anymore. I've had it—no more husband—no more father—just me. I just want to be me." He moved his hand horizontally through the air so I could see him there, levitating, being himself.

"But you are a husband and father," I said, too logically. "That is you."

His look of contempt stopped my heart.

"That's what *you* think. Not what *I* think."

He got up and walked out, and I was afraid another part of me would be left forever sitting in the chair, opposite the ashtray and the Kleenex and the coffee cups, unable ever to move. I knew I could not keep doing that, leaving myself all over the house that way. I knew I could not do that, but I did not know what to do.

There is a type of sadness you have to postpone, and to feel privately. You can only let it emerge in a hidden place and touch it cautiously.

"Please don't pick me up," Robert Kennedy said. He could handle his dying alone, unmoving, but movement would overwhelm him, and everything would be out of his control through eternity.

I acted that way all winter. I was afraid to do anything, to make any kind of move. But grief seems not to disappear. It hides and rushes out unexpectedly, to be experienced anew. Ignorance may be the truest powerlessness, but known powerlessness is the cruelest situation.

Once I had seen a fat lady trying to pick up all the debris of Grand Central Station. She squatted, laboring, disgusted with the litter she could never totally eliminate. I was terrified I would become like her, decayed, passed by by people sitting in brightly lit, fast trains, speeding noisily away so even if I screamed my panic, I could not be heard.

My nails were blunt and on slightly trembling hands, but nails grow even after death.

"Pete, I'm going crazy. We can't go on like this. Please, please tell me what's going on."

"I'll leave. Do you want me to leave?"

"No! Of course not!"

"Then I can't help you. You'll have to go crazy."

"Couldn't we go for counseling? There must be something you can tell me."

"It wouldn't help. It has nothing to do with you."

"Stop telling me that! It has everything to do with me. It's my life."

His face turned white. His mouth tightened, a gash, as he muttered, deliberately spacing his words, with acid diction:

"Your life. Always your life. I don't want to live your life. Just leave me out of it. Leave me to be alone—finally alone. Stop nagging me. Go find other things to do. I don't want to be your husband. I just want to be me."

"What does that mean? How did being my husband ever stop you from being yourself? I don't understand."

"That's always been your trouble. You always have to

56

know everything; you always have to try to understand. You don't leave anything alone; you don't leave me alone. I can't be myself. I told you over and over again."

He began shouting, his face lost in the scarlet of his burning rage: "I don't want to be a husband anymore. Can you hear me? I don't want to be a father anymore. Did you hear? Is it clear? Can you get it through your head once and for all so we never have to have this endless conversation again? Can you ever understand what I want? Can you finally stop and let me be free of this marital trap? Open it up—for God's sake, open it up!"

He hissed. His rigid redness poisoned our living room. Familiarity terminated.

"A clue," I whispered. I could not, would not, give him permission to leave without knowing why. In desperation I reached toward him, trying to brush the redness away, my mind squirreling over the frames of his abrupt departures, silent returns, inexplicable anger, denying, discarding, refusing to recognize the hatred emanating ceaselessly toward the futile gesture of my reaching arm.

He slumped in his chair. His anger evaporated. He frowned at me, discouraged.

"It's no use," he said sadly. "There's no way you can ever understand."

The silence between us deepened across the dining room table. We sat side by side on the couches of our Saturday night visits, separated by increasing spatial vastness. We disconnected, following the routine paths of our coupled world, to an individual side of the bed. We curled, away from each other, in the tense quiet. I no longer asked him where he was going as I felt his body leave his side of the bed to act out the wandering of his spirit, for somehow I comprehended the strange agreement he had reached within himself. He would keep returning until I told him to go.

I waited the winter away, in the disintegrating atmosphere of forgotten love. But spring was rainless. The air became balmy. The daffodils nodded in the sunny weather, reminding me to turn the soil, to prune the rose bushes, to straighten the long vines of the honeysuckle, to prepare for the flowers that would yet bloom.

I decided to take Larry back to college after his spring vacation. It was not possible Pete would let me drive alone such a long way when it was time to return home. Silent or not, he would come for me.

✍ Before: 3

PETE WROTE TO LAURA almost every day he was overseas—thin little V-mail notes. He wrote the thing that made the war tolerable were his buddies. If it weren't for his buddies, he thought he'd go crazy himself. He'd been assigned to work as an orderly in a hospital that also had a psychiatric unit. He hated it, all of it, the groans and screams of the men, the bathrobes, the wheelchairs, the constant stink of infection and death.

When he was transferred to a field battalion hospital he liked it better. He liked best being on the front because then he was close, really close, to his buddies.

One, Mike, was from Jersey City. He was great—always had a big cigar in his mouth and beer in his belly. The guy could drink more beer than anyone in the entire ETO. Once he found the officers' supply of beer locked in a storage unit. He duplicated the lock, carefully removing an evening's supply—"We'd consider it a half-year's supply"—relocking the shed each night so no one knew he was going in and out.

Then Pete did not write for about two weeks, or

Laura did not receive the mail he was sending. When she finally heard from him, he said he'd been kind of low since Mike was transferred but it was Valentine's Day, 1943, and he wanted her to know he loved her.

He sent her a mimeographed GI valentine, writing Shakespeare's "When forty winters shall beseige thy brow . . . ," signing himself Sad Sack. During the day Laura kept it in her office. At night she put it in her notebook as she went to evening classes, having registered for college almost automatically: in September, one went back to school.

Georgie was overseas too, leaving the drugstore abruptly the February after Pearl Harbor to enlist in the army. The allotment he sent their mother was more than he had earned riding the bike and moving the cartons. He looked tall and natural in his uniform. Flecks of dandruff were on his shoulders when Laura and he went to Grand Central where he was to catch a train to Virginia.

Laura held herself stiffly, wanting to hug Georgie and hold herself against his chest, as she did with Pete. Georgie stood too far from her, maintaining a space she could not cross. His mouth was tight and his heavy eyebrows moved together as he frowned, looking over Laura's head, his eyes restlessly scanning the crowded station. As soon as the train came, he kissed her cheek quickly and told her to take care of their mother and Les. The last thing she saw him do, before he disappeared onto the descending steps, was brush his shoulders.

Georgie wrote her mother once or twice a month— short notes of places her mother did not know—Leeds, Sheffield, Anzio, Mt. Something.

"This damn war," her mother complained. "What good is it?" Her mother sat in the dark, listening to the radio, drinking tea. Every once in a while she would wonder why Les was so late.

"Oh, he's over at Aunt Sadie's. He'll be home soon,"

60

Laura would lie, hoping it was true: she didn't want to be responsible for the brother she did not like and never truly saw. Sometimes Laura was aware of an eerie secretiveness about Les. He slipped through a room, standing too quietly in the hallway as she came out of the bathroom; a nervous, beginning smile curving up his lips, a personal tension Les could not, perhaps, express. He would vaporize out of the hall, through the walls, to some world external to Laura or to her mother.

Once Laura watched Les smooth the creases of one of Georgie's letters, patiently, continually, hand-ironing the creases, his pale face blotched in an irregular diagram of pimples and allergic, angry-looking rash, hovering anxiously above the letter, his movements slightly desperate, in some table version of step-on-a-crack-break-your-mother's-back, some litany of faith accomplished by smoothing the creases, bringing your brother war's surcease. In that odd moment, Laura wanted to buy Les an ice-cream pop. When she suggested it, Les flicked Georgie's letter into some cavern in his pants and said he wanted an ice-cream soda, not some jerky pop.

Whatever he wanted was OK with Laura. They walked to the ice-cream parlor under the elevated train and sat opposite each other at a milky-smelling, small white marble table. Les ordered a banana split with vanilla, banana, peach, and peppermint ice cream and lots of cherries. He laughed as he ordered it from the waitress, who wore a dirty red-checked blouse, and he laughed again when she brought him the huge split.

Laura, looking at her primmer chocolate and whipped cream dish, said, "Oh, wow," at the sight of Les's split. Les laughed so hard Laura did not think he would be able to eat the split after all, although she did not think what she said was funny.

She wanted to ask him how school was—Les was in

his second term already. She wanted to know if he had a teacher like Stedman and if he knew the student council president, but Les's laugh got in the way. The elevated trains roared, and his horsey guffaw passed through the roar into the remaining intervals. His nervous, short, explosive laughter made Laura half rise in her chair. After fifteen minutes of it, she did not care who his teachers were. When he asked for a bag of maple creams to take home, she bought them because she hated the whining echo of his, "Ah, c'mon, be a sport, Laura. I'll save some for tomorrow; honest I will. Be a sport. C'mon."

When they left the parlor, Les looked up at her, his eyes just below her own level. He squinted against the nonexistent sun. "That was nice, Laura. I'll write Georgie about that. He'd like to know how the peppermint tasted. I told him I'd try it for him one day and now I kept my promise. Listen"—Les laughed—"if Aunt Sadie ever hears I've got these maple creams and didn't bring her one, she'll give me what-for you can hear a week from next Tuesday. So OK—thanks," and he evaporated.

Jeepers creepers, Laura thought, where'd he get that laugh? She strolled back to the apartment where her mother sat in the dimness, listening to the radio. Maybe her mother did not see how wrinkled Les's shirt collar looked. Laura guessed she ought to iron his shirts herself even if it was so much trouble to get the ironing board out of the small, crowded hall closet. Everything seemed so much harder in the new apartment.

Ever since her mother had begun taking the curtains off the windows of their flat, making all the rooms look oddly small—ever since then, when she had moved jars and tools, when all the wrinkled laundry had been brought up from their part of the basement in large cartons, from that time on Laura felt uncomfortable. Georgie's old boss at the drugstore gave her mother cartons with Sal Hepatica printed on it—or Fletcher's Castoria, or Dr. Lyons Tooth Powder—all the items that kept you healthy and happy—yet her mother used those cartons to strip their flat of its familiarity. She made the rooms empty, the kitchen odd with a jumble of bags, sacks, barrels. Each night when Laura came home from work the flat was less recognizable. She lost her way looking for her talcum powder and reached out to turn on a lamp which was no longer there.

The new apartment consisted of three little rooms overlooking an alley formed by rows and rows of blind, staring windows. Laura's mother put two daybeds in the living room, with a large geranium in a butter tub between them. She gave Les the bedroom, putting an extra folding bed in the closet for Georgie—for the time when Georgie would come home. The kitchen was long and narrow, with the stove and refrigerator on one side and a dark alcove, recessed toward the alley's blind windows, for the table.

Laura could not do anything about the apartment; she did not know how to make herself feel better there. On Saturdays, she piously did whatever her mother asked her to do. Relieved then, she was freer to meet Hilda and Darcy. Laura welcomed the moment when she could say, "See you about half-past eleven, Ma," and go out the door with the funny peephole on it, clattering down the tinny green steps to the street.

She enjoyed the walk to the station, walking past brown apartment houses with identical small semidetached houses sandwiched in between, past the Beautiful Lady beauty parlor, the shoemaker, the luncheonette where someone was always sitting on the stool, drinking something at the counter.

She knew there was no hurry, although she hurried.

Hilda and Darcy got on the train at the Elmhurst station and stood in front of a door so when they arrived at Laura's station they could wave and shout out to her. When Laura breathlessly joined them, they looked for seats. They never found them. The trains were always crowded. So they trioed around one of the white poles, shouting above the noise of the train how swell each looked and deciding what movie to see.

They could see a movie and stage show at the Paramount, at Radio City, or at the Roxy, but if they chose the Astor, there was no stage show. It did not matter too much to them. The movie was the important choice.

Once they decided on the movie, they walked directly to it when they reached the city, directly into the darkness of the huge movie house, without looking up at the gilt encircling the lobby's enormous chandelier. They ate chocolate mints and licorice nibs while they stared in unison at the last perfect kiss, the beautiful ways to die, the sunny kitchens of intact, devoted families. They enjoyed crying at a movie more than laughing.

In all the movies Laura saw during World War II, Pete was the hero. Laura cried if he died, sighed happily when he was able to steal two days from the war in a quaint Italian village. She held her breath as he heroically and unselfishly volunteered for the dangerous action, felt rich hope as the camera panned to the shining clouds of one fine day when peace comes.

She knew that when the boys could come home again, she and Pete would get married. His letters, her letters made it clear each understood there was something conclusive between them, something that made them belong to each other, as members of a family belong.

Laura rarely revisualized the details of the crowded groping moments she had spent with Pete. She savored only her feelings about him, her sense of him. He was the focus around which her other activities naturally fell.

She worked, went to school, spent Saturday night with Darcy and Hilda because she was waiting. She was good to her mother and to Les to ward off any harm befalling Pete. She stopped in to see Mr. and Mrs. Basse at the store to cheer them up, for Pete, to share with them their loneliness and anxiety for him.

She occasionally looked at a small snapshot Pete had sent her. Some foreshortened effect of the camera made him appear squat. His hair, seemingly shaved almost to the skull, appeared stiff, alien. Laura did not recognize the enormous boots Pete wore, nor the tarp-like raincoat. It might, in fact, have been the picture of a stranger, except for the eyes, which seemed to look directly out of the photograph at her.

Pete's eyes promised her familiarity, a sense of sameness. When he came home, she would no longer have to live in a strange place with a brother she did not understand. When Pete came home, she could stop marking time.

Until then, she dreamed, following the movies for her scripts, bending over his still, dead form and sobbing. She liked best when she ran toward him on an unknown field as she recognized his miraculous appearance.

She arose from her movie seat, dignified in her suffering, holding herself erect with head held high. She would not let Pete down. She would keep the faith. The lights she had not seen as she entered the movie theatre she saw as she slowly emerged from her dreams. News bulletins created from blinking light bulbs moved incessantly around the triangular Times Building, dominating

Broadway, drawing attention, forcing the real world back into consciousness.

4,000 ARMLESS WOUNDED TO BE RETURNED....

Laura licked her suddenly dry lips. For a moment, sobbing over Pete's dead body was neither beautiful nor desirable; it became an image from which her mind skittered.

The girls moved quickly, experienced with working their way efficiently through the crowded streets. Bright faces smiled above white-orchid corsages. A soldier was sick on the curb, his buddies laughing around him, smoking, waiting, relaxed. Sailors in heavy blue pea-coats took up the middle of the sidewalk, separating for the girls, "Hey babe—how about it?"

Hilda giggling, Darcy blushing, Laura hesitantly smiling, regrouping beyond the sailors, walking some-what more quickly. Hilda wore ankle-strap high heels. She moved in smooth, staccato beat. Darcy's sandals en-abled her to move one foot more rapidly than the other, obscuring her limp in practiced rhythm. Laura's loafers gave her a flat, easy gait. She could scurry.

They routinely went to a large cafeteria between Sixth and Fifth for coffee and cake after the movie. The cafeteria, too, was crowded. The counterpeople sweated behind the glass-enclosed displays of chicken salad, egg salad, tuna salad, seeded rolls, pickles. Steaming vats of soup, beef stew, fried chicken for the hungrier custom-ers. Row on row of chocolate pie, piled high with whip-ped cream, apple pie, peach pie, brownies, oatmeal cookies. Milk, tea, cocoa. A casual feast for the war-torn.

Laura always had spice cake with chocolate icing. A treat away from home, rich lady eating out. Frequently, rich lady did not have enough money for the cake, although her mother gave her two dollars of her eighteen-dollar salary. Laura did not manage well. If she had the cake, she would not have carfare to get home. But Hilda would always loan her the nickel.

Hilda worked as a switchboard operator for an accounting firm. She listened through headphones, pressed switches, kept in mind who was waiting for a line, kidded with the accountants before connecting them to their callers and earned twenty-five dollars a week. She was terrific.

Hilda managed. She saved, she spent, and she always had enough to loan Laura carfare.

Relaxed in the cafeteria, Laura looked at Hilda's manicured nails, brightening the brown cup she held.

"Bobby said he just hates that Spam," Hilda reported. "I wrote back and told him that was good. Maybe he could keep his weight down. You'd think with all that exercise they have to do, he'd be as skinny as Pete already. But no. He says he's as pudgy as ever."

"Georgie shouldn't be in Italy," Darcy said definitely. "None of them should be in Italy. They should be fighting on a second front in France. I don't understand why you girls don't help me on the committee fighting to open the second front."

"I would, Darcy," Hilda answered, "but I just don't seem to find the time. I mean my mother likes me to go shopping with her on Thursday night, and on Saturday morning I like to get my hair done, and what with work and all, I just don't have any time."

Darcy brushed her hair over her ear and looked at Laura.

"My schoolwork takes such a long time," Laura said defensively, knowing what a weak excuse it was. Darcy worked in a bookstore and went to school at night as well, but she always found time to go down to the little office where people wrote leaflets and mimeographed them in huge quantities and stood in the street giving them out to strangers.

The idea of doing something like that filled Laura with dread—standing in public like that.

Darcy sipped her coffee, putting the cup carefully back on the saucer. She had recently had her ears pierced, and two sterling silver dots twinkled beneath her strands of sunny hair. She looked at Hilda with the stern eyes of a fourth-grade teacher.

"Don't you want to be part of something important?"

Hilda giggled. "I am! And his name is Bobby."

"Isn't that important?" Laura asked Darcy.

"To Hilda, of course," Darcy said. "But in the long run, I don't think so."

"That's what Humphrey Bogart said when he told her to get on the plane. 'It doesn't take much to see how unimportant three little people are in this crazy world.' Do you think anyone will ever send us off on a plane?"

The fourth-grade teacher disappeared as Darcy laughed, "Probably your children—for your twenty-fifth wedding anniversary."

"I'd probably be afraid to get on one," Laura said, forlorn at her fear.

"Oh, I wouldn't. I think the idea of flying is stupendous." Darcy gazed at the vision of herself flying.

"I do, too," Hilda said, enthusiastically. "And I'd wear high heels so my legs would really look swell."

"My stocking seam would be crooked and I'd probably have a run in them anyway," Laura said.

"But you'd be with Pete." Darcy abruptly pushed her cup and saucer away from her.

Going home on the subway, walking alone from the station through the now quiet blocks, Laura was grateful

68

to Hilda and Darcy, grateful for them. They eased the waiting for Pete.

They were all frightened when they heard the second front had actually been opened. Even Darcy was as frightened as she was jubilant. So many soldiers had died. It did not seem possible so many could die and there could still be some left alive.

They sat in Hilda's living room, reassuring each other they would hear soon about Bobby, and after all, Pete and Georgie had been in Italy anyway. They would not have taken them from Italy to France, would they?

"No," Darcy said definitely. "This can only be good news. It has to shorten the war. It has to."

The girls went out for a walk, instinctively following the old route to high school, hoping they were waiting through a shorter time.

They spent New Year's Eve, 1944, together, Darcy and Laura drinking a rye and ginger. Hilda drank a rum and Coke. Their new sophistication did not alleviate their anxiety. So many more soldiers died in the Battle of the Bulge. Who could be left? What were the chances Pete, Georgie, and Bobby were all intact?

They celebrated Passover more solemnly than ever before. If they had been Jews in Germany, in Poland, in Hungary, in Rumania, they would be dead now. They hesitated to speak of their new earrings or dresses.

When Darcy asked Laura and Hilda to contribute to the refugee fund, Laura matched Hilda's two-dollar contribution. Then she enthusiastically joined in Hilda's suggestion that they find a good musical and relax a little already.

After V-E Day, they relaxed enormously. It couldn't be long now!

In August, hot and muggy, irritated in New York's

famous destructive humidity, the girls decided to go to the beach. It was a long trip that required much paraphernalia.

First, shaving—a long, tedious, painful process, razor rasping over legs, under arms, leaving nicks, blood, rash, chafe. Laura patted her hairless self with relief when the ordeal was over.

"Why do you do such a foolish thing?" her mother demanded. "That hair is meant for protection—don't you know that? A smart girl like you?"

The bathroom steamed, generating heat throughout the apartment. Les lay sodden against the couch, listening to the radio, listless in the heat. All week the newspapers had announced Japanese cities were being pulverized by B-29s. Over 1,300,000 people in twelve cities had felt the effects of the bombs. Their apartment seemed removed from all that—an isolated, hot cave, remote from the world. Divided, like the newspaper, into one column announcing the Dead–Army, Dead–Navy, Wounded–Army, Wounded–Navy—and the next column announcing the molded shoulder in a new-look fall suit of understated elegance. If a person willed, a person could see only what she wanted to see.

Laura paused, pushing her suit firmly into the beach basket, next to the towels, the boiled eggs, the already rotting peaches.

"Want to come with us, Les?"

Shake of head. No. Too fatigued to answer.

"I think he's getting sick," Laura's mother said anxiously. "Let him stay quiet, better."

Last night, the girls had seen *Anchors Aweigh*. The movie promised them people did not have to be lonely in a big city. Love could be found everywhere. Paul Whiteman and his orchestra were on the stage. Life could be a rhapsody. Laura hoped Les wasn't going to change those possibilities.

Darcy wore a skirt over her suit, her breasts clearly defined under the tight bathing-suit bodice. Hilda wore a frilly blouse over her suit, the bottom of the bathing suit serving as shorts.

Laura felt heavy, winter-dressed in her jeans, shirt, loafers. "Plain Jane strikes again," she thought.

They took the bus to the subway. The subway to another bus. The buses, the subway, the beach were jammed with people. Sandals thrown on blankets, beach chairs, jars of Noxema, baby oil, large baskets with chicken, iced tea, plums, oranges. Children licked Popsicles, turning mouths yellow, orange.

The girls stretched in a row. Face up to the sun, unmoving. The sound of the waves, constant. Isolated speech, "There is, yes, there is—". A chorused "Ahh." Wolf whistles among the generalized background sounds of speech.

A baby girl, blond, ran to the water's edge, shrieked with delight, ran back to her daddy's arm, clutching her thin red sun cap. Laura, sitting up, watched.

What was it like to be held by Daddy like that? Why can't we remember what it was like?

She lay back, part of the beach life-style, somnolent in the sun. The sun was hot, hotter, hottest. The heat gripped, ground her down into the sand. The particles of shell, gravel, on the blanket melted, ran into the hot sun-stream right to the ocean. Pete strolled by, grinning. He breathed so Laura was cool, refreshed, relaxed. The heat evaporated. The muddy brown waves turned Pete-eye blue.

Laura opened her eyes. Darcy was talking to two soldiers. Their dog tags clanked as they hovered around her. "Hey, that's a nice blue suit you have on there. How'd you know blue was my favorite color?"

Laura thought it must have been last night's movie that made Darcy so friendly. She told the soldier she had picked her suit out with him in mind. The other soldier told Hilda he liked the way they matched. His olive-drab undershirt and her yellow suit.

"My school colors," he said, sitting down cross-legged in front of Hilda as soon as she smiled.

"Where's that?"

"Indiana."

"Never heard of it." Smiling at each other.

Laura closed her eyes again, removing herself.

The first soldier couldn't get off Darcy's blue suit. "Goes nice with your blond hair. A really nice match." More sincerely, he added, "I had a blue car before I was drafted. Same color. Just like that. I loved that car. A Dodge. Nice roomy back seat, too."

Darcy wiggled her hips slightly.

"How'd you find that out? How roomy it was—"

"Hey!" Indiana said. "A live one. A real sharp lady."

Blue Car agreed. Proud he'd found a live one.

The four of them talked, laughed together. Laura turned on her side, away from them. Not right for her to join in. Not while Pete was away still Fighting for His Country, while Georgie was away, while Les didn't feel good. Because she was too plain looking. Because she didn't know what to say.

"Laura," Darcy poked her. "We're going over to the refreshment stand for a drink. Come on with us."

"I guess I don't want to right now." Low-voiced. Embarrassed.

"C'mon, baby. I can handle two," Indiana boasted. "No trouble."

They all stood above her, brushing sand off their

72

thighs, smiling, all golden in the sunlight. Enjoying themselves. They didn't hear vulgarity.

Laura felt dark against the sand. They were easy, natural, a group. She was hard, artificial, other. If Pete were there she could be part of the group, have a soda, kid and laugh with them. Without Pete, she didn't know how.

She watched them go. Blue Car put his arm around Darcy's waist. His hand slid down a little when she limped, slid up a little on the next step. Laura imagined he liked the slippery feeling. Hilda and Indiana kept laughing, her suit a brighter yellow than before.

Laura went down to the water. She sat on the wet sand, digging a hole, watching the water come in and fill it, bubbling spumy in the small indentation. She started to build a castle, packing the wet sand firmly, concentrating on the foundation so the water could not wash it away. She always had done that when she went to the beach, but the water always, eventually, washed the sand away. Finally, she went in swimming, hesitantly moving forward, feeling the coldness against her ankles, her thighs, up to her waist. Never going in deeper, never over her head.

Darcy and Hilda were gone a long time, long enough for all the water to evaporate from Laura's suit, leaving only gritty sand and heat. When they came back, it was almost time to go home. Darcy had given Blue Car her phone number. Laura thought it was dangerous to give a stranger your number. Darcy could not see why. He was a nice enough boy.

In the end, it didn't matter. He never called her. Maybe because the Tuesday after that the newspapers announced the Air Force had dropped an atom bomb on Japan. *The New York Times* said a new age had been ushered in, the age of atomic energy. A tremendous force for the advancement of civilization, or for destruction, was at hand.

Laura cut out all the newspaper articles about it to send to Georgie. She did not read the articles very carefully. She had some vague awareness the A-bomb represented some sort of super power, some technological development, which she relegated to an area beyond her comprehension—something men could understand.

Instead, she studied the lists of returning units. She looked first for Pete's and then for Georgie's and then for Bobby's. Sometimes, she played games and looked for them in reverse order.

Pete's was the first listed for return. She waited for three days by the phone with increasing hysteria. When he finally called, she blurted, "What took you so long?" Pete laughed. She pressed the phone against, into, her ear, because Pete laughed. They arranged to meet at his buddy's apartment before he called his parents so they could have the night alone.

Laura supposed that was wrong, but Pete was insistent he wanted it that way, had dreamed about it for so long that way, she could not say no.

A bowl of white roses sat on the coffee table. The couch was covered with an Indian-print throw with five differently designed pillows: the diamond-shaped blue and white diagonals beckoned them.

Pete threw himself on the couch, his face tanner and thinner than Laura remembered. His eyes gleamed blue-bright as he reached for her, pulling her down into the giving softness of the couch, tracing the outline of her lips, arms, tactile senses evoking the long-imagined moment of their bodies, together again.

They were awkward with buttons and belt buckles, clumsy with need, excitement. They could not be fast

74

enough. With his deadly serious expression, Pete lifted Laura's slip and put his penis in her tight, willing vagina. The diamond shapes diagonaled, extended, penetrated Laura's body in a blue haze of feeling—a bearable-unbearable tension which stopped time, thought, and left her stripped of all feeling but sexual radiance.

Then they held each other for a long time, Pete stretched out on his back in an olive-green undershirt, relaxed, and Laura, cuddled against him, safe and welcome.

They married before Georgie returned. Laura's mother asked her if she knew about sex and Laura said she did. Her mother sighed. Pete's mother thought they were still too young, but she could see, after arguing with them, and crying, they were not interested in an engagement period. She informed them she would meet with Laura's mother and plan a nice wedding for them. Pete said no, they were not very interested in a nice wedding. When Mrs. Basse looked to Laura for confirmation, Laura, frozen in the iciness of Mrs. Basse's controlled, bitter disapproval, murmured agreement with Pete—more in an effort to cease hostilities she could not understand than to express any real wish about the wedding.

Mrs. Basse arranged to have them married in a rabbi's study. The rabbi was a childhood friend of hers whose study was a long way from Elmhurst on a bleak, apartment-filled street. Laura remembered their wedding canopy as concrete, gray slabs without color, heavy, drab. The rings she and Pete had searched for so romantically seemed lusterless in the dusty, strange study.

The rabbi spit at them as he implored them to consecrate their vows. Pete's arms trembled. Hilda blew her nose. Laura's mother touched Laura softly, a gentle, urgent breeze, inarticulate revelation of her loss. When Laura half turned toward her mother, Mrs. Basse told her to look at the rabbi.

Immediately after the ceremony, Pete and Laura left. The ticking meter of the cab, racing toward midtown Manhattan, sounded rhythmically in Laura's head. It bonged with monstrous regularity, *I am Mrs. Basse. I am Mrs. Basse.*

She put a tentative hand on Pete's knee. He put his hand on hers, holding it immobile. She smiled at him.

"Do you think it was nice?"

"It's nice it's done." Pete held her hand and looked out the window. He seemed preoccupied and continued to be serious while he registered them at a hotel, when he settled them in their room, during their lovemaking. Only just before they went to sleep did he repeat, fervently, with passion, "Oh God, it's nice it's done."

They found a studio apartment in Greenwich Village. Their shelves were stacked bricks on which they arranged books and plants and wedding-gift vases. Imitating the scene of their illicit lovemaking, Laura insisted on differently designed pillows over their bedspread. The bedspread fit their bed badly; until then, neither Pete nor Laura had known beds could be queen-sized.

Laura liked the way they fixed up the kitchenette. She liked the cute round table in the alcove near the stove. She liked deciding what they should eat for supper and talking to Pete as they ate.

She even liked to look at the courtyard below their window, at the square of cement down there, despite its being dotted with torn, ketchup-splotchy hamburger bags and discarded, limp, cold french fries.

At night, in the warm, solitary darkness of their

apartment, she particularly liked when Pete lifted her slip and rubbed her breasts and went hastily into her. Although it could never be fast enough for him, Laura adjusted to his immediate rhythm. Then they would lie together, Pete's seriousness replaced by relaxation; Laura, happy and satisfied.

But she was homesick. She was homesick for the house in which they grew up, even though her mother and Les lived in the new place, and Pete's folks now lived in a house on Long Island. Twice she automatically changed trains for Elmhurst before she remembered her home lay downtown.

Everything was so good now. She could not understand herself.

She giggled, alone, on the train, remembering Pete in that silly blue kimono. He was wearing it when he awakened her this morning, a silk kimono that stopped too short at his knobby knees, that clashed with the olive-green Army-issue undershirt he still wore and through which tufts of curling brown hair were visible.

He awakened her by moving a coffee cup under her face. The steam warmed her face, causing misty-morning lightwaves.

"Are you singing?" he asked, sinking in the chair near the bed. "You have to sing," he said. "That's the sure sign of morning-after happiness."

"I'm singing," she groaned, sipping the coffee, her eyes closing and opening languorously, reflecting a slow ebb and flow of echoing sexual feeling. A feather touched her clitoris, and she moved her buttocks against the bed, unconsciously pressed the blanket between her legs.

She sang that they had met and the angels sang. Pete put his hand against her lips.

"Don't sing," he said, his face still winced against her

77

odd croaking, which alternated between soprano and alto without warning. "I'll take your word for it." She finished the coffee. "That was a real nice idea," she said. "You going to keep doing that?"

"It's protective. I've noticed we're not at our most cheerful before coffee."

She grimaced self-consciously. Laura's inexplicable awakening rages were almost automatic. Speaking was physically painful; a thin membrane had to be broken each morning so the first word might get through. Thereafter the other words poured through the small opening, smoothly enlarging it until her throat was again relaxed and she could speak fluently at will.

Once, a small problem with a knotted shoelace threatened to transform her into a homicidal psychotic. She bared her teeth, grunting with fury at the shoelace, finally grabbing the small knot, jerking it back in irritation, in impatience, in total rejection, until she snapped the lace and threw it out the window to be lost among the greasy bags of the courtyard.

Ashamed then, she had carefully washed the coffeepot and changed their sheets.

Pete sat, noticeably patient, watching her prepare for a visit to his folks. She felt the brown skirt had a little too much lint on it. Didn't Pete agree? He did not. She took it off and put on a red plaid skirt. Did Pete think this one made her look too fat? He did not. She was uncertain. She turned around, trying to see her back image.

Pete started to put on the khaki Eisenhower jacket he wore daily, nightly, constantly.

"Can we go now, Lady Jane?" he asked politely, opening the door with a flourish.

Jane Basse's new house was pleasant. There were deep, soft couches with green pillows. A glass-enclosed china closet permitted glints of porcelain and gold to reflect shimmers of light from fragile cups and plates no one used.

Jane put her silverware, one utensil at a time, on either side of the dinner plate, with a napkin for each person, and a glass, all ready, slightly to the side. It seemed more considerate than Laura's mother's arrangement of utensils and glasses in the center of the table. At her mother's, somehow all the forks were being used just when someone needed one from the communal source.

Laura told Pete's family about the arrangement, concluding, "Georgie always seemed to be the one stuck without a fork." Jane moved gracefully between the stove and table, setting platters of corned beef, potato salad, marinated mushrooms, thick, crusty seeded rye at convenient diagonals across the table.

"What do you suppose George will do when he returns?" Jane asked, touching a tendril of her hair tenderly with a light fingertip.

"Go to college, I'm sure," Laura said, watching Pete pile corned beef and mushrooms and mustard to Eiffel Tower height on his rye bread. "All in one bite?" she whispered to him.

"Pete always enjoyed his food," Jane said. "Just like his father." Pete's father worked Sunday afternoons in their delicatessen store. Laura guessed Jane was sorry he couldn't be home with them.

"And what will you do, my son?" Jane asked Pete, sitting opposite him. She focused on Pete's face, her whole body concentrated, momentarily, forward, reminiscent of Pete's stance of controlled eagerness toward Laura. Unexpectedly ill at ease, Laura excused herself and went unnecessarily to the bathroom.

As she returned, she heard Pete saying, "So Laura

and I think law would be best." Turning to her, he said, "Don't we?"

"Sure," she said automatically.

"Your father will be disappointed. He wanted you to go into the business, you know that."

"I know, Mom, but it's not for me. I can't get rid of the smell after a while."

"You don't seem to have any trouble with it now," Jane said, crisply.

"Your sandwiches are another whole situation," Pete smiled.

Jane beamed. "Want to try some of the tongue?"

"Bring it on. I'm your willing taste tester."

"When did 'we' decide law would be best?" Laura asked Pete curiously on the way home.

"When we realized how increasingly important federal regulations would become."

"When exactly did we talk about that?"

"All the time I was overseas, watching everyone's life being decided by number slash number forms. We talked about it almost all the time."

"What did I say?"

"You said, 'Whatever you think best, honey, is OK with me.' And I said, 'That's a great attitude.' But then, I wasn't surprised. I knew I had a great girl."

Laura ducked toward Pete's shoulder.

"Except maybe not in the morning?" she said, a gamine, because she was alone with her husband who thought she was great.

"We'll adjudicate that exception when I learn how to adjudicate."

On the evening "they" decided Pete should return to college and major in prelaw, Georgie came home. Pete and Laura gave Georgie a big, crowded welcome-home dinner in their small apartment.

Georgie, too, was tanner and thinner, but he was friendlier, easier. Laura had no trouble hugging him, even resting against his chest for a minute. She was overjoyed to see him. A pain she did not realize she had in her throat disappeared when she saw him.

Les drank too much wine for a fifteen year old and laughed incessantly while Georgie and Pete sat together in a corner talking about short-arm inspections and fucking majors.

Laura looked quickly at her mother when she heard them, but her mother just smiled, and carried the plates to the sink and started to wash them. Only when Georgie announced he thought he would get married soon, too, and planned to become a teacher, did her mother look at him. She asked Les sharply to lower the radio, shook her head slightly at some unspoken thought, told Laura she was getting to be a really good cook.

Pete asked Georgie who the lucky girl was. Georgie said her name was Lilli and he'd met her in Virginia where he'd first been based. He'd known then he wanted to marry her, but he felt he had to wait until he came home because of the allotment.

Like Pete, he was planning to use the G.I. Bill to go to school. He looked at his mother then and said, "I'll keep sending you what I can, Ma." Laura said she would too, of course. Their mother said maybe she could find a job. They all thought that would be a good thing for her to do, not only because of the money but because it would give her something to do, get her out of the house.

Laura found the idea enormously relieving, and danced around, throwing pieces of cake. Laura's mother collected all the pieces of cake and ate them. "It's good," she said, surprised.

Laura's mother found a job as a clerk. Every day she made herself a bologna sandwich and put it in a brown bag with an apple. She enjoyed working, although apparently she found it very tiring. At night, she sat drinking tea and listening to the radio. Sometimes her sister visited with her. Les stayed home then too.

Georgie acted like a speeded-up film. He searched for an apartment he and Lilli could afford. He registered at City College, bought a suit, experimented with dandruff-removing creams; haunted Klein's until he found a camera of which he approved; personally bought his mother's roundtrip ticket to Virginia and then, after thinking about it for a day or two, returned to buy Les's ticket; resumed haunting Klein's until Les had a well-fitting jacket and nice tie.

"Lilli can put up Ma and Les, but her folks can't handle any more than that." He looked inquiringly at Pete. "It's bad enough I missed your wedding. I hate to have Laura miss mine."

"We can't swing it, Georgie," Pete said definitely. "I know it would be nice, but it's out of the question."

Georgie shrugged his shoulders slightly.

Laura could not think of anything to say.

On the Sunday of Georgie's wedding, not even morning coffee opened her throat. It remained closed all day. She moved privately, tightly around the studio room. Specks of old paint on the baseboard irritated her beyond containment. She sat on the floor with steel wool and rags and scrubbed at the old paint specks, rubbing them incessantly, sometimes scraping with the point of a knife, leaving gashes and nicks behind—but removing the loathsome spots, not stopping until each spot was eliminated before she moved to the next. She clenched her teeth at the more stubborn ones, the ones that resisted the knife, the steel wool, the Lysol. She began to cry in frustration at the spot that defied her control. She knelt before the spot, straining her arms, her back, to reach down far enough to scrub the spot away forever.

Pete came behind her. He moved his hand slowly over her raised, taut buttocks. Laura half turned, surprised, her face swollen with exertion, the smell of Lysol acrid, minute splinters of steel wool staining her knees. Pete brushed at her knees, forcing her face almost down to the floor, plunging into her without a sound, a fore-gesture, uncaring of the wet rags, the dirty water in the pail, thrusting toward ejaculation in solitary passion.

Later, he was exhausted, almost too tired to move to bed, too drained to open his eyes. He had expended some monumental energy, succumbed to some tidal wave of need, which having been met, left him listless, detached.

Laura did not have the heart to disturb him, to remind him she had not had her diaphragm on.

Georgie brought back Lilli and pictures of their wedding in her house in Virginia. Lilli was small, dynamic, charming, with a wide, warm smile. Her smile was the largest part of her. Their apartment was a block or two from Laura and Pete's. Every Sunday, the four of them strolled through the Village, enjoying themselves and each other.

Georgie was very serious about his studies. Wearing his old khakis and a flannel shirt, he went to the library conscientiously every Saturday, reading thick texts and making notes in a hardcovered notebook. He crammed clippings and notecards into it until the threads holding it together split. Then he bought another notebook.

Laura, who always used a loose-leaf for her classes, was ashamed. Her sheets seemed covered with doodles and phrases compared to Georgie's pages and pages of comprehensive notes. She listened while Georgie discussed heterogeneous tracking and the idiocy of rote-memory learning, rarely offering ideas she heard in her classes.

She did not feel what she was doing was equivalent. Georgie and Pete were learning. She was going to school.

Lilli, who already had a BA, was working in an advertising agency. This fact alone would have made her glamorous in Laura's eyes. That she also always wore high heels moved her somewhere near the society set. Yet Lilli made herself accessible to Laura. She showed Laura how to wash silver without scratching it with steel wool. She offered Pete Brandy Alexanders before dinner and advised Georgie on the best organization for a paper he was writing.

They came to depend on Lilli's decisions, feeling more secure because they could rely on her, feeling comfortable in their reliance because she expressed warmth and interest in their well-being.

Laura unhesitatingly spoke first to Lilli when she missed a period. Because Lilli was reassuring, Laura felt more confident when she announced the news to others. Her mother, Hilda, and Darcy squealed identically. Les stared at her abdomen, laughed, and went out somewhere.

Pete's parents said it was wonderful, wonderful, and patted Pete on the back.

Bobby, who had gone into his father's butcher shop, was in the process of expanding it into a supermarket. When he heard about the baby, he asked Pete to have lunch with him. Pete came home tight-lipped and ripped the newspaper when he jerked it open to read. He threw the paper across the room, knocking away four books.

"This room is so damn small! You can't move in here without hitting something."

"You could have done without lunch with Bobby, I gather," Laura said, amused, picking up the books and paper.

"I think I could do without Bobby for lunch, dinner, or late evening snacks from now on. Your friend Bobby is well on his way to becoming a pompous ass. The fat in his tuchas seems to be drifting right up to his head."

"*Our* friend Bobby said something you didn't like," Laura said.

Pete stuck his finger in the air. "On the nose."

"How'd I ever guess?"

"Miserable dumb bastard had the nerve to question me about whether or not I have enough insurance and now that I'm about to be a father, maybe I ought to start thinking more practically."

"Which means, I suppose, stop going to school."

"Exactly."

"Why do you suppose he thinks it's more practical not to get your degree?"

"I told you—because he's a shortsighted, fatheaded bastard who only knows one thing—money, money, money."

"C'mon, Pete, you know that's not true."

"It's almost true, Laura," Pete said, not as angry any more. "I got the whole original You-Have-To-Think-Of-Your-Family-Now speech. The bastard decided if I cared about my family I should go into partnership with him in the store. He has this idea a good delicatessen and a good meat department would make a supermarket really super."

"For someone else, it's not a bad idea."

"The point is, who the hell asked him!"

"I guess he meant well. Don't make such a big thing

out of it. I would really feel bad if there were hard feel-ings between us and Bobby. I'd hate that, Pete!"

"Don't worry. I knew you'd feel that way. I turned Bobby down very politely. I didn't let him know what a jerk I thought he was. I radiated grateful man-to-man fellowship." Pete relaxed against the pillows; then he added, "I'll handle my family my own way."

Laura snuggled up next to him.

"That's good enough for me, honey."

Laura read all about childbirth. Every morning she rubbed her hand over her abdomen, wishing her baby a good growing day. She admired the lush roundness of her breasts. The widening circle of her nipples she be-lieved to be wondrous. She left her skirt buttons undone to accommodate her increased girth, stopped zipping the side panel, finally bought a maternity skirt, investing it with the pricelessness normally reserved for Oriental rugs or authentic Ming vases. She wore Pete's shirts over her skirt, feeling she appeared sporty, casual, disguising from the world her sense of enormous self-importance.

She sat in a warm tub watching the baby move inside her. The slow undulations, the unexpected jab in the steamy relaxing water intensified her relationship with the unseen, unknown baby. "Having a good time?" she asked her abdomen. "Getting enough calcium? Do you have any idea of how much I hate that milk I drink so you can have enough calcium?"

Pete sat on the edge of the tub, smiling at her. His hair curled tightly in the humidity of the room. Vapor covered the mirror over the medicine chest. The ivy plant thrived on the moist, enclosed window. Pete helped her carefully out of the tub and rubbed her dry, looked with obvious enjoyment as she powdered herself.

The sweet talcum odor permeated their hot living space. He paused before opening the door. It was almost as if they were leaving a womb they had comfortably, sensuously shared. The air was inevitably colder outside the bathroom.

When Laura was in her sixth month, Pete borrowed his dad's car and they started looking for an apartment. They decided on a new garden type, just being built in "a location of enduring pleasure and convenience." The garden apartments were across the street from a park.

They found they could not afford a two-bedroom. Instead, they agreed, the baby could have the bedroom and they could do nicely in the living room. Their modern glass-topped table broke when they moved. "It wasn't a good table to have around with a baby anyway," Pete said. Laura concurred it was all for the best. It was clear to them that together all problems could be solved and all clouds ultimately had a silver lining.

They used a bridge table for the kitchen, saving their money to buy a crib when Laura was in her seventh month.

Hilda came. She inspected the two-tier blue and white curtains Laura hung in the bedroom and the bookcase Laura had painted to be used for the baby's clothes.

"You've done a wonderful job here. I don't know how you managed it, but it looks great."

Laura was hesitantly proud of herself. She was not quite sure Hilda meant it. Hilda would not marry Bobby until they had enough money saved.

"You know, I like nice things. I like everything perfect. I guess I'm a fussbudget," Hilda sighed happily, "but that's me."

The green cup from which Laura was drinking was chipped. She hoped the one she gave Hilda was not.

"Of course," Hilda went on, "you and Pete knew so early you wanted to get married. I guess it's different for you. I mean, there was never any question—"

"I thought it was like that with you and Bobby."

"No, I wasn't that sure—at least, not until I went out with some of those beauties from the office. *Then,* I was sure."

Laura laughed.

"Did you tell that to Bobby?"

"Not exactly. I just let him know it's not a good idea to get married until you have a little something to fall back on."

"Well, that's true. It isn't."

Hilda said, too sympathetically, "Listen, when Pete graduates and he's working full time, you'll be able to get what you want."

"Hey—I have what I want now."

"Hmm, well, Bobby says he'll have enough money to buy a car soon."

"Oh, Pete will be green with envy. He's dying for a car. How he hates that subway!"

Hilda giggled. "Did you hear Darcy is seeing this crazy guy who won't go into a subway without an umbrella? Seems he can't stand to have anyone get too close to him, so he accidentally-on-purpose sticks them with the umbrella."

Laura laughed with Hilda.

"Isn't it remarkable how Darcy lives alone like that?" she asked Hilda.

"I can't get over it. My mother would never even hear of an idea like that."

"Would you want to?"

"God, no. Would you?"

"I'd die."

✻ *After: 3*

"WHAT DO YOU MEAN you're going to drive Larry back to school alone?" Hilda was outraged. "Why would you do a thing like that! Pete will have a fit worrying about you."

"I don't think so, Hilda. In fact, I think he'll be somewhat relieved to see me go."

"That certainly doesn't sound like Pete to me."

"I know. I know how strange it sounds—but it's true. Pete's—well—Pete's just not very interested in me right now."

"Is he having trouble with his practice? I mean, if he is, you ought to stay around no matter what he says."

"No, it's me. He's having trouble being married to me."

"I don't believe it!" Shocked.

"That makes two of us."

"Have you talked to him? I mean, Laura, you and Pete, that's not possible."

"I've talked to him—and talked to him—and nothing. He just doesn't want—doesn't seem to care."

"That doesn't make any sense. It's crazy."

Miserable, I repeated I knew.

"There couldn't be another woman," Hilda said, convincing herself. "Pete wouldn't do anything like that. I know Bobby always said if he ever was attracted to anyone else, he'd come right home and tell me about it. And I'm sure Pete would do the same thing."

I remained silent. The winter had been so long. I could not explain the impact of the long winter to Hilda, so Hilda could understand Pete might do something neither I nor Hilda could ever understand.

"Well, I think you're making a mistake," Hilda decided. "I think you ought to just stay put and not make waves. He'll come to his senses."

"I appreciate your advice, Hilda, honestly, but I feel I just have to go away for a little while."

"Well, if you're decided. . . . Don't worry. We'll invite him over for supper. Bobby will call him. We'll keep an eye on him for you."

I told Darcy, "So I've decided the best thing to do is go away for a few days."

"Makes a lot of sense. It will give you a chance to see things in perspective, to decide how you want to handle this."

"I'm nervous about the trip—afraid, really. I'm not sure I can drive it all alone."

"Hell, Larry will be with you going. By the time you come back, you'll know the way. You don't have to worry. And after a few days Pete will realize how much he misses you."

"Do you really think so?"

"Hasn't he all his life?"

"But people change—their feelings change."

"Not like that. Not just overnight."

"It's been going on for a while now."

"'A while' is relative. For you and Pete, it's got to be overnight."

The long winter, one (endless) night?

"Whatever you think is best," Lilli said. "Just remember you can call us anytime if you want to. I'm sure you will be all right, but if you run into any trouble—or even just want to talk to someone, just call. Promise? Now, just a minute. Georgie wants to talk to you."

"What the hell is this all about?" Georgie roared.

"It's a little complicated to go into—but cutting through to the closing—it reads, 'Kid, I've had it.'"

"Just like that?"

"After the requisite screaming."

"Throw him out. What are you going away for? Let him pack his things and get lost."

"But I don't want him to!"

"That's logical. You don't want him to go, so you go instead."

"I'm not going forever. Only for a few days."

"So what's all the fuss. Go and come back. Buy him a present. I don't care what he says. Pete is not going to walk out on you after all these years. A guy does not just leave his wife and kids. Where would he go anyway, at his age? Who would put up with me but Lilli? I could never go through breaking in another woman. Too much trouble. It's not worth it."

"If you say so—"

"I know you feel bad, kid, but don't go overboard. Take your little trip and you'll feel you've done something. So you'll feel better. You don't have to be a doormat all your life, you know."

"When was I a doormat!"

"Don't get upset. You're upset enough. Just have a good trip and call me if you need anything."

Before that trip, before I drove Larry back to college, had I ever been alone? Was there ever a night no one was in the house with me? Was it possible I had lived for almost half a century and never been without people around me?

It was not possible that it was possible.

If Pete did not hold my hand, how could I pass the dog? Why had my mother not taught me to walk to school alone? Why had Georgie not taught me to ride a bike and deliver prescriptions?

I cursed those who loved me for protecting me. I dreamed Pete would come for me, hating him because I needed so badly to have him come and get me.

I despised myself because my whines told me I was doing the same thing again, because my questions required answers from other people, whose responses I could not direct.

❧ *Before: 4*

FIVE-THIRTY WAS A quiet time in the courtyard of their garden apartment. The neighbors' kids were inside watching TV and the girls were making supper. Ella, next door, was frying fish. The odor sickened Laura as she sat enjoying the tranquil privacy of the court.

They had just returned from visiting Georgie and Lilli at a summer camp. Georgie was working as a science counselor and Lilli as a crafts counselor. Their summer, in comparison to Laura's and Pete's, seemed youthful, fun.

Laura felt old, sleeping on the bunk bed. It was too narrow for her wider girth, too narrow for her to sleep with Pete. The trip home had also been tiresome. She usually enjoyed the timelessness of the road—the routine of coffee stops and lunch served by strangers—but her back hurt in the bus, and her vague tension about possibly delivering prematurely made her anxious to be home and done with the trip.

Pete felt it and resented her for it, she knew, but there had been no way of alleviating her feeling. They had unpacked silently last night. He had gone to school withdrawn. He felt cheated, she guessed, and it made her guilty.

She looked at the trees in the park, wishing it would get a little cooler. The heat made her lethargic. She decided not to make a salad but just to cut up some tomatoes. She wondered exactly when the baby would be born and what it would be.

Sunny came over with a glass of lemonade in one hand and her chair in another.

"Hi, honey. I've been meaning to stop in and see you, but the kids had dental appointments this afternoon, and then Leo wasn't coming home for supper tonight so I took them to the movies. I've got such a headache I feel like my head will burst—and they're in the house watching television. They'll be blind by the time they're twenty, I'm sure. And it'll be my fault. How do you feel?"

"Just fine. It was a lovely trip. Lilli is great and Georgie seemed to be enjoying himself. I don't think kids ever stopped coming over to fool around with him. I'm a little tired, of course. . . ."

"Well, I think you were crazy to go," Sunny said as she settled her chair so it would not hit the grass. "It's hard enough for you now, just to move around."

"Oh, come on, Sunny. It's not necessary to sit and get fat, you know."

"Well, you'll need all your strength when the baby comes and there's a good deal to be said for the old-fashioned ideas."

"I suppose so," Laura said, not really caring. She felt dulled, and she wished Sunny would go away so she could sit in a vacuum.

"I remember when I had my first," Sunny said, pursing her lips in reminiscence. "Leo was so nervous I

94

couldn't wait for him to get out. And of course we were only three blocks from the hospital but he just hung around. Not that I cared much what *he* was doing at the time. Of course that was in wartime, and everything was so crowded they rushed me out four days after Jimmy was born. My mother insisted I have a nurse for four weeks, and believe me, I didn't move a muscle, I was so sore. I had eight stitches you know, and I felt every one of them."

Laura didn't say anything. Her back hurt her, and the baby began to feel like a heavy stone pushing her insides down.

"When Cindy was born," Sunny continued, enjoying herself, "it was better. I was more frightened because I knew what to expect, but Leo was busy with Jimmy and he had gotten over the idea it would take only five minutes, so it was less hectic all around. Oh, but I'm glad that's over with. I was in labor forever, twenty four hours you know, and they thought they'd have to cut me, but thank God she was born and everything was all right. And I was so thrilled to have a daughter. You know, it's true, a boy will leave you when he gets older and has his own wife. But with a girl, you can take her shopping and she can be a real friend."

"Are you so friendly with your mother?" Laura asked tersely, feeling a little better. "I think it's nice to have a boy first."

"Well, I did, didn't I?" Sunny said defensively. "Besides, it's nice for a man to have a son."

"I guess we really don't have much choice, do we?" Laura said. She looked over to the driveway to see if Pete was home yet. It was getting late for him. The heaviness was back with her again. She didn't know how she would get the dishes done. Maybe she'd just leave them for the morning.

"Well," Sunny said, getting up, "I'd better be getting back. I'll have to get them something for supper, though how they can eat after all that junk they ate in the movies is beyond me. Kids. I can't ever remember being like that." She went back to her apartment, leaving her chair behind.

Laura watched her go, wondering what it was like to be a mother with dental appointments and supper to get. It seemed so far away from her life. Anyway, she was too tired to think about it too much.

She saw Pete coming up the stairs from the driveway, and for a moment she tensed, not really knowing why she did. He looked hot and tired as he walked slowly, carrying his jacket over his shoulder. She could not remember anymore what it was like to go to school.

He smiled when he saw her and sat down on Sunny's chair.

"Whew, what a day. I thought it would never end."

She smiled faintly at him, suddenly frightened by the gnawing pain in her back, thinking in panic that it was too soon.

"Hi, cutie," she said, sighing a little as the pain went quickly away. "Anything new?"

"Yeah, I met my Evidence professor. He told me how well I did on the exam—after he told me how fat I was getting. Listen babe, mind if I take a shower before supper?"

"Of course not. Go ahead. It's all ready. Just let me know when you're finished."

"You bet." He started up the stairs to the apartment. At the door he stopped and looked at her a little sheepishly. "How do you feel, honey?"

She smiled up at him, a warm tenderness washing away her lethargy.

"Just swell, honey. Just swell."

When he'd gone in, she wondered why she'd said that. She didn't feel swell at all. In fact, she felt lousy. Maybe she was going to be one of those Pollyannaish women who suffered silently and then sprang cancer on her family.

Ella's second son, Stevie, in pajamas, came to the screen door of his apartment and looked out at her. Laura smiled at him, wishing he would go away so she wouldn't have to talk to him.

He didn't go away, just stood there looking at her. Finally she asked him if he was ready for bed, feeling fatuous.

"Nope."

"Had your dinner yet?"

"Nope. And I'm not going to eat it either. I hate fish!"

Laura wondered what you did when your child didn't like the supper you made.

Stevie looked at her silently for a while. She couldn't think of anything to say. Finally he said sharply, "Are you going to get a baby?"

She smiled. "Oh yes, next month, I think."

"How do you know?"

"Well, the doctor told me."

"How does he know?"

"He goes to school for years and years, just to learn that."

"I've got a hundred ninety-seven baseball cards."

"That's wonderful," Laura said, weakly, unsure of the relevance of his information. "You'd better get away from the door though. I think you might catch cold standing there in your pajamas." What a hypocrite I am, she thought.

The gnawing pain in her back returned. She wanted to lock herself in her bedroom. She wondered if she ought to tell Pete about it.

After a while, she felt better. Pete was singing in the shower. She put the iced coffee on the table, and the plates and the roast beef. She sliced the tomatoes in a round circle on the plate and turned off the oven. She did not think the potatoes would get cold in the short time before they sat down, and the kitchen was too hot with the oven on.

She felt the gnawing pain again, and she was very frightened. Her hands began to shake. An unreal feeling blanketed her. She thought of the old joke about the woman in the labor room who said she'd changed her mind; Laura did not know how she would go through with it.

After a while, she felt better. The unreal feeling persisted though—she could not remember what time it was.

Pete came in and they sat down and began to eat. He had Stevie's clean look. She tried to think of Dr. Klein's telephone number.

"You're pretty quiet tonight, Laura," Pete said. There was some ketchup on the side of his mouth, which nauseated her. She looked away quickly and said, "It's been a quiet day. I dusted and slept mostly. You really didn't get your money's worth today, I guess."

"I will very soon," he said, smiling warmly at her.

"There's ketchup on your lip," she said, getting up heavily. "Pete, I don't feel so good. I think I'll lie down for a while."

"What's the matter?" he said, anxiously. He jumped up, spilling his iced coffee. Laura watched it run over the side of the table, but it did not concern her because there was a burning cramp forcing her insides down to the ground and she wanted to lie down and curl her knees up against her stomach. "Look," he said, breathing forcefully, "suppose I call the doctor."

"Oh, for God's sake, Pete," she burst out, "what are you going to tell him? I'm tired! I'm going to lie down for a moment. Don't make such a damn fuss about everything."

He started to sponge up the spilled coffee, not saying anything, angry at the circumstances that made him unable to.

She went in and lay on the cot they had put in the baby's room. It was beginning to turn dark out, and the thought of dusk reminded her of the times she had visited her father. She felt inconsolably sad, as though she were mourning his death for the first time.

The burning pain went away, but her back hurt her. She could not find a comfortable position. Some slight stiffening in her abdomen alerted her to a coming contraction. She sat up quickly, fighting the spasm. "Rain, rain, go away," she murmured. She turned to the clock and saw it was just seven-fifteen. She turned the face to the wall. She made time disappear.

She accepted the fact labor had begun. She knew she would have to do something about it, but she was still too afraid. Her heart beat rapidly and she wanted to go to the bathroom. Instead, she went over to the mirror, urging her image to show a little courage. All she really had to do was put herself in expert hands and let them and nature take its course. She really did not have to *do* anything.

She got back into bed, but just as quickly sat up as the burning pain radiated from her abdomen to her back. She was encircled and going under. She needed time after all. She turned the clock and saw it was seven-thirty.

"Pete!" Help!

He came in, hesitant to speak, watching her for some clue.

"I guess this is it."

"OK. I'll call the doctor. Do you think we have enough time?"

"How the hell should I know! Call the doctor."

"Well, what should I say? Maybe you better talk to him. I mean, are you sure it's a contraction? Maybe the roast beef, and the heat—"

"I'm sure," she interrupted him. "I'm positive."

Great, just great. He was scared, too. Laura sat down on the bed, staring at the clock. Her back hurt constantly, and saliva began to fill her mouth. She spit out into a Kleenex and dropped the Kleenex under the bed. Then she thought, "Suppose I don't come back? Everyone will talk about what a slob of a housekeeper I was." She picked up the Kleenex and threw it in the wastepaper basket.

Then she went into the kitchen and took out the cleanser and scrubbed the sink. Pete never washed the sink when he finished, but no one would know he had done the dishes. She threw out the old SOS pad and pressed her head against the cold faucet as the live girdle squeezed her torso again.

"I couldn't get the doctor. Answering service said they'd try to reach him. Why don't you lie down again?"

"I'd rather walk around. I'm not sick, you know. I'm just going to have a baby."

"We're going to have a baby, Laura. Relax. It's a great thing."

He came close to her and put his arm around her shoulder. "You've got a family, Laura. It happens all the time to hundreds of women every day, but not all of them have someone like me around."

She heard him only dimly. She was trying to remember whether or not her new bra was dry. She could not go to the hospital with this one. The straps were all twisted, and there was blue dye under the arms from the time she'd worn the blouse under her suit and it was too warm at Darcy's. She would not take off the jacket that night because her stomach stuck out too much. She almost laughed at the idea of once having worried about her stomach. She should have been watching her back. It was threatening to break in two.

She saw Pete looking anxiously at her, but she did not have time to tell him she heard him and to thank him for trying to help.

"I'd like to change my clothes and get washed. Why don't you make sure Sunny's car has enough gas?"

When the doctor called, he told her to go on to the hospital. He sounded quite cheerful, and she hated him for being so casual. The word hospital had conjured up visions of knives and needles and unbearable lights glaring down on squirming figures.

She turned off the lights and went out, leaving the door unlocked. Relief washed over her when she saw the courtyard was empty. Privacy seemed crucial.

By the time she joined Pete, she was feeling quite relaxed.

"Wasn't it nice of Sunny to have the car ready for us? Isn't it nice to know it will be over soon?"

Pete smiled at her, but did not say anything, looking straight ahead, driving with tense concentration.

"Don't be sore, Pete. I know you're there. Who else would be with me but you!"

"I'm not sore."

"Yes you are."

"For Christ's sake, Laura, do you have to tell me every step of the way how I feel? I know how I feel. Just talk about how you feel."

"To tell you the truth, I feel great. Maybe it was all a false alarm."

"Oh, God, I hope not."

They both laughed. She stroked his arm.

"Move closer," he said.

"Wise guy," she said lovingly.

There was a traffic jam on the bridge. The red lights sparkled in front of them. Laura watched the spectrum of cars fan out in front of her, curving gracefully toward the toll booth. The skyline was etched in the black smoke of the sky's expanse. They were specks in the panorama. How could anyone know they were in the middle of a momentous occasion?

They made good time after leaving the bridge. The streets were fairly quiet. The hospital's parking attendant told them to use the emergency parking spaces. But when the car stopped, Laura did not want to get out. She was afraid she would not be able to control her fear and would run in panic, grotesque in the street, a woman having a baby, acting like a baby. So she got out rapidly and walked straight ahead, without waiting for Pete. He caught up with her at the reception desk and held her arm tightly.

A nurse took her up an elevator. Laura had a sense of a very old building. She thought the elevator would break down. As they left the elevator, she heard women crying and smelled iodine. She held herself rigidly, willing herself forward, praying she would not disgrace herself. Her legs felt heavy, detached, so that she had to remember consciously how to move them or they would never get her to the room to which the nurse was leading her.

"OK, Miss." Miss! "Get undressed and get into bed. Don't go to the bathroom. Dr. Klein will be here soon to look at you."

As Laura lay on the bed, she could see the traffic light

outside. Sometimes she had some pains only when it was red, and sometimes only when it was green.

The nurse came back and shaved her vaginal area. Laura, thinking she would die of shame, never took her eyes away from the window. There was nothing else in the world she could ever remember doing except looking through the window at the traffic light.

The nurse gave her an enema. Laura had to go to the bathroom—she couldn't wait; she had to go—but the nurse ignored her and continued. When Laura finished with the bedpan, the nurse left. Laura sneaked into the lav, afraid the nurse would come back and tear her away.

She was weak and shaking when she got back to bed and could not believe ordinary girls had undergone this experience more than once, and knowingly. A feeling of amazed respect came over her.

An intern came in, spread her legs, and pushed a finger into her. She willed herself to be less fearful.

"Who are you?"

"You've got a ways to go yet," the intern told her cheerfully, ignoring her question. "You'll be all right. Want something to keep you comfortable?"

"No, I'm OK, thank you. Where's Dr. Klein?"

"He's been up half the night and all day. We'll just let him rest for a while. Why all you girls decide to have your babies at the same time. . . . Anyway, we'll call him when it's time. OK?"

"Sure." Goddamn it! Why do I have to be the understanding one! Why can't I be the girl he's up half the night for. . . .

The evening assumed a routine. Face the pain, go with the pain, beg the pain. She watched the traffic light grow larger and larger, the red swallowing the room. She felt the unironed gray of the sheets chafe her back, stick claws between her legs. The shaved area of her vagina burned, stank of antiseptic, distended unbearably. Her water broke and she howled in her mind, alone forever in terror.

The intern came back and told her sternly she should have called him. He was irritated with her. He gave her some medication, and she awoke to pain and slept, aware she would be called back only too soon. The night wore on, moving into infinity, and she lost her fear, her self-consciousness, and forgot why she was there.

She dreamed she moved from one reality to another. As she moved into each, she forgot the one that had passed and she did not know of the one to come, until she came to a reality in which she did remember and did know. She awoke, terrified, as Dr. Klein came in. She was dumb with anguish for unremembered reasons.

He told Laura she was a good girl. Obscure pride moved sluggishly beyond the pain. She felt elated: they did not know; she had kept her privacy.

When they moved her onto a rolling cart, she was aware of a momentum beginning, a hurrying sensation. The people around her were occupied, knowledgeable, busy. She did not want to interfere with them so she curled up, hiding herself from the swirling storm that was bending shadows up and down the halls and around the bright glares of light.

"Move down, Laura," Dr. Klein said harshly. "I can't go chasing you up the table." She moved down, re-experiencing pride in obedience, and studied the whirls of blackness that pressed against her vision. She felt the colossal strain of her abdomen, the bulging, muscular agony of delivery, and wondered why it was so quiet. It was as though the movie had ended and the only people left in the theatre were some stragglers, their voices louder in the empty area than they realized.

She opened her eyes and looked at the baby on her abdomen. It was wet, its black hair saturated against its head.

"Do you want something while I take a few stitches, Laura?" Dr. Klein asked.

Terrified of returning pain, of the needles and knives of the hospital in her mind, she said, "No, I'm OK."

"Well, so is your son, Laura. Everything is perfect."

Laura watched the rubber-gloved nurse pick up the wet baby. She moved her head to look at him, and when Dr. Klein told her not to move for a moment, she ignored him. A maniacal joy had begun to seize her, the dim sense of pride returned in huge waves, clearly etched. She put out her arms and the nurse gave her the baby. Total pleasure overwhelmed her.

The baby's squeezed-shut eyes, fat cheeks, quivering mouth were hypnotically fascinating. She could not stop staring at his face. He was the most interesting human being she had ever seen.

Laura awoke and looked at the lady in the bed opposite her. The lady was talking to her.

"Tommy stepped right on that rusty nail and it's just made a mess of his foot. I don't know how Drake will be able to manage with Tommy having to be carried around like that. That kid's been nothing but trouble since he was born. I hope this one isn't like that."

"I had a boy, too," Laura said. Shut up, lady. I want to think about my son.

"Well, this is my third and it's no bargain, believe me. Having them isn't so easy, but bringing them up is even worse.

"What time is it?"

"Almost five. They'll be bringing up supper soon."

"When do they bring the babies?"

"After visiting hours. I wish they'd skip that feeding. It would be nice to visit and just read until morning. We'll have enough of them soon enough."

Visiting hour. I wonder if they told Pete. I wonder how he felt. Pete—a father, The word was there, but the idea was alien. Everything seemed so strange. Laura tried to remember what it was like sitting in the court before dinner, but it all seemed too far away. She was in another world, and she did not know if she could get back to the one she had left so abruptly.

The metal covers on her dinner plates made her feel odd. The only time she'd ever been served with metal covers was on the train down to Philadelphia to meet Pete's army buddy. The whole time she had felt odd with the two of them, totally excluded from an experience they remembered, of which she had no real knowledge.

When Pete came in, she began to grin stupidly. She could not stop even when he kissed her and put some roses down.

"How was it?"

"Not bad. Did you see him?"

"Yeah. He has a lot of hair, doesn't he?"

"Um."

"He's cute, isn't he?"

"You said it!"

"Just like you, huh?"

"Think you're going to be all right?"

"No question. And you?"

"Well, I was pretty tired at the deli today, but I'll go right home and get a lot of sleep."

"Did you call your folks before you got there?"

"Oh, God, yes. They'll be here the first thing tomorrow. And I called your mother. She was cackling away. I'm surprised she's not here already." He started to laugh. "It's insane, you know. I can't stop wanting to laugh. I never felt so wonderful."

"I know just how you feel. I can't wait to look at its toes."

"Do you think they're all there?"

"Wouldn't they tell us if they weren't?"

"They're all there."

Pete took Laura's hand and counted her fingers. "Like mother, like son," he said. He hugged her.

Pete's mother and father visited the next day. Jane sat regally, lush, immaculate, perfectly arranged. Laura sweated, wrinkled, in contrast to the cool, starched woman.

"We thought you might consider staying with us for a while, Laura."

Where would I hide my bras?

"It would give Pete a chance to save some money and get ahead a little. I mean, it's so hard for him to have to support a family and maintain your apartment and keep his mind on his school work. I mean, we have so much room. . . . Of course, the decision is up to you two, but if I were you, I think I'd want to make things easier for my husband."

Laura looked at Pete, waiting for him to answer. If he was as angry as he had been when Bobby raised the same consideration, he gave no sign of it. The silence lengthened. Pete's father smiled nervously and cleared his throat. Pete's mother sat in icy tranquillity.

Laura had once seen a Sargent painting. The painted woman sat permanently graceful, nuanced by white on white, her beauty overwhelming the already beautiful room of the museum. Laura thought of the painting and the fascination she had felt with the baby's face last night.

"I don't think—that is, we appreciate the offer—but

you know, a baby. It's bound to be messy. There are so many things. . . ."

"Laura, you seem to forget I had a child. I know just what's involved; perhaps even more than you—"

"Jane," Pete's father said, "don't rush them. We've been talking it over and figuring it out, but they haven't had a chance to talk about it or figure it out for themselves. Give them a chance. There's no rush, is there?"

Pete shifted closer to his parents. It seemed to Laura the three of them were moving beyond a wooden panel, upright in their chairs, studying her, judging her. She knew she would be found guilty.

"We have to give the baby a name," she said to Pete, urgently, irrelevantly. "We have to decide it now."

"I thought we had decided on Emanuel, after your dad, if it was a boy."

Laura looked timidly at her mother-in-law, but Jane was determinedly not going to interfere.

"Emanuel it will be then. Emanuel Basse."

"It's a nice name," Pete's father said. "Manny, we'll call him Manny. It's friendlier. Oh, won't we have fun with Manny. Won't it be fun to see him come running when Grandpa comes home. Hey, Pete, Jane—that sounds pretty good, doesn't it? Grandpa."

"And how does Grandma feel?" Pete asked, smiling fondly at his mother.

"Perfect," she said.

After they left, Pete said, "So what do you think, Laura? Think we should move over there?"

"How could we be natural? Manny couldn't even get to know us because we couldn't be ourselves. How could we relax and just talk and fool around, you know. Just be ourselves."

"I don't see why not, Laura. It isn't as though we really planned to have him. It was kind of a shock at first, wasn't it? You can't turn around now and say we should just settle into accepting it when we've been given a second chance, you might say. And why couldn't I be natural? They're not strangers. They're my mother and father, for God's sake. That's who we're talking about. My mother and father."

"Well, they're not my mother and father. And they're not Manny's either. Can't you just see your mother washing and ironing his polo shirts every five minutes? Suppose he wants to play outside and it's muddy or something. How do you think we'd feel about that damned ironed polo shirt?"

"I wish I knew where you get your ridiculous ideas from. Don't you think I ever got dirty when I was a kid? You act as though my mother were some kind of Craig's wife. There's nothing wrong with wanting to be reasonably clean. Maybe we don't feel as strongly about it as she does, but that's hardly a basis for making going to college so damn hard—and the money—God, the money. Be practical, Laura. Don't be so childish. We're talking about a second chance to get started. Besides, you saw how pleased Dad was. They'd love having us. It couldn't be bad for Manny to grow up with love, could it? Look at it that way."

"How do you think my mother would feel? It would be like she's an outsider."

"I'm thinking of you, Laura. I'm thinking you're not so crazy about doing housework and you're always worrying you're not doing it right. I'm thinking it would be just great, great, just great to have some money again. . . ."

"And what do you think for Manny? Don't we owe him something?"

"Even you can't feel my folks' home is a bad place for him. He'll have more than we can ever give him."

"It's not right. It doesn't seem right. It doesn't feel right."

"That's not an answer. That's a reaction."

"But that's the way you live, isn't it? By reaction. '

"Not for big things—unless you're a kid. For important things, you've got to figure it out."

"You sound just like your father."

"Well, it's not a bad way to sound. He's always done right by us. He made a good living and worked hard."

"Is that what you think I want from you?"

"It has to be a big part of it."

Laura suddenly felt very tired. "All right. If you want to move over there, we will."

Pete looked at her coldly.

"That's just like you. Never finish—never really solve the problem. Just give in all of a sudden."

"I didn't know I was like that."

"Well, you do now," he said bitterly. "And you know you don't want to move. You'll be sullen and unhappy. Who needs that! We'll stay where we are."

Laura could not quite follow what happened. One moment she felt Pete's fury, and the next she saw him relax, slouch confidently in his chair.

"It was the money, Laura. The money was getting me down. I don't really want to live with my folks again. Let Manny live with his own imperfect parents, and if he runs to Grandpa, let it be because they're coming to visit."

"Are you sure, Pete?"

"No, of course not; but I know I'd have trouble making a pass at you in my mother's house. So with money on one side, and you on the other, and Manny in between in any case, I guess it's decided."

"You don't seem too happy about it."

"It's not perfect."

When he was going, Laura was unexpectedly afraid he would not kiss her and talk about coming back. The enormity of the problems she would face without him shocked her into crawling for his reassurance. She hated herself as she clutched his arm and whispered, "See you tomorrow?" She hated him when he shrugged his shoulders and said, "I guess I have to." Even his smile did not soften the words.

Emanuel did not seem to enjoy his bottle that night. He took a few sips and cried. Laura put him over her shoulder and patted him tenderly, but he continued to cry. She patted him a little harder, but he could not belch. She had an impulse to throw him against the wall and visualized his head spattering, membranes, hair, mucous. Horrified, she cradled him against her, crooning to him, rocking him.

When the nurse took him back to the nursery, Laura got up and washed herself. She changed her nightgown and put perfume on. As she went to sleep, she thought about the day and the night before, and dusk in the court before labor; but she hid the memory of her impulse from herself.

After: 4

NERVOUSLY, I DROVE Larry back to college. In defense at my tension, I guess, he slept most of the way. We had a quiet trip.

I waited for two days, pretending to explore the campus, but Pete did not call. He would not, after all, come for me. Clearly, I would have to return alone.

Agony obscured my view of the yellow-lined, black roads. I saw the Pennsylvania farms, beginning green—the silos, silent against the cloudless horizon—only in postscript. My pain was punctuated by the machinery of American travel convenience at twenty-two-mile intervals. Gas, Fresca, gum; wastepaper baskets rarely used.

I passed a Buick and saw children fighting in the back seat. I saw barefoot young people in a red Mustang. I could barely see a waitress at a snack bar, hearing through a tunnel her "Have a safe trip."

At six, before darkness set in, I stopped at a motel—inspected for cleanliness—convenient to the turnpike—the strips of paper guaranteeing toilet sterility—the motel-wall painting guaranteeing unity of monochromism—fifteen to twenty-two dollars for the privacy of emptiness—direct dial phones, TV—with the full understanding the management claims no responsibility for personal loss.

I: not knowing what to do.

I had an image of a heavy truck behind me. The driver was slowly shifting gears, ready to move into third. The cab was too high; his view was too constricted. He could not see me. It would be easy for me to slow down, to be crushed beneath the massive, uncaring wheels; yet I moved, obediently, automatically out of his way, so he could accelerate and go where he had to go.

The next day, I left the highway. I drove the side roads and stopped near one of the still farmhouses. I looked at the landscape, rolling out quietly as far as I could see. I drove, following the meandering roads, safe in sunshine dryness, empty of other transportation.

The hurt never abated. I was desolate.

I stopped again at a motel and sat for a long time on the edge of the empty bed. I realized no one knew where I was. Only I knew. I could see what the restaurant looked like. I could taste the food. I had the opportunity to have the experience. I would have to be courageous.

I took off my skirt and blouse, put on stockings and high heels and my green dress that never wrinkled. I sprayed Givenchy on my wrists. Never quite ready, I self-consciously walked into the restaurant. It was a bright restaurant decorated with sprays of plastic greenery. I wanted to dust the dull green plastic in this first restaurant into which I had ever walked alone.

I ordered a chicken-salad sandwich and a Bloody Mary, the most adult order I could imagine. I choked slightly on a piece of lettuce. The gratuitous potato chips were arid; their coarse salt dehydrating. I gulped at the Bloody Mary, wondering if the silent, commonplace couple opposite me thought I was a drunk; wondering how one found a way to speak to strangers during a long, long trip; wondering why, when we celebrated Georgie's last birthday in a crowded French restaurant, seated immediately next to strangers, I had noticed no one but our group, heard only our conversation. I moved to feel Pete's thigh next to mine, but there was only empty space.

I carefully figured out the tip before paying my bill, leaving the coins in an orderly pyramid of nickels and dimes.

As I walked back to my motel room, I decided I would go directly home the next day. I could not avoid the clear knowledge of our separation any longer. No matter how strange, how unbelievable, how irrational, Pete and I were separated. No husband lets his wife walk unprotected into a restaurant.

I cried for a long time that night, hiding my face with the pillow so no one who might be in the next room could hear me. I slept, and dreamed I was driving around until I parked the car by the side of a field. I walked into the grove nearby. My heart pounded. I could not understand why I wanted to go into the strange place.

A Pete grows on every tree. His tight curly hair is the bark, seaming and browning the trunk. He hangs, a shrivelled apple from one tree, a one-eyed blue monster on another. His phallus writhes in weeping-willow formation, overhanging a frothy stream.

I move through the forest directly toward the phallus. Pete's hands reach up from the moss and ferns to trip me. His legs kick, his toenails scratch my arms, my neck, my eyes. Momentarily blinded, I panic and falter.

114

I reach out to keep myself from falling. The hairy bark is slippery. I cannot grasp it.

I pull my hands away, arching my back to maintain balance. A current of pain sends my back muscle into spasm. I cry out with pain. The Pete trees' branches blow in the sudden wind. They whip my sounds away. My screams are silenced.

A cloud covers the Pete forest. Dark silence. I keep moving, scratching through the Pete twigs and moss and hairy leaves to the phallus. It writhes out of my reach. The tree cringes against the frothy river, away from me. In the silence. In the dark. In the nightmare shapes of Pete transformed.

I awoke. My body was drenched with sweat. My back ached. Real shapes emerged. The lamp, my own shaking hands. The shade hit the window as a rainy breeze misted the sill.

I thought the shade was the only sound in the room. Then I heard my breathing. The bed squeaked as I turned painfully on my stomach. The sheets rustled slightly. I moved my legs against them, listening to the sound. A bird whistled sharply. A dog barked. The clock ticked. The ceiling creaked. It was not silent after all.

I showered the nightmare away, but the images lingered so that I did not want to call Pete to tell him I was coming. I did not want to hear his voice. I just went; and that's how, I think, I found out, finally, why he did not want to be a husband and father anymore.

I arrived home about two. The smell of burnt coffee saturated the kitchen. A loaf of bread and a milk container were open on the table. There were unwashed cups on the stove and in the sink. A hamburger congealed in a frying pan on top of the refrigerator.

Upstairs, the bed was unmade. The blankets hung

crazily over the foot of the bed. Pete's socks and underwear were on the floor. One slipper was exactly in the middle of the bathroom. The shower faucet was dripping.

I was disgusted. I went downstairs to clean the kitchen first. I opened the refrigerator and threw out bits of moldy cheese and tightened the mayonnaise jar lid and moved the half-unwrapped butter to a covered dish. Then I went upstairs and made the bed and scrubbed out the bathtub. I dragged out the vacuum cleaner and cleaned behind the bureau and on top of the drapes.

Then I methodically went through every one of Pete's suit pockets and every one of his bureau drawers, looking coldly. First I found a box, hidden under his red polo shirt. The box had a safe-deposit key in it. In another drawer, I found a bottle of champagne.

I put them both on top of the bureau, studying them. Then I went to a back closet where I kept Pete's old clothes, and there I found a white jumpsuit and a blue shirt with ruffles on the wrist. I took them out and put them on the bureau with the key and the champagne bottle. My heart started to beat erratically. I felt cold, bitterly, hurtingly cold, and perversely I started to sweat. For a minute, I went back to the Pete forest.

I could hear Pete saying, "I don't want to be a husband anymore." I looked at that white, probably clinging, jumpsuit and tried to see what man would wear it and where.

So when Pete came home, I said to him directly, "You're a homosexual."

"Yes," he said, and lay down on the couch and closed his eyes.

116

❧ *Before: 5*

AFTER PETE GRADUATED from law school, he spent much of his spare time shopping. He came home with thin brown bags filled with button-down shirts and ties and belts. He and his father went to buy suits at a store to which his father had always gone. Laura could not tell why one shirt was so different from another. She saw fabric and color, but not cut. Pete assured her each suit was quite different, and well worth the price, which, thanks to his father's friend, was always at least 40 percent less than it should have been.

Laura enjoyed watching Pete fuss with himself. He studied a small pimple on his face, squeezing it firmly. It must go. She squealed, he would give himself an infection, experiencing a maternal, what-a-little-boy-you-are, glow.

She felt somewhat less pleasure as he bought a tie to match his brown shirt, another to match his tan shirt, a third to match his beige shirt. The shade differences were so tiny. What difference did it really make?

Pete's weight was a constant topic of conversation.

He was too fat. Where? Where was he too fat? Look at that bulge. Just pinch above his waist. How could you miss it? Laura missed it, but she learned to count calories and assured him his whole, entire meal was maybe one thousand calories. Nothing for such a growing boy.

"Don't be such a wise guy," he said, pushing the baked potato aside.

"It's filled with potassium. Healthy. Good."

"Spinach is better."

"I suppose. But meat and potatoes—bread and butter. Those are the basic dishes of mankind."

"That kind of man I don't have to be. He's too damn fat."

"I never saw you fat."

"That's because you see what you want to see. Skinnies like you don't know how careful people have to be."

Pete and Hilda had a wonderful time talking about their diets. A pound off was a pride gained. Bobby, who of all of them should have dieted, munched away at peanuts.

"They could get boring," he said to Laura.

"They are boring," she said.

"But they are beautiful, aren't they?" Bobby pointed out.

"Why does everybody in the United States of America feel they have to weigh ten pounds less than they do?"

Pete and Hilda knew why. Bobby did not care.

Pete and Laura played their own version of Jack Sprat in another arena. As meticulous, careful, fussing, even rigid as he was about his appearance, Pete was careless and slovenly about discarding items. He carefully hung up his slacks at night, checking for stains, tears, catches on the fabric. Then he left his socks under the bed. He threw his shorts on the window sill, left a coffee cup on the bathroom floor.

"Who goes to the bathroom with coffee? It's contradictory," Laura complained.

"It's a long sit. Gives me something to do."

"Why don't you read magazines like everyone else?"

"Interferes with my thinking. I get my best thinking done in the bathroom."

"Coffee in the bathroom. The new thinking man's drink."

"The new man's thinking drink."

"What makes you a new man?"

"All that thinking."

"What is it you're thinking about?"

"The new man."

"I haven't even found out about the old man yet."

"I'll wait for you to catch up."

Laura took Pete's coffee cup to the sink. Sweet man. Always waiting for her.

She didn't leave her cups or stockings or underthings on the floor. She put everything away immediately. On the other hand, she never knew she had a stain or tear in her skirt until she put the skirt on. Pete's ways were better.

Laura wore turned-up dungarees and Pete's old shirts and sweaters. She had one pair of black high heels for which she bought a matching good dress. She rarely bought lingerie. Her jewelry consisted of two pairs of earrings and a pin Pete bought her for her birthday—a green stone in an antique ebony setting. Because she did not like green and black, she wore it only occasionally.

They both bought clothes for Manny, and books, and toys. He liked model cars and trucks, liked to line them up across the living room into the bedroom.

When Sol was born, Laura hemmed Manny's overalls and Cloroxed his old polo shirts. When Larry was born, she could buy new ones.

Pete and Laura bought a two-story stucco in an older neighborhood of Long Island. On a slight incline, pachysandra and steps curved up to the front door. At first, Laura and Pete gave Manny and Sol the large front bedroom and Larry the smaller one, reserving for themselves the bedroom next to the hall bathroom. When Larry complained he was lonely at night, they moved him in with the other boys. When Manny complained it was too crowded, they finished the third floor and gave him a dorm room. Sol thought having one's own room was a terrific idea, so he opted to take the one Larry vacated. Ultimately, Larry enjoyed the solitary splendor of the largest bedroom in the house.

Occasionally, Pete thought it would be a good idea for him and Laura to switch bedrooms with Larry. By that time, no one had the energy to move the furniture and clothes, pictures, and plants, around again. Thus the room arrangements were final, if not perfect.

Pete set up the TV in the basement, and Laura decorated the downstairs front windows with asparagus ferns, huge geraniums, wandering Jews, begonias that bloomed all year with delicate white and pink blossoms. Pete put up a basketball hoop over the garage door, and Laura planted a lilac bush, roses, and honeysuckle along their long side yard. She planted a pussy-willow tree so it was in direct line from their bedroom window.

Pete and Laura shopped for weeks until they found a dining-room table that could remain stationary to seat six and open to seat twenty. When Laura looked at the rich brown table with oddly shaped natural knotholes on it, she said they had found the end of the rainbow. Pete

120

said it was an expensive end. Then he put his arms around Laura and held her close to him. Laura felt they were very happy.

They planned a party.

"We'll only have champagne," Pete said. "We'll bubble our way into the New Year. Let's invite the whole neighborhood."

"I'd rather have a smaller party, Pete. Close, you know, intimate."

"So—that means my folks and your mom, Hilda, Bobby, Lilli, and Georgie. Think Darcy will come?"

"Yes—but—let's leave the old folks out."

"Well, I'll have to run over and see my mother early in the evening then."

"I know. I thought you could take the kids and that would give me a chance to get everything ready— including my face."

"Um—we'll see about the kids. I can move faster without them. It'll be less complicated all around."

"Well, not for me."

"Oh, yes, it will. What's good for me is good for you."

"Of course."

At the New Year's Eve party, Bobby drank six glasses of champagne and lurched at Darcy. She semicircled away from him. He fell clumsily on the couch, from which, dazed, he looked at them.

"Darcy is really very pretty," he said, solemnly.

"Oh, for God's sake," Georgie said in disgust.

Hilda giggled. "He never stops. Big talker, that's my Bobby. He'd drop dead if he ever caught her." She smiled affectionately at her big talker. "Go take a nap, Bobby. You're going to be a mess, as it is, tomorrow."

Bobby obediently wavered upstairs.

Darcy picked at the hem of her skirt.

"Don't you mind?" she asked Hilda.

"He doesn't mean anything by it," Hilda said. "He's just playing."

Laura admired Hilda's good nature.

Pete proposed a toast to the lechers of the world. Georgie thought that was not very funny. Lilli thought Georgie ought to stop being such a prude. Darcy thought they ought to drink to Lillian Hellman. Pete said it was easy to admire her but difficult to lech after her.

Laura said they all ought to eat something. Pete said enthusiastically, "And we'd better have something to drink with it. Her cooking is not entirely trustworthy, you know." He took a bottle of champagne, put it between his knees, and started to pop the cork.

"Watch out," Darcy said nervously.

"What for? Let the corks fall where they may. It's a new year!"

The cork flew, with a great noise, onto the bookcase, ricocheted off the side wall, and hit the fireplace screen, pushing it into the fire. A spray of embers bloomed.

"Fourth of July in winter," Pete said happily.

"Maybe he ought to go to sleep with Bobby," Hilda suggested.

"Did he wear a black lace bra?" Pete asked.

Hilda snapped her fingers. "I knew he forgot something tonight."

"Too bad," Pete said, "maybe next year."

It was the time of their lives when no one questioned there would be a next year.

The year brought trouble to Georgie and Lilli. He lost his teaching job because he refused to sign the loyalty oath the school system demanded.

"My loyalty was proved in the war, damn it. No one is going to tell me if I'm loyal or not.

"Stinkin' bastards. They really just want me to be too

afraid to organize the union. They're not interested in loyalty—they're interested in money!"

Pete's mother and father, tight-lipped, asked Pete if he intended to keep seeing Georgie and Lilli. Pete told them never to ask him such a question again. Laura's mother said that's what comes of butting into everyone's business. She told Georgie and Lilli to move in with her until they got back on their feet again.

They stayed with Laura's mother for a couple of months. Lilli's smile shrank and Georgie's hair looked thinner, dryer. Dandruff flaked his shoulders. He brushed at it constantly. Eventually Georgie took a job selling real estate in New Jersey. He and Lilli later moved to one of the new split-levels in an area everyone now referred to as suburban.

Georgie would not speak of the situation, but Lilli told Laura he had no intention of stopping the fight for democracy. He sued the school system and persisted in litigation, using the union's lawyers. Laura was ashamed at her relief Pete did not have to be involved.

Darcy said Georgie was a true hero. Laura, agreeing, knew she was a true coward.

Pete taught the boys how to ride bikes, running alongside them, laughing, until they found balance and he could throw himself down, satisfied. He taught them to hit a ball and to steal an extra base. Ducking for apples with Sol's friends—at what became an annual Halloween party—he almost drowned. He thought the whole thing so damned funny. At Christmas, they invited everyone they knew for a huge Good-Housekeeping reciped buffet and gave out Vogue-wrapped presents.

Laura's mother baby-sat for them, watching TV with the kids in silent pleasure, while Pete and Laura drove into the city and saw Rodgers and Hammerstein musicals and Arthur Miller plays. They went to the Washington H.S. chamber music concerts with Darcy. They met Hilda and Bobby in Italian restaurants. They visited on alternate Sundays with Lilli and Georgie, and Pete's mother and father.

Georgie thought it would be a great idea if Pete and Bobby would join him and two other guys for a biweekly poker game. Lilli and Hilda, Darcy and Laura, could play bridge together so no one would feel left out, and the boys could play as late as they liked. It was a perfect arrangement for everyone.

Except Pete hated it. On poker nights he grumbled, "If I have to hear about Bobby's dumb night watchmen once more, I'm going to send Bobby to an eternal night." He did not want any more real-estate investment tips from Georgie. As for the obnoxious guys Georgie called friends, if he were Georgie, he'd become a hermit.

When Hilda and Bobby suggested it might be a good idea if each couple put in two dollars a poker night until they had enough for a night on the town, Pete said sure—fine idea. The next poker night he had to work late. He had a stomachache the newly scheduled night. He had to rewrite a brief suddenly, after that date. He didn't think it was a good idea to leave the kids with a baby-sitter with Larry still feverish from an ear infection.

"So we'll ask them to play here," Laura said, guilty she had not considered Larry's condition.

"No, it's too far for Georgie and his friends. It's not worth the trouble."

"What are you talking about? You do it all the time."

"Yes—and it's not worth the trouble."

"You mean, you want to let it go. You don't want to be part of the group?"

124

"That's right. I don't."

Laura felt someone had taken her candy away. "But why? It's so much fun to be all together, to look forward to a night on the town."

"If you want to go to town, I'll take you. Only I don't want to pay for it through long hours when I know what everyone is going to say before they say it." Pete suddenly stretched his feet out. "Oh, God, why didn't I find a job where I could sit like the rest of you do," he smirked, falsetto, imitating Bobby. "Sure," he said, in a louder voice, brushing frantically at his shoulders, "I sit on a chaise lounge showing the Ralstons their latest mansion." Adding gratuitously, "Your brother. We-ell, maybe I'll just see you," he parodied, "maybe we'll just up the stakes a little—say ten dollars. Separate the men from the boys."

Pete brooded for a minute. "Why do people think ten dollars—even one thousand—can separate the men from the boys?"

"You take it too seriously, Pete. It's just a game. It's a way for people to have fun."

"I don't think you take it seriously enough, Laura. It's not a game. It's a group process."

"I don't understand why you have to be so mean. You're going to spoil the whole thing."

Angry and disappointed, she spent a day or two slamming things around and not talking to him. Pete didn't seem to care much, so after a while she cooled off. Wanting to make up, she asked him, "Which are you in the Great Separation—man or boy?"

Pete's twinkle delighted her.

"I want to be a man but be counted as a boy."

"How do you do that?"

"By buying a little yellow convertible when the first

125

wrinkle appears—and speeding around a lot. Of course, no one will see your wrinkles then because you'll be hiding your face and screaming at me to go slower."

"Maybe I'll be used to it by then. You can't tell."

"Afraid I can."

Caught up in the gossamer of everyday routine, they were unaware the wisps were becoming threads, the threads ropes. The grocery budget burgeoned into a monster of cookies, soda, roast beef, fruit, washing powder. The doctor became a pediatric specialist for Manny's broken toe; the dentist, an orthodontist for Larry's misbite; Saturdays, an endless series of errands.

It seemed to be happening to everyone. Appointments had to be made weeks in advance because baby-sitting arrangements were required before anyone could get together.

Hilda stopped working, searched for a house, found one to her satisfaction, and nine months to the day they moved in, had a little girl.

Georgie and Lilli adopted a little girl at about the same time, and two months later, Lilli was pregnant. Laura's mother never stopped smiling.

Darcy bought a bookstore in partnership with Patrick, a heavyset, middle-aged man with a deep, reverberating voice. They conferred with Georgie about location, Bobby about the bookkeeping, Pete about the legalities of partnership. By the time the conferences were over, Patrick was an established part of their group. He was naturally invited to the briss for Georgie's son.

"No wonder you Jewish men are so close to your mothers," Patrick boomed, "they could arrange to have you done in before you were two weeks old. It would be all over right then."

Laura thought he was stupid. Pete thought he was sympathetic.

"What's to be sympathetic about? It's such a minor thing. It's the symbolism that's big, not the—" Laura didn't know how to finish. Pete did:

"Cutting. That's the family jewels being cut. If you were a man, you'd know what a big thing it was."

"Anyway, it isn't the mother who decides it. It's the men who are in charge. I never even heard of one mother being there when it's done."

"Ah—but you're Jewish through the mother. She tells the men—make this one a Jew. Put the mark on him: cut him!"

"Circumsize him is more what a mother would say. She'd never say 'Cut him!'"

"That's because you're a softie, Laura—and I'll grant you, so is Lilli. But Darcy I'm not so sure about—and any number of the other women. Lots and lots of them, in fact."

"I'll be damned!" Laura said. "I never dreamt you felt that way."

One week's routine was broken when Pete told Laura he would be going to Maryland for three days for the NLA's executive meeting.

"We'll miss you, honey. Do you think you can get back in time for dinner Friday night?"

"I don't think you realize what an honor it is to be asked to serve."

"I'm delighted for you; I just wondered about Friday because your folks are coming over."

"Well, I can't be sure. I'll try to get home by late afternoon, but you know how it is. A group always gets together afterwards. Sometimes I think more real work is done there anyway."

She really did not know. There were no association conferences in her life. Laura was embarrassed by her lack of knowledge, sophistication. Pete was growing, awarded honors she did not know were honors.

She began to consider finishing her work for her degree. When Larry started kindergarten, she asked Pete to teach her to drive. She was incompetent, jerking the car to a stall, shifting too slowly from second to third. Pete told her every idiot in the country could drive and so could she. She asked him to buy an automatic shift, but he said driving an automatic was too boring. Somehow, though, she passed her test. Knowing it was a fluke, she transferred her credits to a college within suburban limits.

She went to classes two nights a week, after the dishes were done, driving herself, peering forward toward the windshield, rigid, so that her neck muscles hurt her for weeks. Sometimes it was nightmarish. The juxtaposition of courses with mealtimes, arranging for a sitter, checking weather reports lest she be trapped on a snowy night in school.

Laura sat in the attached desk and chair in the classroom, fighting sleepiness, striving not to think about the rash Sol was developing. She read the assigned material over and over again, listened to the voice of the professor, tried to understand.

The classroom lights cast sallow overtones. Everyone seemed to have dark circles under lusterless eyes. Papers were an insurmountable burden. Work in the library was difficult to arrange. Often getting there and back took longer than the time she could actually spend when she finally arrived.

It always seemed to be cold. The wind blew across the dusty campus, flinging papers at the raw wood and aluminum of the new buildings constantly being erected.

Isolated from the young, with their life buoyancy, she persisted doggedly; her mind moved cautiously through the material presented to her. She questioned and found no answers and finally learned not to question. After that, she enjoyed her classes. Because she found she had a strong aptitude for languages, she majored in Russian and German literature.

She sat doing her homework while the boys did theirs—books, papers, pens, dictionaries, records, notes, in a happy mess on the table with milk, coffee, and cookies so they could all snack and study.

She worried about every exam and studied carefully for each. She handed in her term papers on the due date, fretting until the papers were returned. Why had she handed it in with such a stupid statement on page 4! such a clumsy translation on page 10!

Late at night, after the boys were asleep, her housework and school work done, she and Pete read in bed, talking about his clients or the superior he did not like at the firm.

"Why don't you open your own office?" Laura told him. "I'll be working soon."

"You—how much money can you make? Between the sitters and the clothes you'll need, you'll bring in enough to pay the telephone bill, that's all. And then we'll need another car for you sooner or later. It's hard enough now when you use it."

Laura felt guilty and moved closer to him. "I guess we did do a lot backwards. Even Hilda saw that before Manny was born. But won't it be nice to have the degrees and the kids and the cars some day. We just weren't very orderly, I guess, but we'll still get it all."

"Let's go to sleep."

"Do we have to?"

"Yes, I've got a long day tomorrow. I've got to see my mother in between the Johnsons' tax problems. She's worried about my Dad again."

"I'm sorry."

Laura wanted Pete to stroke her back and her breasts, but she did not know how to tell him. It seemed wrong now.

They had sex on weekends, after the parties or the theatre or the dinners. Laura did not feel much like sex then. She often awoke Sunday morning sensuous, restless, with confused dream-memories of huge rooms with tiled floors and far-up windows. Pete liked to get up and play tennis. It was unfair for her to move against him then.

Darcy bought Laura a copy of *Fanny Hill.* "I never thought I'd live to see the day this was on public sale," she said. "Maybe progress is possible after all."

Laura read it secretly, feeling ridiculous as she hid it behind the emergency canned food shelf. She did not know what to do with it. It never occurred to her to throw a book out; yet she could hardly leave it in the bookcase for the boys to see.

She remembered the details of the book, though, and one day she went into the college bookstore and bought a marriage manual. She only had the nerve to do it because it was on the recommended list for a course on The Family.

She read with great interest of the various positions described, especially the hints about prolonging foreplay. With some trepidation, she read it openly one night to Pete.

"Have you ever heard of this before?" she said, reading aloud a section describing ice on the testicles for shock sensual value. "Can you imagine getting an icebag before getting into bed?"

"Sounds disgusting."

"Don't you think it might be fun to try some of these other things though?"

"Don't be such a kid. That's only fantasy. People don't really do those things."

"They don't?" she said, disappointed.

"Of course not."

Subtly, she did try to prolong their foreplay—not turning when Pete caressed her; feeling backhanded for his penis, stroking him more slowly, less rhythmically. Inexorably, though, his rapid, terribly serious urgency would trigger her own need, and she would turn over involuntarily, reaching for him, putting him into her, and he would thrust and she would lift and they would come together.

Always, afterward, his total relaxation, his loving gestures while holding her, his murmured endearments brought her an equal, enormous pleasure.

Sometimes it struck her as odd that after all their years together, she still could never tell Pete directly she was feeling sexy but had to wait for him to initiate their lovemaking. Perhaps in sublimation, she hugged and kissed Pete during the evening. She liked to touch his hand or walk so that she was slightly behind him, pressing against his shoulder. One day, he told her fondly, "Honey, nobody in the world could ever give you enough affection. You're a little neurotic, you know that?"

She did not question his judgment, and she believed she was honest when, surveyed for a course, she checked off sex life as highly satisfactory.

Pete's father continued not to feel well. Pete's

mother, always regally plump, started to lose weight. Her shoulder muscles hung in flabs as her weight drained in response to Pete's father's illness.

Pete drove his mother and father to the doctor's office for X rays and blood tests. Often he could not, as a consequence, be home for dinner. Laura and the boys did not feel at home when Pete was not there. It was as though an arm had been pulled from its joint. They felt, in fact, disjointed, with Pete's chair a blind socket.

When his father was hospitalized, Pete visited his mother every day. Frequently, he slept over. "I just can't leave her alone now."

He busied himself with the running of the delicatessen, as well as attending to his own practice. He checked his father's will for loopholes without mentioning anything to his mother. He was always tired. He sat sometimes on the edge of the bed trying to work up the energy to undress. Laura knelt before him and unlaced his shoes. He did not seem to notice.

Laura felt hurt, shut out. She went to the hospital with him whenever she could arrange for a sitter, so she could be part of it. It seemed to make no difference to Pete whether she came or not.

He sat in the hospital room looking at his father. His father was swollen with edema. His urine flowed brown-yellow into a bag. His eyelids fluttered. He appeared to breathe through his swollen belly.

Once, Pete took his father's hand, but his father pulled it away. He needed to scratch his face. Pete brought his father soft cotton pajamas the morning his father died. Pete looked at the unopened box in his hand.

"My father never opened my present," he said.

He stayed next to his mother all the time. His mother screamed to his dead father, "How could you do this to me! I never thought you would leave me like this." Pete sobbed while trying to stop his mother's hysteria.

132

Once he spoke of his feelings to Laura. On the anniversary of his father's death, as the stone was unveiled, Pete murmured, "We were just getting to know each other. Now it's too late."

Laura said nothing; she thought Pete knew his father quite well.

Pete's mother said, when they were almost finished with the mourning period, Pete should not sleep over anymore. Pete and his mother talked a long time in the kitchen. They decided to sell the store and organize a trust for her so she need never worry about money.

Pete found her an apartment near them. He moved her himself, renting a drive-yourself truck. He said he did not want any stranger handling his parents' things.

Pete's mother became hysterical again on the day of the move. This time Pete did not sob with her. He constantly assured her he would always be around, always be available. He kept his arm around her, helping her into the car, making sure she was safely in, before going around to the driver's side.

"It would have been nice if you said Laura and I will always be available," Laura said, later.

"Don't be so petty, for Christ's sake," Pete said irritably.

Laura apologized.

Pete did not make too much of a fuss about Laura's graduation. "We all knew you could do it," he said, kissing her, while simultaneously relegating her work to easy, automatic, foregone conclusion.

Manny bought her a record he liked to hear. At dinner Sol gave her a Hostess cupcake "for the graduate with the mostest"; Larry gave her a music box. Lilli called and said they were proud of her. Her mother asked her if she had to take any more classes. Hilda said she admired Laura. She knew she never would have found the time. Darcy gave her the name of a university press that needed a line editor who could also act as translator from time to time.

Laura went to work in a small, dusty office. She had a desk, a leather chair, and bookcases. She put a grape ivy on the bookcase and a philodendron on her desk. Every morning she checked their moisture and rotated them toward the small window. At lunchtime, she walked across the campus to eat in the cavernous dining commons, made cheerful by the green salad, and red apples next to yellow bananas.

She made friends with the Chinese translator, Soo, a diminutive young woman, who spent her solitary nights writing short stories in Chinese and sending them for publication to Hong Kong. She met Christine, an assistant professor of Slavic languages, a huge, solid woman with incongruous Veronica Lake gray hair falling over one eye. She had lunch occasionally with Jay, the head of accounting, a shortish man with large brown eyes who complained incessantly of his insomnia. Jay ate prunes for dessert. No matter how carefully Laura watched, she never saw him spit out a pit. They materialized on his spoon. Then he solemnly placed them on the side of his plate, five precisely spaced dots.

Laura tolerated the editing and relished the translation: working on the general pattern of meaning first, then fussing, searching for the specific, closest nuance of an individual word.

Translation assignments stimulated her for days and kept her patient with her other duties, while waiting for another.

Assignments were made by her supervisor, Fred, a tall, gaunt man with a vague resemblance to a beardless Abe Lincoln.

She cooked Sunday nights—meatloaf, chickens, pot

roasts, so dinner was easy to prepare when she returned home from work. She got up early to do the laundry before she went to work. She was careful not to leave dishes unwashed before she left for work. She spent Saturday morning marketing, shopping. She reminded the boys of their music lessons, their dental appointments. She went over with them, carefully, how they were to get there and when they would be home.

Laura had little stories to tell Pete about the crazy bookkeeper who nailed his back office door shut because he could not stand people cutting through from the campus yard anymore; and the memo sent out one day from the publishing department, informing them, in six different languages, the quota for useless memos was not being met that week.

Pete told her about the embezzler he uncovered while arranging a merger of two companies and of his odd feeling of guilt at having to be the one to finger the embezzler. He told her how upset he was, in court, watching people waiting to be called; how they did not understand what was involved, were not really adequately protected. He volunteered part of his time to legal aid. Sometimes, he asked Laura to translate Spanish notes from Puerto Rican clients.

Laura was touched by his caring nature. She was not surprised when he brought home a stray dog. At first, she cringed away from his arms, smiling anxiously at the puppy he carried.

"There's no reason to be afraid, Laura. He just wants to be friends with you. I don't think he's had any friends lately."

The puppy craned its neck toward Laura, then toward Pete, its tail thumping against Pete's chest. Laura timidly reached out to pat its head. She patted its tail instead. The puppy bounded toward her. Pete laughed as she screamed. The dog ran between Pete's legs, cowering.

"He's afraid of *you*," Pete said. "Look, you terrified him."

Laura knelt down, looking at the quivering puppy mass. "He doesn't want to hurt me," she whispered.

They called the puppy Laddie. He became part of their family, thumping his tail ecstatically at anyone's presence, following Laura around routinely. She learned to avoid turning too quickly when she was cleaning because his body would be curled a speck from her feet. The family laughed when Laddie threw himself at her lap if there was a thunderstorm. Laura could feel his heart thumping hysterically as she stroked his head, trying to soothe him.

"It must be nice to be so open about one's fears," Pete said.

Laura felt Pete taught her to care beyond herself. She always knew what the answer would be when Manny asked if he could have a gerbil, or when a cat just walked in one day, and after regarding Laddie, decided he was certainly no threat. Because of Pete, there was always room for something else in their house.

When they met Hilda and Bobby, it seemed as though Pete did all the talking. There was so much to tell, so many experiences to report, to wonder about. They could not get over the insanity of the people he told them about: the wife who sued her husband because he gave a desk to his nephew, the man who shot his neighbor because he could hear him snore on a summer night.

Darcy and Pete argued about the welfare system when she came to dinner. Laura and the boys listened to them, to the passionate conviction of their loudly expressed opinions; and the days blurred for Laura into voices, words, chores, and Pete's warm, nightly, cuddling kiss and the rapid sexual satisfaction of the weekend.

They began to think it might be possible to plan a trip to Europe, but Pete was hesitant because he could not find a secretary he could trust. Just when he felt she knew the routine, she did something so stupid, so crass, he had to fire her on the spot. He could not look at such a dumb broad every day. For two or three years, he'd come storming home, furious with the about-to-be-fired secretary.

Darcy told him in no uncertain terms it was bosses like him that made an office workers' union so necessary. Pete wanted to know if she'd like the job. He would give her all the union benefits she wanted. She told him cheerfully to go to hell. He said he would have to find a decent secretary first so he could dictate his last will and testament. Laura would not be able to manage a week without instructions. She did not even know how much was left to their mortgage.

Laura started to say that was not true at all, when Darcy interrupted to ask if the insurance would not cover everything. Pete said he did not believe in it—it was a waste of money. He had no intention of going before the house was paid off and surely not before they got to Europe. And for that he needed a good secretary. Darcy still refused to take the job.

Finally, Pete went over to the law school. He checked out all the night students who might want a day job in his office if they could type and take shorthand. "Knowing how to spell is more than I can expect," he said. A tall young man took the job. He held himself very straight, ramrod-fashion, when he met Laura.

"At least I don't have to worry about you two in the office," Laura said.

"No, you don't have to worry in the office," Pete stressed. "Outside, I don't promise. Keep worrying. I like it."

"As long as you like it, I guess I don't really have to worry."

"True," he said, "and that's forever, you know. Forever. Let the lines on your face be from laughing, not worrying."

Laura studied the crow's-feet beginning to appear around her eyes.

She put herself on *Cosmopolitan's* ten-day beauty regime.

"What do you think now?" she said, sleeked up for Saturday night.

"I can see you have a great sense of humor." Pete kissed the lines around her eyes.

"God, that's nice," she said.

When Pete decided they could go to Europe, he studied *Europe on Five Dollars A Day* and announced they would spend no more than a thousand dollars on the trip. He wrote for hotel reservations, planning their itinerary through Rome and Florence and Paris. They packed the kids off to camp. Laura clung to Pete all during the plane trip, terrified. He laughed at her and held her patiently, reassuring her she was probably safer than when she was driving herself.

They ran through Rome, Laura chattering with anyone who would speak to her, exhilarated by the language, the semantics of gesture properly wedded to word. They looked at the Vatican treasures with an almost childish awe and sat in silence as Michelangelo's ceiling emerged, poetic, from their concentrated gaze.

They bought copies of the touching hands, and in Florence, one of the nude David with his penis grace-

138

fully part of his muscular, exquisite symmetry, although Laura was not sure they could hang such a frank picture on their wall at home.

It was very hot when they arrived in Paris. Laura's stomach started to bother her. Pete wanted to go for a long walk on the Champs Élysées. Because she did not want to disappoint him, they walked, in the heat, although she became increasingly uncomfortable, needing badly to go to the bathroom and then to lie down.

Pete said Montmartre would be cooler, insisting they should experience the walk up the steep hills to the cafés on top. They sat overlooking the Utrillo rooftops. Pete drank wine with obvious, total pleasure, his body in its after-sex, triumphant posture. Laura sipped at Perrier water, feeling guilty. She was wasting their time and place and opportunity to enjoy it all. When they took the funicular down the steep hill, Laura started to feel faint and clammy. Pete became upset, asking her if she was all right. She said no, she was sorry; she was not.

He called a taxi and they went back to their hotel. Laura had diarrhea and a temperature that gave her a dull, insistent headache. She sweated and shivered and thought she would die of homesickness. She wanted her own bed and she wanted to see her children. She did not tell Pete. She only said, "I'm sorry."

"Well, do you mind if I go out tonight? It looks like you'll just have to sleep this away and there's nothing much I can do but watch you."

"You're right. Go ahead. I'm sure I'll feel better in the morning."

"Sure you'll be all right?" he said then, anxiously, illogically uncertain.

"Of course. It doesn't make sense for you to waste a whole evening in Paris for this."

She snuggled down, relieved to be able to sleep, to

not make the effort to move. Pete went out quietly. She thought how different men and women were. No matter how sensible it was to realize this was no major illness, she never could have left anyone in the family to be sick alone.

❧ *After: 5*

I LOOKED AT PETE'S closed eyes, at his immobile, familiar length on the couch, at his remembered hands casually flung up against the pillow for comfort. It was not his homosexuality which stunned me. It was his withdrawal, his lack of concern for the devastating terror flooding me, his passivity to the death facing us, his manifest unwillingness to stop the destruction, to protect us.

He opened his eyes. Hard lapis lazuli on Icelandic tundra; vast empty expanses of frigid earth.

He yawned and closed his eyes again.

"God," he said, "I'm so tired."

I understood the holocaust. I had already been banished from his living world. I had already stood in the jammed, suffocating train, unknowingly moving to the extermination camps, looking at his hand pointing to the crematoria; he too bored already to give my fate any thought, the decision long since made in his head.

My voice, my smell, my movements, my hair, my mouth, my hands: the physical elements of all our years, days, moments, seconds were annoyances to him. He wanted them gone so he could sleep and, refreshed, go about his own business unhampered.

The immobile me, the stick figure forever standing upstairs in the bedroom, laughed contemptuously at the ugly nuisance looking at her husband/stranger, still not accepting that she was so unimportant, so unattractive that of course she could be left without a backward glance.

I finally realized it.

I began to howl; razors cutting my nipples; legs, yanked apart, distorted, cement jammed into my vagina; a revolting spectacle, sickening to anyone who saw me; causing anyone to edge back, away, away from the ugliness.

I was an animal, making the noises of an animal, slavering, ready to grovel; yearning, stretching to lick the hand that hit me.

Still with his eyes closed, Pete said, "I'm sorry. I can't help myself. I didn't want to hurt you but I have no choice anymore. If I have to keep living with you, I'll go crazy. I can't do it anymore. I won't do it anymore."

"Whoever asked you to do it?" I raged. "Whoever forced you? You volunteered, didn't you? Twenty-five, twenty-six years ago. A quarter of a century!" I screamed, "Why, now, suddenly?"

"I fell in love. I never fell in love before."

I became rigid. "How dare you say that to me!" I whispered.

His lack of response frustrated me beyond containment.

"You mean it was OK to use me and not tell me as long as it was convenient for you, and now I have to take the consequences of your decision?" I was appalled at that realization. An earthquake of shock reverberated through my being.

"Why didn't you tell me! How could you not tell me! What right did you have to make such decisions for my core, my . . ."

Pete sat up, impatient.

"You know very well I couldn't tell you—or anyone else. You know it as well as I do. Why don't you just stop all this? It won't do either of us any good. I found someone I can love. I can be myself, the real me, and I'm going to. I'm not living this farce a minute longer. I'm not going to be a hypocrite and live with your rules."

I looked around for the judge, bewilderment stopping my hysteria. I became calm, almost intellectually curious, anxious only to understand this unthinkable thinking.

"What are my rules?" I asked, leaning forward eagerly, a student, ready to learn.

"Come home every night, for one," Pete said promptly. "Buy dull gray clothes for another. Remember Mother's Day. Match the curtains and rugs. It's boring; it suffocates me: I don't want to be part of it anymore."

"I don't understand," I said helplessly, a retarded student after all. "Those hardly seem such terrible 'rules' that—"

"You'll never understand," he interrupted. "Just leave me alone. That's all I ask. Is that too much to ask? You can have anything you want—the house, the car, anything. Just leave me out of it."

I jumped up, filled with an energy I could not handle. I started to walk aimlessly to the dining room, walking with increasing speed around the dining-room table. As I accelerated around the table, I went down to the basement, rummaging behind the washing-machine powders where a thick, knotted rope lay. I trod boldly behind Pete's insufferable relaxed body and flung the rope around his neck, a surge of strength rendering him helpless, unable to move anything but his arms and legs, futilely flailing as I garroted, strangled the throat from which his words had emerged, cutting them off through eternity—silenced forever. Still walking around the table, in a half trot now, I found a cleaver in the second kitchen drawer and hacked, vicious cuts, slashing, chopping until I dug out his Adam's apple and jammed it into his ear so he could no longer speak and only he could hear his aborted words.

My heart pushed out of me, thumping across the room, a small tornado, smashing, into his heart—breaking his heart into unimportant, minute pieces of flesh, insubstantial drops of blood staining him, while his fingernails tore at the gaping hole where his heart had been, trying to stem the flow of diminishing life: turning blue, putrifying; dying, dead, vanquished, a forgotten plague.

Horrified by the reality of my murderous impulses, terrified they were out of control, I ran outside, running past the houses on our block, ducking the gypsy moths on the trees. Gasping, I slowed to a walk, found myself on the avenue, looking at furs displayed in a window incongruously located next to a pizza place. I went into the library and read a magazine I did not see. I walked to Macy's, stopping in the men's department.

I touched the white handkerchiefs and green ties. I ruffled through the sports jackets, the flannels, the dacrons, until I saw a leather, fringed jacket. Then I started to cry, and I kept on crying: walking back, blowing my nose, looking down at the pavement, at my shoes coming one after the other into blurred view; sitting on the steps of my house; in bed, holding the unsigned note telling me he would not be back, huddled, in fetal position, against an atavistic terror, until the incessant tears were transformed to gritty irritants: a sick, cold, nauseating fear that the Falcaro dog could somehow break into the house in which I now cried alone.

144

✎ Before: 6

PETE AND LAURA'S HOUSE was always crowded. Every day, each boy had a friend or two visting. Dinner invitations were extended without hesitation. Laura's sons assumed it was all right with her, although they told her in a questioning way, willing enough to understand it might not be possible that night. Laura rarely had a reason to say no. It was their friendships, their relationships. She hardly felt she had any right to determine the nature of them.

Sol fell in love. Sarah was Gatsby's own golden girl: tall, slim; straight, fine, long hair shining on her shoulders. She was a constant visitor at Sol's insistence and clear delight. They sat in his room, listening to records, talking, talking, until Sol's buddy, Steve, came over. Then they would go down and watch their favorite programs. Laura saw them straddling the brink of childhood's end and adulthood's beginning as they ridiculed what they simultaneously believed.

They drank endless quantities of soda, leaving cans under the couch, on the television set. They ate fruit and potato chips and made roast-beef sandwiches before dinner. They were ravenous. Rabelaisian in their need to feel, taste, use their high sexual energy.

Manny sat more quietly with them, troubled by summer-school homework he should do and did not want to do. His friend Al was pimple-faced, tense; his friend Len was exuberant, crew-cut, militarily brisk. Len spoke for the three of them, arguing with Steve during commercials, about the new Vietnam war separating momentarily from the group, easily reintegrating when the sitcom continued.

Larry sat on the floor, his newly long legs difficult for him to handle in the smallish room. His friends came in and out, still more restless than the slightly older group; suddenly going out to ride their bikes, capriciously returning for lemonade, cokes; thirsty, hot, used; stopping only for a second, in the flowing, infinite moments before them.

Pete more frequently came home early in the afternoon, smiling broadly at the cries of "Hey—here's Big Dad," moving slowly, almost rhythmically through the grouping, pulling at his tie, throwing his briefcase down with a sigh of relief. They turned on a ball game and yelled at plays, Manny now perking up, becoming dominant, quoting statistics, reminding them of plays from three years ago.

Sarah joined Laura upstairs in the kitchen with the count of dinner-eaters that night. The kitchen table was not large enough to accommodate them all and Laura wanted to use the dining-room table, calling down for one of them to please put another leaf in the table.

"Just a minute!" An intense silence from downstairs revealed an important play in action. Laura and Sarah waited until it was over so they could set the table, put out the bread, ketchup, butter, horseradish, glasses, bottles of soda, milk, iced tea.

They cut salad companionably, sitting at a kitchen table covered with celery, lettuce, tomatoes, radishes, scallions, green peppers—a harvest time, echoing farm fairs, hot hours digging roots, faces squinted upward to the sky.

Laura checked the stew, stirring it until it defrosted from her Sunday freezing-for-the-week, permitting the meat and vegetables and potatoes to grow hot, waiting for her family and their friends to be ready to eat, pleased she was prepared for them.

Usually their general conversation at dinner was pleasant, small talk affectionately exchanged. Sometimes, though, an unexpected bitterness silenced all but the participants.

"I think," Sol said once, "blacks have a natural superior ability to play basketball. All you have to do is watch them. They just move differently than we do. You can see it."

"Bullshit," Pete said. "That's bullshit."

"Think it's transferred through the genes," Laura asked, "the complete rules?"

"The trouble with you, Sol," Pete said, "is you don't know enough. City College had the best basketball team in the country—and they were all Jews. It's poverty that makes them move."

"You've got to stay agile not to be defeated?" Laura asked Pete.

"Damn right."

"Nice metaphor."

"We're not talking words, Dad, we're talking bodies," Sol said. "You can tell by just looking."

"Try that method and you're going to be fooled by a lot of people," Pete warned him.

But the bitterness dissipated by the time dinner was over.

Laura and Sarah cleared off the table, soaking the dishes, pots, forks, spoons in hot, soapy water, Laura looking at the window as she washed, at the pussy-willow tree growing steadily next to the honeysuckle.

The boys drifted back, helping to wipe the dishes, putting things away for Laura, getting a piece of fruit from the refrigerator. Sometimes during the summer, they settled down for a game of Risk, the moths beating against the lighted screens, as though they, too, wanted to join in.

Pete went back to his office for a while and Sarah and Sol went for a walk. Larry went back to the sitcoms and Manny told Al and Len he had to do his homework now. He went up to his room, and Laura and Steve visited comfortably. When Steve left, Laura curled up on the living-room couch to read the newspaper, surprised it was so late.

When Pete came home, they went to bed, both very tired, and kissed goodnight, nestling close for a moment or two, until Pete said, "I have to turn now." They turned on their sides, away from each other, Pete patting Laura's hip a moment; and they slept.

One September morning, Laura had a discussion with Fred because, as supervisor, he was ultimately responsible for the work issuing from their office. The problem was about *ricco* (rich) or *ricchezza* (riches).

"Do you think I should add *overly* to the original? He said merely *rich* but the context doesn't quite carry the nuance. It might be confusing in English, standing alone like that."

Fred rubbed his mouth, touched his tie—his habitual gestures of thought.

"No, I really don't think so. That's on the verge of rewriting. It's almost a breach of ethics with the author.

He trusts us to convey what he said, not what we think he should say."

"I understand that, Fred. Your guideline does not appear to apply here, though. We owe it to the author also to convey the intention of his word."

"It strikes me as an infringement."

"Perhaps you're right. Perhaps I should err on the side of caution."

Fred sat back in his chair; he appeared to be looking too intently at Laura's forehead.

"It's a pleasure doing business with a reasonable woman. In fact, everything about you is a pleasure. You're always the same—not moody."

Laura bent over her work, almost confused.

"Well," she finally ventured, "that's a nice thing to say. Thank you." She paused. "Is your family moody?"

"My wife, you mean?"

"I guess so."

"Yes—quiet, very quiet. She does not like to talk much. Withdrawn, really. Mostly she eats. That's no family secret. All you have to do is see her to know."

"That sounds a little hard for you."

"It is, but I don't let it get me down. I like to drive so I go up to Vermont and back—drive three hundred miles a day. Sometimes I take my Dad along for an outing. He smokes his cigars and fouls up the air, but he enjoys it so much, I end up enjoying it too. Anyway, I can wash out the cigar smoke when I get home. Gives me something else to do."

"But what do you do when you get to Vermont? You just don't turn around and come back, do you?"

"No, we always find something to do. Usually we pick up a couple of bottles of Jack Daniel's. It's a hell of a lot less there. Then we come back."

"And drink it?"

"That's almost the best part."

"I'd never think of doing that for an outing," Laura realized. "It's a good idea, really. I suppose you could pick up bottles for gifts and always be prepared. I wonder why we never thought of it."

"Maybe you'd like to come with me sometime," Fred said.

"I don't think my husband would like that."

"So we won't tell him."

"I never could keep a secret."

"I'll teach you."

Laura returned to her work. When she got home that night, the house was too crowded. She wanted to go to their bedroom and lie down, and relish the conversation the way she had saved a maraschino cherry in her fruit salad, for the last spoonful, so it was a noticeable last taste. She wanted to hold Pete closer, longer, when he came in, wanted to tell him she was feeling a surge of love for him, that it was strange how there always seemed some new current.

Instead, she rushed Larry to the emergency room because he stepped on a nail and left a thick, red blood course from the kitchen to the den. Larry assumed an invalid's role immediately, happily putting his bandaged foot up and asking if she would mind bringing him down a Coke.

She divided her time between catering to him and getting dinner on the table. Random images of Fred's oblique glances floated in and out of her mind.

When they went to bed, she said to Pete, "Do you think, if Larry's foot is healed enough by Saturday, we could spend the weekend in New York? I'd love to go to the theatre and have dinner at a really good French restaurant, and sleep in a hotel and have coffee brought up

Sunday morning with the *Times*. Don't you think that would be fun?"

"Probably, but not this weekend. I promised the boys I'd take them to Yankee Stadium Saturday afternoon."

"Well, that's OK. We could still drop them off. They could take a train back."

"But then I would miss the game."

Laura dared to bend down and kiss the tip of his penis, barely revealed through the gap in his shorts.

"We could play some games of our own," she said.

"It will never replace the Yankees."

He bit her neck gently, nuzzling against her. "Nothing personal," he said lightly.

Laura believed him.

Patrick appeared to be somewhat more than Darcy's business partner as Laura and Pete met them at the bar, waiting for the others. His hand was too casually resting on Darcy's shoulder. A recorded Elvis Presley sang, "You ain't nothin' but a hound dog."

"Think it's the people's music?" Laura teased Darcy.

"Well, there are some definite folk qualities beneath the commercialization—"

"Folk—what is that?—another word for screwing?" Georgie, behind her, said. "Let's not have a bunch of intellectual bullshit about crap," bending to kiss Darcy's cheek.

"I think we'd better get our table," Lilli said, amused, "because if that's going to be the topic of conversation, the shots we're about to get from Mr. Soft-Tones here, well—one better be seated."

She smiled the waiter into finding them a table. By the time Hilda and Bobby joined them, Lilli's smile was more fixed than fond. Apparently, Elvis represented obscenity, coarseness, vulgarity, sheer idiocy to Georgie and Patrick. Darcy and Lilli thought he was not for them, but he was not such a threat as the men seemed to think. Laura could not understand why folk quality could only be expressed through double negatives. Bobby thought the music was just plain ugly. Pete and Hilda found it rather cheerful. "Sort of makes me want to dance around," Hilda confessed. "I don't really think it's any worse than 'Mairzy Doats' was. And anyway, it can't be very important. It's just a fad."

"That's true," Lilli said. "Beethoven will outlast him, and so will Ella Fitzgerald for that matter."

"I think he may be important, though," Pete said, pressing the tines of his fork into his napkin, "the way Freud was important. Even if you don't read him, you're influenced by him because so many others are influenced. By the time you're affected you may not recognize the source, but you'll see things differently."

"I don't think this guy wants you to see things differently," Georgie said through a mouthful of Italian bread. "I think he wants you to feel it right in the groin! No mistakes about what effect he wants!"

"That's ridiculous!" Hilda was outraged. "The guy belts out the song so you want to get up and dance!"

Patrick's "The hell he does want you to *dance*—" started the decibel acceleration. It went on among them all through the pasta and veal—but it never made it to the spumoni.

"We *must* request you leave now," the manager said, holding the check on a tray that trembled with his anger. They laughed their way out, although Laura's cheeks burned with shame.

At Georgie's birthday party that year, everyone gave him an Elvis record. "Very funny," he muttered as each was unwrapped. His daughter squealed with delight as he silently handed them over to her. "Now I'm going to have to live with that. Thanks a lot. Great gag."

Fred's reports of his activities were doing something to Laura's ideas. He not only drove to Vermont, he went to dances, he watched television at bars, and he went sailing alone whenever he could.

"But why?" Laura asked him. "Isn't it lonely?"

"Of course not. It's the opposite. It's nice to talk to the guys and there's nothing nicer than the wind and water and sun all in one dose. Why don't you come out with me sometime?"

"Oh, God—me! On a boat! Never in a million years. I'm the smoke-filled café type."

"Did you ever try it?"

"No. I'm afraid of deep water."

"So you'll wear a life jacket. Everyone does, anyway."

"I don't think I'd like it."

"You'll never know until you try."

"I know."

But Pete thought it would be fun when Fred asked him one night when he and his wife came for dinner. Laura thought Fred asked Pete to go sailing just to fill in the vacuum caused by Fred's wife. For Fred's wife dominated the room with her silence. She sat heavily, beady black eyes stolidly in a puffy-flour face. Unsmiling, she watched Laura, appeared to listen carefully to Pete, never spoke directly to Fred. She moved only toward the dip and vegetables on the table in front of her, eating steadily. Chomping, crunching, her mouth moving below the expressionless eyes, she saturated the room with her intense, obese presence.

Pete and Fred returned from their sail, sunburned and whiskery.

"You should have come," Pete said, giving Laura a sweaty kiss. "It was terrific."

"Maybe I should have."

When the university press accepted a special Russian science contract, Fred hired Janet Lovella to do the translation. Janet was a lively young woman with a frequent smile. She wore brightly colored kerchiefs. Whenever Janet moved, there was a small rainbow.

Laura liked her immediately. They ate lunch together. Several times, Janet and her husband had dinner with Laura and Pete and the boys.

Janet was enthusiastic about Pete.

"He's so goddamn smart," she said, "and funny." Janet's voice was slightly hoarse.

"I enjoy him, too," Laura said smugly.

"But I don't know how you get the patience to wait on them like that." Janet lit a cigarette, throwing the match onto her plate.

"I guess it's just the way we're used to. I don't really think of it as 'waiting on them' anyway. They'd help if I asked. It just never seems necessary," Laura said, almost proudly.

"Bullshit," Janet said.

Laura winced slightly. The word seemed so unnecessarily vulgar from a woman.

"Bullshit," Janet repeated. "Everyone's old enough to share. You work all day too, you know."

Laura thought about it. She did hate to market. The basket was always too small for all the items she needed. Somehow the check-out line she chose always moved too slowly. Maybe Janet was right. Maybe marketing was a good place to start. Laura left a shopping list on the kitchen table one day, addressed To Anyone. She attached fifty dollars. When she arrived home, the money was gone but the list was still there.

154

"I took it," Pete told her. "I needed some cash anyway. Sorry, I didn't have time to do the shopping for you."

"That's OK, honey. It wasn't urgent, really. But how come you needed the cash? Didn't you just cash a check yesterday?"

"The fuel pump went again, and you know how our favorite service station feels about checks."

"I don't know why you stick with him. You're too loyal, that's your trouble."

Pete kissed her. "You're really observant," he said.

When Laura told Janet about the shopping list, she never even remembered the money.

"You see, it's routine," she explained to Janet. "I think that's the way families function. Everyone sort of knows what everyone else is doing. So we don't get in each other's way, in a sense. We can all be busy without a lot of trouble."

"Everyone doesn't *sort* of know what to do, Laura. It's more what you've been conditioned to do. You don't see alternatives. There really are no other ways for you to think about."

"You've been translating Pavlov too long."

"Having the kids was a conditioned response, nevertheless."

Laura moved impatiently. "I always wanted kids. I like having a family. In fact, I probably would have had two or three more, but Pete wasn't so crazy about the idea." Laura thought a little, and added, "Which makes sense since he's the one who's had to support us all. Do you feel you're conditioned because *you* want to have children?" Laura thought she was making the killing point.

"I don't, though."

"Really not?"

"Really not."

Laura dismissed the statement. She thought Janet was probably having trouble conceiving. She did not want to hurt Janet by piercing her defenses, so to change the subject, she complained about the new deadline system Fred had introduced, and never raised the question of Janet's babies again—nor even considered Janet might have told her the truth when she said she did not want children.

At home, Sol's records bothered her. She did not like the melodies and found she could not hear her own classical station because his records were turned up too high.

"For God's sake, lower that damn thing," she called up to him.

He yelled something but she could not understand him. Finally, she ran upstairs in an irritable fury. "I can't hear myself think!" she fumed. "Cut it down."

"It is down, Mom. That's what I just told you."

"That's down?"

"Yes!"

"You're going deaf."

He mirrored her irritable fury. "Why don't you just listen to it instead of automatically knocking it. You yell it's too loud and still you can't hear it."

"It's ugly. Why should I bother to listen to more ugliness?"

"You never even heard it. You don't know."

"I know!"

As she said it, Laura seemed to hear her voice echoing, "I know, I know, I know." She calmed down.

"OK, Sol. Maybe I am getting to be a know-it-all. I'll listen to it carefully."

She sat down and looked at her son, and listened conspicuously.

"Well?" Sol asked when the song was ended.

"It's ugly."

She started downstairs, but then she turned and called up to him, "But the words are interesting."

At dinner, she noticed Manny had stopped shaving. After that the bathroom sink seemed always clogged.

"I think you're either going to have to stop washing or shave your beard off," she told him. He laughed and did neither.

Then Sol stopped shaving. "We're going to have to buy stocks in the Drano company," she remarked to Pete.

"It's the style. In fact, I'm thinking of growing one myself."

"Settle for a mustache. On you a beard would just look religious."

"Why? Do you think I'm beginning to look old?"

"Not to me; but I guess to your sons. . . ."

"There you go again, rushing us into old age."

Laura was insulted. "When did I ever rush you into old age?"

"I don't know how. I just know you do."

"Everyone seems to know everything these days."

"I don't know what you're talking about."

"I know you don't."

But neither of them claimed to know what to do when Sol said he wanted Sarah to sleep over the weekend of his high-school prom and made it apparent he wanted her to sleep in his room.

"What does her mother say?"

"C'mon, Mom, you know she's not going to tell her mother."

"Well, when she is in this house, we're *in loco parentis*," Pete said. "So I guess Larry will sleep in the den, and she'll sleep in his room. Of course, what goes on after everyone's in bed is your business."

"What kind of suggestion is that?" Laura asked, annoyed.

"You remember when I came home from overseas...."

"What happened?" Sol grinned.

"Nothing! For Christ's sake, Pete. What a thing to say."

Pete looked at Sol. "I was only kidding. Your mother was, and is, a square."

"In a round-peg house," Laura said, still annoyed.

"It's all right, Mom. It's none of my business anyway." Sol put his arm around her shoulder. "Just as what goes on with Sarah and me is none of your business."

Laura looked up at Sol. "How the hell did you get so tall?"

Pete sighed.

"It's OK," Sol said to him, "you're still the only one who can pick up a chair by holding one leg."

"Don't patronize me, sonny."

"I'm not, honestly. In fact, when the day comes I can do it, I'll go outside and cry."

"You read that somewhere."

"Yeah, but the tears will be real, Big Dad."

Hilda and Bobby came to dinner the night of Sol's prom. They could not get over how cute Sol and Sarah looked. Pete and Laura exchanged amused glances at the fond gushiness: Sol's terse "Thanks" suggested he was not too comfortable with it. Sarah glowed.

"Well, you've really got something to be proud of there," Hilda said comfortably, stretching out her legs. The checks of her slacks had irridescent threads that made shimmering waves as she moved.

"It makes it all worthwhile, doesn't it?" Bobby said. "All the heartaches, all the troubles, when you see them like that. It even makes me forget my feet for a while."

They all looked at Bobby's molded shoes solemnly.

"One hundred fifty dollars I paid to have these shoes made for me," he said, "and they don't make me feel as good as seeing that boy did."

"You're a good friend," Laura said.

"Well, that's what it's all about, isn't it? Kids and old friendships."

"God forbid," Pete said. "God forbid, that's all it should be about."

Laura noticed the typists were wearing slacks when they came to work. She thought it must be very comfortable and wished she were daring enough to wear a pair, too. She ultimately bought a Glen plaid slack suit and tried it on with a fine cashmere sweater Lilli had given her for Christmas.

"What do you think?" she asked Pete, as she craned her neck to see herself in the mirror. "Think I can go to work this way?"

He studied her carefully. "They're too big on you," he decided.

"I don't like them too tight."

"They'd look better."

She wiggled her hips. "Better for what?"

Pete did not answer; Laura was uncertain whether he had seen her suggestive movement because he was rummaging for something in his bureau, his back turned to her. She felt obscurely ashamed.

After: 6

"I DON'T EVEN KNOW what a homosexual is!" I screamed at Dr. Summers.

He looked at me with hooded eyelids.

"It's a mirror image," he said calmly. "Your sex partner is yourself, so you can do to him what you want done to you."

"But all he had to do was tell me what he wanted and I would have done it. How could he not know that!"

"You could not, though. You have no penis. That's the turn-on for him—the penis. You don't have it."

"But I have breasts. I smell nice. My skin is—"

"So does every other woman, but it doesn't turn you on, does it?"

"No," I said bitterly, "but other men's penises didn't either."

"They could have. You just did not permit it."

"Because I thought that was the right thing to do. I thought that's what we'd promised each other. Be faithful, I thought. Be faithful and you'll be treated faithfully."

"He couldn't help it. It was overwhelming."

"Goddamn, I'm paying you thirty-five dollars an hour for these stupid conversations and all you do is defend him."

"I'm not defending your husband. I'm just stating what the situation is. He must have been going through hell all these years. He couldn't handle it anymore."

I grabbed at the Kleenex as the by now familiar ghastly gnawing started somewhere below my chest and mucous suffocated me.

"I could not be much of a woman," I mumbled, miserable. "If I had been prettier, or more luscious. These goddamn bony hips!"

"I don't think it's that simple. Do you really think that's what it is?"

"But how could I not know!"

"He related to you heterosexually. You did not know because he treated you as a woman. The important thing now is that you treat yourself as a woman and not let him decide your life for you."

"You're impossible. You don't understand—he is my life."

"Romantic, but untrue. He's part of your life. He's left a big gap and you'll have to learn to live without him. It's difficult but you can do it. You're attractive, you're bright, you make friends easily. You can do it. I like you. Others will too. You can find ways to find that out."

"I can't."

"You can."

I saw Dr. Summers every week so he could remind me I could.

He gave me some medication so I could stop crying, but he had no medication to prevent the gnawing, and the suffocating mucous.

"Try jogging. Exercise. Work. Don't sit around."

"Why don't you write a book on positive thinking? Your advice is about as helpful."

"Jog."

"I can't."

"You can."

I wandered around the house at night, listening to the emptiness. Sometimes I stood in the middle of Manny's room. His bed was smoothly covered, an unliving peculiarity; his bookcase sparse looking from removed books; his clarinet case covered and dusty in the corner. He was so far away, a Peace Corps worker, leading a life unknown to me, beyond my stretch for aid.

If I walked into Sol's room, I saw his collection of Tarzan books waiting, neatly stacked by me. His Phillies pennant hung limply; none of it any more than a childhood memory to the young man in his Sarah-shared apartment in L.A. Happy in love, unaware of my situation, he was light-years from understanding assistance.

I sat in Larry's large room, crowded with Beardsley posters—mauve, brown, blackly etched designs of curling lines, going ultimately nowhere, trapped on the borders of heavy-rag stock paper. An old pair of sneakers lay under his bed, the frayed rims reminding me of his constant need for movement—and of his last move to the familiar dorms of the University of Wisconsin. A student of chemistry, worried by exams, analyses, experiments, new friends, new activities. He could not be dragged away from his growth to my despair.

One night, I whirled looking for Laddie. I called, listening for him. He was not there. Pete had brought him to our house and perhaps Laddie felt he now had to go too. I never found him.

I did not cry. I whimpered: the sound of defeat.

*　　*　　*

I took to washing the kitchen floor, scrubbing the baseboards, rearranging the cabinets at three in the morning.

"Good!" Dr. Summers said. "No need to brood in bed. Keep moving."

"But I'm so tired. I can barely drag myself to work. I don't even have the energy to invite someone for dinner. I can't get through the marketing."

"You can."

The nights continued too long. I washed my panties, bras: prewashing, rinsing, hanging them to dry. One night I looked at the dinginess of them. I pulled them off the line I had strung across the bathtub. I crammed them in a plastic bag and threw them all out, running out to the garbage can in the dark night, barefooted.

Then I went through drawers and closets, throwing blouses, skirts, sweatshirts, stockings out. I went to a bra shop the next day and asked the lady to fit me. "I think I don't know my size," I confessed. "You don't," she said, looking at the shoulder straps, pulled up too high, knotted.

I bought six snow-white lacy bras and embroidered panties. My bureau drawer had never seemed so full.

"I can't really afford it, you know," I told Dr. Summers.

"You can," he said.

"There isn't even anyone to see them."

"You see them."

I stopped marketing regularly. I bought egg rolls and steak and peppers and egg foo yung and fried shrimp and ate Chinese food all week; at eleven o'clock at night and two in the morning, whenever I felt hungry.

"You're getting the idea of what you can do," Dr.

Summers said. "We might even get a couple of pounds on you yet. You'll look wonderful."

"It's a selfish way to live. It's a self-centered, childish, impulsive existence."

"Stop making up rules. Do whatever maximizes your good feelings."

"I can't seem to stop."

"You can."

I gave up reading the paper Sunday morning and went walking instead. I had images of couples waking up and making love, and I walked faster. I saw people going to church and getting together for family luncheons and felt sorry for myself. I went back home and did not know what to do with all the hours suddenly mine.

"Find your interests," Dr. Summers said.

"I don't have any."

"You have."

I took bridge lessons and played duplicate bridge with harsh, noncommunicative people, watching ringed hands turn cards, manicured nails tap tables. I checked for wedding bands, furtively studying the woman who had one. Why had this huge-breasted, unsympathetic woman kept her husband while mine left?

I drove myself home, sick with gnawing pain and mucous, reading in bed, eating in bed, remembering in bed; unable to grasp the reality of being the only one in the house.

"I'm getting so sick of always being blue," I complained to Dr. Summers. "I'm so tired of being tired. I can't stand myself anymore."

"You're getting better."

I started to cry. "And I'll never stop crying, damn it!"

"You will," he said.

*   *   *

I met Darcy and Hilda for lunch. It was a relief to be
in a situation of such comfortable familiarity. Even if
Hilda was plumper, she was still perky. Her hair had a
Miss Clairol reddish tinge, her curls bounced merrily as
she chattered. She wore a large ruby, encircled with
diamonds, on her small, graceful finger. Her wedding
ring was almost covered by a square sapphire. She glit-
tered light.

"We're all looking for someone," Hilda said. "I check
out every party we go to."

"Maybe," Darcy suggested, "you ought to try to answer some of those singles ads." Darcy pulled her chair
closer to the table, the heavy gold necklaces she wore
jangling as she did so. Her golden-hooped earrings
moved in rhythm to her words. "I know it sounds crazy,
but I have a friend, a really nice, intelligent woman who
just couldn't find any male companionship. So she figured, 'What the hell.' She went into the bookstore and
bought lots of newspapers and magazines and just happened to buy the singles newspapers too. And do you
know, some of the ads sounded absolutely straight. So
she put in an ad of her own. She didn't lie about
anything—told her real age, weight, everything. Do you
know what happened? She received ninety answers!
Can you imagine? And such a nice group—a dean of a
community college, a surgeon and lots of engineers—
engineering seems to be a very lonely profession. Well,
to make a long story short—she's now been living for six
months with a guy she met that way and they're planning
to get married."

Darcy smoothed her still-lovely blond hair. "You
might consider it. I bet you'd meet a lot of interesting
guys that way."

We were in a pretty tea room, and I did not want to

cry in such a public place. I was afraid I was going to because I could feel my throat muscles tighten and the mucous swelling, the globs of misery beginning their suffocation.

I knew Darcy and Hilda meant well. I appreciated the concern they felt and wanted to let them know I appreciated it; but I could not. Overwhelming my appreciation was an inexplicable anger, almost a rage. They made me feel demeaned. It did not make sense. I knew they were only saying what I, too, felt. Of course I had to find a boyfriend, a lover. Only somehow, when they talked to me that way, it was as though there was nothing else to me. A guy in my life was such a clear, absolute necessity, the number one issue. It was almost too critical.

"I just can't imagine having sex with anyone but Pete," I said. "I mean, getting undressed in front of a stranger!"

"Don't worry," Darcy assured me. "It will be easy when it comes. It will feel natural—although honestly, Laura, I still cannot believe all this is really necessary. I'm positive you and Pete could—"

"Stop," I interrupted.

"Be sensible, Laura," Hilda said. "What Darcy's telling you is what we all think. We know if you would just forgive Pete, just send him the word that whatever he did, you'll forget—we know Pete would jump at the chance to make up."

"Please," I said. "Leave it alone. Please."

They looked at each other. "Well," Hilda sighed, "maybe it will blow over. Maybe he will make the first move. But God," she burst out, "I'd hate to be in your shoes. Believe you me, I'm going to take good care of Bobby."

166

Did I not take good care of Pete? Did I take bad care?

Darcy and Hilda still looked expectantly at me. They wanted me to give them some details. I could not. I could not tell them about a male thirty-two-year-old interior decorator with styled hair and too much men's cologne on. I had even met him once in a theatre lobby, not knowing then he was anything more than a passing acquaintance of Pete's. I had only been aware of an intense discomfort that seemed to emanate directly from the ruffled cuffs peeking from under his jacket sleeve, and had noticed that Pete pulled his own cuff-linked sleeves below his jacket sleeve, as though to show that he, too, had finery.

"My wife," Pete murmured.

Ruffles nodded and moved on.

"Who's that?" I asked as Pete watched him walk away.

"Just a guy I play tennis with once in a while."

"With—or against?"

"With."

Pete turned to look at me. His eyes were cold. "I have to go to the men's room. See you back at the seat."

It was my turn to watch someone go. "Wonder what's bothering him?" I thought, not too seriously.

And now that I knew, I could not force myself to tell my friends, although I wanted to, kept trying to find the words to tell them, so they could understand my separation from Pete could not just blow over, could not be settled by even the most well-meaning of friends, could probably not be settled by anyone.

"Maybe," I said to Dr. Summers later, telling him about the lunch, "maybe that's how Pete always felt. Unable even to say it out loud, holding it in, hiding."

"It must have used a great deal of his energy."

"You mean fighting your instincts to get out—using your strength to chain yourself in the closet instead of trying to break the chains?"

"Precisely."

"I could almost feel sorry for him. I do, I guess. I mean, I felt how not telling Darcy and Hilda separated me from them when I only wanted to be closer. He must have felt that way sometimes."

Dr. Summers and I were silent, thinking of the chained Pete.

Then I continued, "I don't, however, think that could excuse all the lying and cheating he did. I mean, in the end, it's one problem to be a homosexual without letting your wife know; it's quite another issue to be such a traitor to someone who loved you. And he asked me to love him, didn't he? I lived up to my promises to him. I didn't go out and screw around behind his back."

"You ought to try to remember that. You'll find some lucky man who will appreciate you, who will get a 100 percent commitment from a wonderful girl."

"Do you think I ought to go searching around resorts, too?" I said sarcastically.

"No. I think if you do that you're only setting yourself up for disappointment if no one suitable is there. I think you ought to pursue your interests. If you go to a resort, go to relax, swim, enjoy the food, socialize generally. If you keep doing that, sooner or later, you will meet someone. You can't miss."

"So you, too, think meeting someone is the bottom line?"

"That's for you to say."

I looked at Dr. Summers's thin, sincere face, at the dusty old brown shoes he habitually wore, feeling the odd rage I felt at lunch recurring.

Dr. Summers waited, silently.

168

"There's something wrong with it," I said slowly. "It is the bottom line, I guess, and I don't like it. It makes me too dependent on some quirk of fate. It makes it seem that everything I'm doing is a substitute while I'm waiting to find Mr. Right."

"If you don't like to feel that way, why don't you change your perspective?"

"I can't."

"You can."

"You mean going to dinner with a woman friend can be just as satisfying as going to dinner with couples, part of a couple?"

"You'll have to find that out for yourself."

"Will you come for dinner Saturday night?" I asked Janet, a funny tremor curling upward from my stomach to emerge as a palsy of my right hand. Janet's face revealed nothing but natural acceptance as she said she and her husband would love to.

Darcy volunteered to bring a pita bread hors d'oeuvre she'd just discovered. She assumed it was OK with me if Patrick came too. I found it was. I asked Soo, Fred and his wife, and Hilda and Bobby. Hilda and Bobby couldn't make it.

My body willed what my mind could not. Hands automatically fingered tomatoes, tested cantaloupe, peeled carrots, potatoes, carried ice through the kitchen door from the freezer, whisked cold water and stock into a creamy gravy, pulled the table cloth down until it hung evenly on all four sides of the table, impatiently rewashed spotted knives.

My voice greeted Soo. My arms hugged Fred. My eyes marveled again at the girth of Fred's wife. My feet took Janet's coat to the closet. Fred's wife was an intolerable guest as she immediately assumed her silent eating-the-whole-dip-until-finished role, but Fred was great. The smooth bartender, he added a rye-soaked lemon twist to Soo's ginger ale, whispering to her he intended to get her drunk and have his way with her, "whispering" so everyone could hear. Soo said unless he could do it sideways he was no good to her. I think I was surprised Soo knew the stupid old joke about Chinese girls.

Janet's husband never stopped looking at Fred's wife. He seemed hypnotized by a pin she wore. A somewhat tarnished silver actor's mask of comedy, the pin nestled on the mountain of her right shoulder. As she moved forward to dip a cucumber in avocado cream, the pin disappeared. As she breathed back against the couch, the pin reappeared, glinting in the lamplight, moving up and down in acquiescence to her chewing mouth.

She gave the lie forever to stereotypes about fat ladies. She did not have a pretty face. She was not jolly. She was probably, in fact, withdrawn and depressed, hidden behind the wall of flesh she kept strengthening with every passing bite.

Fred kept trying to keep everyone cheerful. His wife remained remote—the encased Princess. Suffocating between pounds, densities, thicknesses, slabs—ultimately stifling Fred's exuberance by the literal, and metaphysical, weight of her presence.

"I guess it's time for us to go now," Fred said quietly. "It was nice, very nice, of you to ask us."

I moved the chairs back into place and emptied ashtrays, and did not want to go into the empty bedroom. I lay down on the den floor and looked at the blue and yellow fibers of the rug. I heard a faucet dripping but I did not want to turn it off. I never wanted to get up again. I wanted to lie there, looking at the rug, and never hear advice on how to find a man. I did not want to let anyone ever see me again, to see that no one wanted to live with me, that I was unwanted, that the answer to *Who cares?* is *No one.*

I started to cry and kept crying; the mucous swelled, inflamed, suffocated me with burning. Imperceptibly, the image of myself emerged: I spectated. I saw myself crying on the rug. How long could I stay there? Who would come to stop me? I could cry for the rest of my life. Would it matter?

No one knew what I was doing or feeling. No one was going to change what I did. A repetitive drum—no one, none, persona non grata—or otherwise welcome.

So I got up and washed my face. My back hurt from lying so long on the floor. "You're too old for this," I told myself in the mirror. "You need a bed and a good night's sleep. You can't be fooling around all night like some Greek tragic heroine." I said out loud in the empty house, "A chopped liver on rye would do you a world of good."

I settled for an English muffin and a murder mystery.

❧ Before: 7

LAURA STOPPED IN to see her mother. She found her making a cup of tea. Her mother boiled the water in a small pot, although there was a large teakettle on the back burner. Then she walked around the kitchen, holding the pot of boiling water while she talked to Laura. She opened the refrigerator to get some lemon, still holding the pot.

Laura glimpsed the empty, shining racks of the refrigerator just before she jumped up to get the pot from her mother. She was afraid her mother would spill the hot water. For a minute, it was a Marx Brothers scene, her mother in turn jumping, startled.

"What is it!"

"The pot. Why do you walk around holding the pot?"

Her mother looked at it.

"I forgot I was holding it."

"Well, let's have the goddamn tea already. . . . So, Ma, are you OK?"

"Well, I feel better today. Yesterday—was it yesterday?—maybe a couple of days ago, I got so dizzy. I was trying to push the window down, and then I got so dizzy I just had to hang on until it passed."

"And did it?"

"Yeah, but Laura, I was so tired, you can't imagine. I just had to stop everything and take a nap."

Laura stood up and put her arms around her mother. Her mother was so small, a yellowing leaf drifting in a random rain puddle.

Several years back, she and Georgie had noticed how painful it was for their mother to go to work in the cold weather. Her toes cramped and burned; she had red, festering blisters around her mouth all winter. They persuaded her to stop working and enjoy her apartment.

"It's not right," Laura murmured to her mother.

"What?"

"Your living alone so long. You should have had someone with you all these years."

"Don't talk like a child, Laura. Who would I live with after Dad died?"

"But that was so long ago."

"What difference does that make?"

Her mother had no expectations. There could be no changes: only extended time. Laura shuddered.

"Maybe now, we should try—" Laura did not know what they should try.

But her mother had not expected any suggestion.

"I don't want to give you more problems. You have enough to do. I'm all right."

"Come, let's sit in the living room."

Laura's mother leaned her head against the couch a minute. A sudden embarrassed smile.

"I like to watch *The Dating Game.* It's on now. I know how dumb it is, but I enjoy it so much, you wouldn't believe it. Funny how you enjoy even though you know it's dumb."

Laura studied her mother's room while her mother watched the program. Her mother did enjoy the program. Her laugh was girlish, pretty, in contrast to her living room. The room still had a certain furnished-room quality to it, probably caused by the linoleum. Laura could never quite get used to her mother's partiality for linoleum rather than a rug.

Her mother had put a faded print cover on the couch, thrown a maroon, blue, and black comforter over the chair. A painted waterfall, framed in white and gold, was too small for the wall's expanse. It mocked beauty rather than reflected it.

A sweet woman with no taste. Laura's mother lived in an ugliness she did not see. She laughed at *The Dating Game,* somewhat ashamed of herself. Maybe that's the way she coped, doing things she found enjoyable, accepting some slight shame about it all—some mediocre, inferior status. She let Laura and Georgie feel superior, in control.

For the first time Laura wondered if her mother had permitted them to feel that way, understanding it made them feel better, enabled them to act. Her mother had after all moved away from the sink on her own. Perhaps only in retrospect had she sat too long, too still at the table—until Laura and Georgie felt they had to do something. They might only think they'd all still be sitting, waiting, in that kitchen.

Laura called Georgie.

"I don't think she feels too well. She's getting so forgetful. I'm afraid she'll put something on the stove and not remember."

"I know. Lilli noticed it too. But we couldn't think of what to do . . . "

"Maybe Les?" Georgie suggested.

"Are you kidding?"

Les. Laura could never get close to Les. For such a long time he had just been a responsibility to avoid. And then, when he moved to Florida, working in a department store, there had been too much distance. Laura met Les and his wife, Arlene, when Les came to see their mother; but the stout, pimply-faced Arlene, with her slow, drawling voice, was an alien—out of Laura's context, unknowable. And Les laughed when he spoke, prefacing most of his remarks with a guffawed "to tell the truth." Visiting Les and Arlene left Laura with aching teeth and strained jaw from the clenched-mouth position she usually maintained in their presence.

Pete had long since established, "He's *your* brother and she's *your* sister-in-law," so Laura saw them alone, and any visiting without Pete was emptyish. She went to her mother's apartment to see them, knowing she would stay as short a time as decently possible.

So when Georgie said maybe they ought to think of Les, Laura really had no idea if he could or could not help their mother. She did not know Les. Sometimes she wondered how it was possible to have a brother and not know him at all.

"You speak to Les, Georgie; maybe a long visit where it's warm would help her. Who knows?"

"You know she'll never go for a *long* visit."

"She's right in a way, I guess. What could she do there all day? How would you like to be stuck with Arlene?"

"If your mother-in-law weren't such an iceberg—" Georgie began.

"Lost cause," Laura replied crisply. "Jane brags about what she does for the kids, and it ends up making Ma feel she's not their grandmother as well."

"So we're back to square one. What to do?"

"I guess we'll have to be even more careful one of us calls her every day and sees she's busy at least one day of the weekend."

"No problem, Laura. Incidentally, I increased the amount of money I send her. I thought she needed a cost of living adjustment by now."

"So, what's my percentage increase?"

"Well, one hundred eighty dollars and seventy-five cents won't take you out of the second-class range. You'll have to go at least over two hundred to make first-class."

"I'll take no chances. I'll go for two hundred fifty and be firmly in the first class."

"You're a good kid, Laura."

Laura's mother worried that Georgie and Laura could not afford to send her money and asked, anxiously, if Laura was sure it was all right with Pete. Laura assured her and reassured her: it was her own money she sent and it was all right with Pete. Laura's mother said, "Well. . . ."

Laura was certain her mother had the same conversation with Georgie about Lilli's feelings, and she was equally certain Lilli felt as Pete did.

One warm Sunday afternoon, while visiting Georgie, her mother became dizzy. She was too dizzy to stand up so Lilli put her to bed; but even in bed, Laura's mother was dizzy. She clung to the side of the bedframe and groaned and she did not have the strength to go to the bathroom.

Georgie called an ambulance to take his mother to the nearest hospital. It was chrome modern and spotless, and it broke Laura's heart to see her mother lying on the white, gentile sheets. Her mother had had a stroke.

Georgie contacted Les as Laura sat next to her

176

mother, watching her breathe frantically into an oxygen mask, her small body heaving on one side, the other side heavy, inert from the neural damage.

Les stood at the foot of the bed and nervously guffawed, "To tell you the truth, she doesn't look too good." Laura kept watching her mother, consciously breathing with her, as though by doing so, she could prevent her mother from stopping. Georgie ran out of the room and called Lilli.

When Lilli said there was no point to their sitting around in the hospital, they went back to Georgie's house and sat around there. Lilli gently gave them coffee and tea, and when Pete came, he and Lilli spoke together softly in the kitchen. When Laura heard Pete making phone calls, she knew her mother was going to die.

She curled herself up in a corner of her mind and she would not come out.

She held Pete's hand tightly during the funeral, unaware of anything else. Later, at Georgie's house, after the funeral, she noticed Sol unknot his tie and open his shirt. She saw how much less somber Larry looked once he had removed his gray suit and put on jeans.

"Where's Manny?" Laura asked Pete.

"You know he's still in the Peace Corps, honey," Pete said. "Don't do this."

"Yes."

Laura walked over to Georgie and sat close to him on the couch. Lilli favored crowded shelves. She had hundreds of miniatures around: fat granny dolls with inane smiles and gold-rimmed eyeglasses, Indian dolls of the Caribbean, of Peru, of Arizona, in calico skirts and red bandanas. The drying straw of the dolls contrasted with the variety of huge, flowering plants, hanging from baskets above the couch, crowding the baby-grand piano.

Silken-stone pastel ceramics froze in dance position, in sheep watch, in embrace, in cuddling a child. Without people, it was a peopled room.

When Hilda came in, Georgie and Laura moved to make room for her. They became an audience, watching the others move around: eating candy, drinking coffee, whiskey, talking in small knots of people.

"She was a lovely woman," Bobby said, his face serious with sincerity.

"Take comfort in the fact she had a natural death," Darcy directed them. "She did not die somewhere from brutality as so many have."

"They always made room for her in their lives," Lilli told everyone. "They always took care of her."

"Time heals," Pete said. "Give it time."

Of all the stupid things people say, Laura thought momentarily back in her mind's corner, that has to be high on the list. There may be something else, but it does not replace what was. There's a hole and there's a supplement. They exist side by side, not in overlay. She wanted to express that thought to everyone. But all that came out was, "Well. . . ."

Her abdominal muscles ached: she was holding herself rigidly prepared for someone to say, "It was a lovely funeral." Arlene supplied the inevitable text.

Les beamed proudly at his wife. "To tell the truth, it was." Laura wanted to shake him, to get behind the nervous laughter, to feel the blood they shared.

"Do you want to come with Georgie and me when we go through Ma's things, Les?"

Les did not laugh as he said coldly, "To tell the truth, no."

When Laura and Georgie went to pack their mother's belongings, they found a suitcase filled with plastic bags and a drawer full of broken costume jewelry, shards of colored glass and tarnished gold.

"It's an odd inheritance, isn't it?" Georgie said ruefully.

"Do you think our kids will think what we leave is significant?"

"Only if it's real property."

"And preferably cash."

"And preferably cash."

Georgie brushed at his dandruff—which had long since been cleared up. "Whatever we leave, Laura, won't matter," he said seriously. "They'll have to do for themselves. We can't take care of them forever." And when they were in his car, driving her home, he said, "Wouldn't it be great if we could just freeze time. Just stop the frame."

"Where would you stop it?"

"Somewhere when the kids are between nine and fourteen; somewhere in there while Ma is still enjoying them and they come home every night."

"I don't know, Georgie. Maybe when our kids have kids, we'll be happy time did not stop."

"Well, anyway you slice it, we're the older generation now."

"I'll have to take adult lessons."

Laura sat in her backyard, near the pussy-willow tree and the heavy-scented honeysuckle, listening to the hum, humming of the bees hypnotized by the sweet largess of their nectared feast. Her mother had rarely offered advice after the basic "Be a good girl." She was meticulous about reminding Laura she was a big girl now when the time came, and probably had performed an act of heroism, breaking through her ingrained deep inhibitions, to tell Laura about menstruation.

Her truest expression of conveyed femininity had been to worry about her.

Her mother's flat, square figure appeared in memory. Wearing her green and brown daisied housedress, Laura's mother's image tacitly demonstrated what was important. Cleanliness first. Concealment second. Her mother had no breasts, no curves. Her mother's bunions denied sexuality.

Pete's mother's high heels were not without sex. She was rounded, a Rubens next to Laura's mother. Lush, warm. But Laura's mother's smile was sweet, her eyes soft, and Pete's mother's smile was tight, her eyes greedy.

Laura never thought she had missed something by not wearing a creamy-soft gown and veil on her wedding day. She had never before considered it. Her wedding band was plain gold. She had never chosen a silver pattern, special chinaware.

"Put more blue shadow on your eyes," Pete told Laura when they went out.

"It smears," she said. "It makes my eyes itch."

Hilda had bottles with six different colors of nail polish. She had creams, lotions, foundation makeup, moisturizers, perfume bottles, crowding her bathroom shelves. Laura used a can of talcum powder and a deodorant.

Lilli had belts. Belts of suede, leathers, gold chains, silver chains, white plastic belts with blue and white bows, linked brown braided belts with specks of green woven in. She had shoes to match bags, housecoats, dressing gowns, drawers of soft colored sweaters. Silken fuzz clung to the side of the drawer—soft mists of feminine apparel.

Once, twice, three times as each son was bar mitzvahed, Laura had spent time with detail. Shoe color exactly matched to handbag of proper size. Raw-silk suit appropriate for the mother. High-collared blouse. Beige, ivory tones—neutral, bland.

Pete, in light-gray wool blend, tie sparkling with orange, yellow peacocks; not so neutral, not so bland. On him: right. The Star. Luminescence. Still. Laura told him then. Admiring. In love.

An obsession with appropriateness, with what was considered the right thing to do. Playing the role, checking out the way it was played, beginning with her mother.

Images, absorbed by life's osmosis; from the screen, television, books; flowing first from her mother's brown and green daisied housedress.

"Pete," Laura asked, "will you teach me to be the older generation?"

"Sorry, my exuberant boyishness disqualifies me."

✒ Ever After

AFTER PETE, AFTER THAT, for a long time, I did not know what I was doing. I seemed to lose chunks of time. I would realize I had been driving for hours, remembering a fragment image of an old New England cemetery where the stones were so thin all grief was gone, with no idea where I had seen the graveyard.

I bought books I did not remember rereading until I saw I had three copies of the same title. I had trouble remembering the day of the week, the time of the day. If I watched the six o'clock news, I felt I had never left the house. I could not connect my sitting there with an hour earlier when I had been in my office, checking a last-moment sentence with Fred, or pinching the geranium.

I lost the connections which made me one person. I split into disparate roles I could not integrate. I spoke cheerfully on the phone one minute with Sol, sat idly the next, wondering after a while why the radio sound was so blurred. I started to go for a walk, stopping, surprised to find it dark out. I looked at my watch and saw it was three-thirty. I remembered I should go to bed.

182

I was frightened all the time.

I thought I was a terrible waste of space and ought to give it to the living. But whenever I thought of suicide, I thought how many problems it would cause everyone. I grew tired trying to solve those problems. I was afraid Fred would find me. It might be a week before he decided to break the door down, to find out why I had not come to work nor called in. Then what: The smell of rot would shock him, and disgust him. I could not bear to think of disgusting Fred through eternity.

In any case, I could not do anything so revealing, to so expose my private feelings. I did not want to announce that, yes, it was true, no woman could live alone very long without either going mad or killing herself. Yet I could not very well leave a sign that said "For this woman only—don't generalize."

I did not want Larry to call and, listening to the unanswered rings, hang up, satisfied I was out, active. I did not want to disappoint him. My sons seemed to take such pride in my not being home.

"Jesus, Mom, why don't you remember you're an old lady and sit by the fire once in a while. I've been trying to get ahold of you for a week at least." Happily, because if I were not sitting by the fire, I had to be OK.

And I, feeling like a sneak, compulsively:

"When you speak to your father, is he home by the fire?"

"No. He's even harder to get than you."

"You try hard?" I ask jealously.

"Not very. No."

For a minute I am happy my sons are punishing Pete by not caring very much. I like to think he is hurt, too; but I am not sure he is.

In fact, I think otherwise and it drives me crazier. I think he is happy, at home in his new home, in a Brooklyn Heights apartment with his lover in a red-brick living room. He is in the middle of sophistication and new passion and I am mundane and bitter. I hate myself because I am ordinary and I hate Pete because he is queer.

Nothing makes sense and I return to wanting to die, to escape the senselessness.

Fred, irritated one Monday morning, threw a manila envelope on my desk. "I wanted you to get started on this Sunday—but you—you're never where you're supposed to be."

"I'm sorry, Fred. I—" I stopped. I could not tell him I had been sitting in a museum most of Sunday, ostensibly looking at a Sargent, while internally I was talking to victims, mentally interviewing, one by one, the haunted.

In the city of Cracow, in 1939, a little Jewish boy was taken from the street, and a big Jewish boy was ordered to throw hot coals and ashes on him until the little boy died of burns and the big boy screamed his remaining hours away in an irrevocable insanity.

"What did you say to God?" I asked the little fellow.

"I dared not ask. It was not suitable for me to ask. I had to assume He knew what He was doing."

"Why would you assume that?"

"Because I certainly could never understand it, whatever the reason, so it's best to leave it as something, mysteriously, God's will."

The little fellow looked at me through his charred eyes, red flesh puckering in terrible wounds around the burned eyeballs.

"Don't compare yourself to me," he said.

"Of course not," I whispered.

The black spectre strolled by as the little fellow disappeared. He sat down next to me and said, conversationally, "I first saw him when he was eating breakfast.

184

Such an ordinary human thing to do, don't you think? And after that simple, routine action, he grabbed me, chained my hands, put an iron collar around my neck, attached that collar to the man in front of me and the man in back of me and dragged us all away—far away—where I still don't know—but a place where my wife and children were not, so that I never saw them again, never knew where I was without them, and I couldn't die no matter how I longed to because I could not shake off the chains nor move without my master's permission."

"But that was 1827," I argued, with him, and with myself.

"Do you think time has made it better? I was broken; I never escaped. And you," he added, "are you so broken you cannot escape?"

"I don't know."

"You look pretty whole to me," he said bitterly.

"I don't know how I could ever trust that I knew another human being."

"Why not? You understand now."

"But it's taken my whole lifetime to find out!"

"You're not talking from a real grave, lady. Your lifetime seems to be still continuing to me. I'm talking from the grave—a black, hopeless hole of memory—but you're sitting there breathing, in front of a doorway leading to wherever you want to go."

The big Jewish fellow came back, raving.

"What, what is with that woman? What does she want? Is she smelling gas—is she suffocating with someone's nails clenching her back for safety that doesn't exist? Throw her down the stairs!"

I jumped up.

"Ha! You don't want that, do you?"

I hurried toward the door.

"You want to survive after all, don't you," he roared after me. "You don't want to die at all. You're playing, playing foolish self-pitying games."

The black spectre said, "Now you can survive."

He was the expert.

I went to Georgie. "When they blacklisted you, when your profession was aborted like that, did anyone come forward to help you?"

"You mean outside the family?"

"Yes—like your colleagues, or supervisor."

"No. No one."

"Were you bitter about it?"

"They only had to do it once. I never gave them another chance."

"It?"

"Turn their backs to me."

"Then you're bitter?"

"No. I know what to expect. Everyone's entitled to the benefit of the doubt once. But once is all."

"And how did you go about handling your hurt?"

"Easy. Beat the bastards at their own game. Get richer."

If Georgie were in my position, he would never forgive Pete. He would find a way to get even.

Was it enough for me to know Pete could not depend any more on even the minor courtesies from his sons?

How empty would an empty mailbox seem on Father's Day?

I did not know. I could not assess Pete's present any more than I could his past.

Then I became a listener. For if I had missed so much about Pete, been so ignorant of his feelings and actions, been so blind in the long intimacy of our marriage, how much else had I missed?

186

Hilda told Bobby and me, relishing every detail, about a woman she saw in the bakery. "A tall woman, in a green Saks suit yet, bought three cinnamon Danish and four custard éclairs. The clerk put them all neatly in a box and tied a string around the box. Only she forgot to break the string. So there goes this classy woman, walking imperiously across Lexington Avenue, pulling the string right across and, as far as I know, right to her Park Avenue apartment." Hilda laughed heartily. "It was a regular movie."

Bobby laughed with Hilda. "My wife sees everything," he told Laura proudly.

I heard the good-natured cheerfulness of their household, their pleasure in the minutiae of their lives. What appeared so unimportant to me was the foundation of their stability.

I went to Tanglewood with Darcy and Patrick. "You turn right here," Darcy told him. "Move into the left lane now. We'll come to the next turn soon."

I thought the directions annoyed Patrick, as they certainly would have Pete—or at least I think they would have. I cannot ever be really sure of anything about Pete anymore. But then Patrick asked Darcy to which toll booth he should go, and I realized, with surprise, he liked the directions.

Darcy knew a French restaurant two miles from Tanglewood. The owner came out in a high white chef's hat and wished us all good appetite.

"What are you having, Darcy?" Patrick asked, studying the enormous cardboard menu.

"I understand the duck is wonderful. I think I'll try it."

"What do you think I should have?"

"Why don't you try the trout? That way we can taste a

little of everything." Darcy turned to me. "Why don't you order the beef—"

"Of course," I said.

At the concert, Darcy felt chilly. Patrick went back to the car to get her sweater. Had Pete ever done that for me? I think it would have been assumed that if I was the chilly one, I would get my own sweater. I doubt it is important what the reality was. I thought I would have not expected Pete to run the errand. With Darcy, it was otherwise. I admired her for it.

As I listened to Georgie and Lilli, I heard how many superlatives they used. "The greatest!" "The absolute best!" It must be tiring to reach the extremes all the time, I thought.

But they seemed to listen, too. "No one ever just goes to a doctor," Georgie said. "He goes to the top man in his field." And another time, "People always tell me I look great now. Last time I didn't look so good; now I look much better."

I saw how Georgie and Lilli frequently engaged in private conversation; hugged each other; stayed near each other in the room. Georgie asked Lilli what restaurant they should go to and she said, "Whatever you're in the mood for, dear." He asked her if she liked what she was eating, and Lilli said it was a little too salty. "Don't eat it," Georgie said. "Order something else."

"No, it's not necessary. How is your cutlet?"

"The greatest," he said.

"He always makes the best choice," Lilli told me, ruefully pleased.

I went to the beach. I lay in the hot, still air, listening to the family settled in next to me. Their radio blared rock, monotonous, repetitive beat. The father lay dozing,

188

his hat over his eyes, a dead cigar in his mouth. His hairy belly sucked in and out. His wife read a magazine, calling suddenly, "Jamie! Leave her alone!" A teenage boy lay with his ear next to the radio, looking into the sun.

Two nubile, preadolescent girls sat together, eating cherries, throwing the pits on the sand.

"I bought the white pullover for Ginny," one told the other. "I think she'll like it, don't you?"

"I know I would." A seal of approval, obviously, for the youngster smiled happily, revealing heavy gray braces crowding her mouth.

I closed my eyes, feeling the gritty sand and smooth sun. I liked the contrast and was quiescent. I told myself I was not lonely, although alone. I had been there once in a family group. Then going to the beach had meant detailed packing—towels, dry pants, sun oil, fruit, chicken, napkins, balls, a first-aid kit—and my panties carefully hidden at the bottom of one of the jammed tote bags.

Pete took a long time to go into the water: standing ankle deep, bellowing about how cold it was, and then abruptly diving headlong, hidden for a moment, then emerging, snorting, calling out to me to come on in because it was wonderful. And immediately swimming off, alternately diving under and coming up with a roar; shaking himself briskly when he came back to the beach, asking what there was to eat, and throwing himself, wet, in the sand; unconcerned as the thick sand layer became magnetized to his wet body, arms, legs stretched out in total submission to the sun.

Getting a tan was a very serious business to Pete. He held his face up stiffly, not wanting to miss a ray. He turned over reluctantly, accepting the necessity for doing his back. He rarely talked much at the beach.

Maybe that's why I thought I was not lonely. We had always experienced it separately.

I sensed people were having experiences I had already had. It was not necessary for me to be part of it again. I'd been through it and was at a later stage.

But I could not transfer that feeling to all situations. I was tormented by the idea I had been cheated of some kind of just reward.

I felt I had done everything I was supposed to do. I had not neglected my husband for the children. I had been aware of him, interested in what he was doing, helpful when I could be, letting him help me when he could. When I had a flat, I called him, tearful, lost. I reserved time for us to be alone, to stroll together, window-shopping, relaxed, without pressure. I remembered every birthday, searching for the tennis racket he really wanted, inscribing gift books *yours, always*.

I had not sat and grown fat and stupid. I had studied, learned a profession, added to the conversation, kept myself thin, clean. According to the *Redbook* quiz, I was a good wife, a good mother.

Why then?

I argued my case interminably. Always I was right, had been grieviously wronged, dealt an unjust hand. I whined my anger.

Nothing changed.

I learned from my listening that people made arrangements among themselves which were only partially articulated. Most of it was lived out, not worked out, certainly not totally communicated.

If I were going to make it, I had to keep doing something—although the "something" might not be very satisfying nor, if it was with someone, totally understood. With Pete gone, there could be no total anything.

I tried to do things I had always done, living automatically and routinely, so the quality of living was apparent, if not substantive.

It did not work. Even such a customary act as going to the theatre with Hilda and Bobby made me unhappy. I did not know quite where to walk as we strolled to a restaurant. I was not sure how I should analyze the play. "It was swell" was not enough for me, and that's all Hilda might want to say.

I started to make dates with Soo, but she always wanted to go to the early show so we would not get home too late. I found it depressing to eat in almost-empty restaurants at five-thirty. When we came out of a movie, the lines of people waiting to go in seemed the in-crowd, the partygoers. I felt like a wallflower.

At lunch one Tuesday, Soo said casually she could not, after all, go to the movies with me Friday. A friend of a friend had introduced her to a guy. She was going to the movies with him. She knew I would understand.

I understood meeting a new man was more important than meeting a woman. A woman you could get to any time. Nor was I surprised that I didn't see much of Soo socially after that, but I was surprised to realize women exploit other women emotionally and then drop them when a guy turns up.

"My husband was my best friend," the widow said sadly. "Why did I need anyone else?"

So what else is new? I thought.

Labor Day weekend was coming up. I received no invitations, and sometime in the middle of August, I realized I would likely spend the three days alone unless I did something about it. I had to do something. I knew that because the idea of those three days filled me with a dread I had only experienced when I visited my dying father.

I returned from work each night all during the rest of August, worrying about the Labor Day weekend. I could not sleep, anticipating the bottomless, infinite void of those three days.

I checked through my phone book, looking at the names of my friends and relatives, trying to decide whom I might invite over. I was even more anxious about calling someone and hearing the person say he or she was busy. I felt brittle, emaciated. I was afraid to risk hearing the word no. It would shatter me.

I methodically called the museums in New York City, and kept visualizing the return home, knowing a museum would suffocate me and there would still be two more days. I could manage Sunday morning, but the afternoon would never end. I would spend the rest of my life waiting for Sunday afternoon to end, sitting downstairs, while the immobile part of me haunted the bedroom.

I decided I must find a place of anonymity, where no one would notice me, would see I was alone, unsurrounded by loving family: unloved. I decided to go to Las Vegas.

It took me eight hours to pack. The white blouse I wanted to take had a yellow spot on it. The housecoat was too large. I could not go without low shoes, blue high heels, black high heels, slippers, a bathing suit. But all the shoes made the valise too heavy. The bathing suit would be wrinkled beyond wearing.

I knew I would be unable to carry that bulky, bulging heavy suitcase through the airport.

If I found a porter, how much did I tip him?

"What the hell difference does it make?" I told myself. "Go and find out."

I went.

A blister hurt my hand from the overcrowded valise

and I may have tipped the porter ten dollars because I started to sweat and wanted him to go away fast, but I ultimately found myself in a hotel room that was clean and large and private.

I wandered around the casino, moving idly from one slot machine to another. All around me there was noise, sudden shouts, bells ringing, clanging coins, cigarette smoke; and the red cherries, the purple plums, the unexpected 7's flashing before my eyes. No one bothered me. No one isolated me, so that in my isolation, I was free, mobile, able to eat alone without embarrassment, to join a group at the roulette table without shyness, to sleep alone, unidentified.

I flew back at the end of the Labor Day vacation, moving briskly, assuredly through the mobbed waiting room where no one waited for me and entered my empty house, relieved and happy to be home. I had survived the three-day weekend.

I nodded once to the leftover me in the middle of the room and said, "Fuck you, Pete," as I unpacked and prepared for the coming week's work.

When Manny returned from his overseas Peace Corps duty, he only knew Pete and I had separated. He asked no details, which surprised me. Were I he, I know I would have been unable to wait until I was told. "If the person wants to tell me, she will" was not something I could live with, no matter how I recognized the exquisite tactfulness of the attitude. I would hint, and nag, possibly cajole, until I knew.

I had done that with Darcy. Why hadn't she married Patrick was a question I kept raising and returning to until she told me, irritably, because he was already married and his wife countenanced no divorce. So I knew.

My idea of being exquisitely tactful was to make no further comment.

Manny was emaciated. He had been hit hard by dysentery and hard work and maybe sheer growth. He was also poised, much more confident, and easy, easy to be with. Relaxed, comfortable—and unquestioning.

I waited impatiently. I wanted Pete to tell him. I wanted someone other than Dr. Summers to know how unjustly I'd been treated, what an innocent victim I was, how deserving of comforting and loving. I wanted people on my side.

But Manny was cool. He did not let me know for several weeks he knew about his father. Manny was busy organizing his life, finding an apartment, enrolling himself in law school; resuming, reconstituting his own social life.

Or perhaps he merely wanted to avoid the conversation. I never know for sure any longer.

On the morning of my forty-ninth birthday, he called to invite me to dinner. "You always said it was your heart's desire to meet your children in a restaurant. So this is the day your wish can be fulfilled; that is, up to nine dollars' worth. After that we'd have to do dishes anyway, so we might as well not go out at all."

I was pleased. The restaurant he chose was New England lovely with wood beams and soft rose lights. Fresh white snapdragons graced each table, and sitting opposite him I felt filled with grace too. I ordered carefully, respecting the nine-dollar limit apparently too obviously. "It was only a joke, Ma," Manny said patiently.

I had an odd feeling of distortion, looking at us through the funny mirror of time's passage. I knew all the intimate physical details of this person, from the carefully counted toes of his birth day to the pulsating softness of his baby skull. I had taken his familiar hand

194

when white, tense creases revealed his terror at a carousel he badly wanted to conquer when he was two years old. I sewed tags in sweaters that became too small for him in the two months he was at summer camp, and I avoided looking at stiffened streaks of semen on his late-adolescent sheets. I had seen him walk quickly, and without looking back, to an airplane, to go to an unknown country, for an unknown length of time—and now he sat, amused at my dimwitted literal response; and I no more knew him than I had known his father.

I gulped down the iced water at my setting as though I had just passed years in the Sahara, as dismay at my ignorance emptied the well of my being. I could not bear another reminder of the known abruptly transformed into the unknown.

Yet, there he was, opposite me, smiling at my awkwardness, and I did not know how it happened that he learned to sense tension and to assess it and to determine his reaction to it.

His reaction was characteristically kind: an attempt to alleviate my uneasiness. But Pete loomed between us, and I realized I could not be easy with Manny until we did something about that.

And while I was trying to find a way to say what I never seemed able to say aloud to anyone but Dr. Summers, while I was brooding in my inimitably futile, inadequate way, Manny said, "I've seen Dad."

"And?"

"And he told me, if that's what you're asking, and I guess it is."

I waited.

He frowned. "It was a shock. OK, it was a shock. I think Dad was pretty tense about it, too. I mean, he never sat down and just talked to me or anything. He said he wanted to talk to me, but he didn't really. We were in his motel room and he was packing. He just kind of moved around and kept packing things and told me."

"What did you do?" I studied him, trying to feel his feelings, trying, for once, to be in someone else's emotions, person. He smiled faintly at me. "I didn't do anything, Mom. What was there for me to do? I told him I wanted him to be happy—as, of course, I want you to be happy—and he had to do what he thinks best. That's what I told him. And what I told myself was I'm not going to think about it. I'm just not going to let it have anything to do with me."

I was disappointed. I moved my chopped steak around in its onion gravy so it would be good and saturated with the sauce; and I kept myself really busy doing that because I did not want to let Manny know sometimes it helped a mother to have a child take sides no matter what all the goddamn books said, and despite the patent reality this was no child.

Manny continued, "He's my father, Mom, and he always will be. That's my business with him—father and son. And nothing else."

"Don't expect he will be willing to spend much time at it," I said, hearing Pete's "I don't want to be a husband and father any more" in hollow memory-echo.

"Don't be bitter, Ma."

"I didn't mean—" I said, resentful.

"It's not something we can talk about too much, is it?" Manny, the stranger-adult said. "I'll try to relate to him as I remember him—as my father. I did tell him I don't ever want to see him with his, uh, his friend—and I won't. I'll meet him and see him when I can and hope I keep remembering what he was like when I was a kid."

"I hope you can work it out that way, honey."

"As long as the Yankees keep playing, I guess I'll be able to."

"Not much, is it?" I said, sadly.

"About as much as I want, Mom."

"Do you think he's told Larry and Sol?"

"Well, I haven't, that's for damn sure," Manny emphasized. "Can't we just drop it for now? In fact, now," he said, lifting his wine glass, "let's just wish you a happy birthday and many happy returns."

"I appreciate your sentiments, son," I responded, resisting my impulse to speak ironically.

"He's an immoral bastard!" Sol shouted over the phone. "Sue him for every goddamn penny he has and ever will have. I don't want to hear from you until I hear you've got a lawsuit going that will wipe him out. Threaten to let the ABA know. Have the son of a bitch disbarred if he so much as argues with you."

"Easy, easy," I soothed.

His fury made me feel queasy. I wanted Sol on my side but I did not want him to hate so much. His anger was an acid that could corrode all our relationships.

"It has nothing to do with you, really," I reminded Sol. "It's between your father and me—"

"Cocksucking fags ought to be wiped off the face of the earth."

"Sol!"

Idiotically, for a second I was as shocked by Sol's language as by the new fact of Pete. But Manny had reminded me Pete would always be their father and I did not want Sol all mixed up. So I told him the cheating was done to me, not him. His father had not cheated him. He had treated Sol as a son, as a son he loved.

"Don't give me any of that New York Jew liberalism. Fags are destroying the moral fiber of this country. There's too goddamn much permissiveness. If it weren't permitted by your bleeding heart sops, it wouldn't be so prevalent. People like you are just encouraging all this shit."

I trembled. The phone shook so much I laid it down on the couch and lay down with my mouth to the speaker. The bed shivered with me. The mucous suffocated me, growing thicker, more impenetrable than ever before. I opened my mouth and gaped for air like a fish. My legs moved up involuntarily so that I cringed in a fetal position, trying to speak into the receiver without touching it, trying to connect to the Sol who had once promised to cry if his father lost his dominance.

"Fuck him, Ma. Do you hear me?" Sol continued shouting. "Don't let him get away with this. Destroy him—now—like the rat he is."

"Sol," I pleaded. "Stop. Calm down. You're talking about something he couldn't help. It's like telling a person with diabetes not to have sugar. It was out of his control—but he's still your father. You've had years of fatherhood from him. Try to remember that. You don't have to wipe it all out."

"He is wiped out. He's dead. Gone. Finito. Got that? And now you get every penny you can. You got that, Ma? Every cent!"

He hung up. I continued to lie there, gasping, trying to get through the mucous. *New York Jew Liberal* had come from my own son's mouth, and I was adrift again in a world peopled only and forever with strangers.

After that, I not only did not dare to ask Larry if he knew, I dreaded what might happen when he did know. I wrote nothing except what I was doing, and Larry said nothing when he called except what he was doing. The impasse ended when Larry came home for his last spring vacation before graduation.

"We're going to make it an M.O.," I informed him, "a really Momentous Occasion. Sol is going to come in with Sarah, and Manny said he's thinking of introducing us to a very, very fascinating young lady he's learned to love studying law with—her name is Betty—and I gather it's more than law he loves studying with her—and I have already bought a perfect oyster eggshell-white pure silk suit from Bonwit's and intend to be photographed with the most handsome graduate of the class of '72."

"You might have some trouble finding this handsome graduate. He doesn't intend to be at the ceremony. He thought he'd spend the occasion getting stoned with his friends, like any other normal red-blooded American boy."

"Oh, c'mon, cutie. I've really been looking forward to this reunion. We've all been so separate. . . ."

Larry helped himself to a box of cookies. Typically, while the rest of the world dieted, he consumed sweets and carbohydrates constantly and never gained weight. I complained about that.

"Genes," he said. "Brilliant genetic selection." He ate a few more cookies, thoughtfully. Then he looked directly at me. "I don't want Dad there."

I lowered my eyes and studied my hands. "I think my freckles are becoming the liver spots of the aged," I observed. "I wasn't so careful about my genetic selection, I guess."

"Don't stall, Mom. No Dad. Agreed?"

"I'm not stalling, Larry. I didn't know it was up to me." I blushed. I don't like to lie and really I had hoped Larry would ask Pete. I kept having this fantasy that we would all be together and then Pete wouldn't want to leave and Sol would break down and cry and ask forgiveness and we would all live happily ever after.

I stopped studying my hands and studied the skinny cookie eater instead. "Did you know Sol doesn't want to see him again?"

"Yes."

"Do you know why?"

"Yes."

I was enormously relieved. I dared, now, to ask, "Do you feel the same way?"

"Of course not. I don't know where Sol's getting all that moral fiber crap from. He must be hanging around some of the Jesus freaks in L.A. No, I don't feel any of that, but—"

"But—?"

"I don't like to see Dad. He makes me uncomfortable. All of a sudden he calls and starts to play The Father. How much money do I have? What do I intend to do when I graduate? Then he disappears into silence for another two months. He doesn't know a damn thing about me and doesn't want to know. He only calls so he won't feel guilty. It's his feelings he's bothered with, not mine." Larry grinned wickedly. "I oblige him. I always tell him I need some money. He always says he'll send some. And after another couple of weeks, he sends half of what I said I needed. I guess he's not guilty enough, huh?"

"Well . . . ," I said, "were you upset, Larry, about his decision to live a homosexual life?"

"You make it sound so formal, Mom."

"I suppose I think it is. Like a decision to become a Jesuit. It is a major decision after all."

"It's not such a big deal."

"It's not?"

"Nah. I always knew anyway," he added casually.

"What are you talking about? What do you mean you always knew?"

"I don't know. I just did. From the time I was about fifteen on, I think."

"How could you know and I didn't!"

"You forget, Ma—or maybe you never understood—half the kids I grew up with had weird parents. One of my friend's mom used to call for him at ten in the morning, right in the middle of class, because she'd be so loaded already she'd think it was time to drive him home.

"Half the fathers used to make passes at the girls—when they weren't borrowing joints off us."

"But your father wasn't like that. He was so—fatherly," I finished lamely.

"Not for me. Not really. In fact, he made me uncomfortable all the time. He paid so much attention to my appearance. I felt something was wrong. Something was awry. You'd ask me how school was and Dad would say the belt I had on would look super with a buckle he'd seen at some store." Larry took time to think. "I guess I never thought he was having fag sex. I never went that far. It's just that he fussed about my looks like my fag friends, so I thought of him that way." He stopped again. "I wasn't so crazy about it, of course."

I wanted to hold him, to tell him adults really were not so weird, that his father was an aberration—a one-in-a-million shot. And then I feared Larry's truth might be closer to reality than mine, so I told him I guessed, in the end, we have to accept everything human and he agreed we did.

A few days later he mailed me a quote from Alexander Pope:

> Were there all harmony, all virtue here
> That neither air nor ocean felt the wind;
> That never passion discomposed the mind.

> But all subsists by elemental strife
> And passions are the elements of life.

So I guess Larry really did agree.

We had a wonderful time at Larry's graduation. We took pictures of each other: of Betty, sweet, soft, friendly; of Sarah, golden as ever. Manny, Sol, and Larry joked with each other and patted each other every once in a while on the shoulders. Everyone ate too much and drank chilled wine in nongourmet, but definitely Basse, characteristic fashion.

We even played a short game of initials, leaving Sarah and Betty out as my sons and I too quickly guessed B.R. was Branch Rickey because Manny was giving the initials, or F.D. was Fyodor Dostoeyevsky when it was Larry's turn. N.R. was shouted simultaneously by all of us to Sol. Even Sarah guessed he would choose Nelson Rockefeller to think of first.

But no one ever ventured P.B., although I think each of us must have thought of Pete sometime during the day.

Pete sent Larry a Mexican sweater and a seventy-five-dollar check for his graduation.

"It's nice." I said.

"You don't think I'd ever wear a sweater like that, do you?"

"Well, send a thank-you note anyway. Be gracious."

"Maybe. When I get around to it."

"That's gracious?"

"I hate to be forced into being involved with him. I don't need his presents."

"Maybe he wanted to come to the graduation and—"

"If I promise to send the letter, can we forget about him?" Larry interrupted.

He left the sweater on the hall table when he went

202

home. For a few days, every time I saw the sweater just lying there in the white tissue paper, with the red ribbon that had been tied outside the box resting limp on the tissue, every time I saw that discarded gift, I felt sorry for Pete. He had once mourned because his father had not opened his gift. Now his son had opened his and did not want it.

After a while, I threw the sweater in the Goodwill box outside the supermarket.

My lawyer grew impatient. She needed a financial statement from Pete in order to prepare the necessary papers, but she had no one to call to get it. In any case, she felt there were so many details Pete and I ought to go over, we really ought to have a conference.

I jumped at the chance to call Pete legitimately. I could not remember his voice or what he looked like, so that the gnawing ache and suffocating mucous seemed to exist independently of any cause, an unattached pain I experienced without reason.

His voice made me homesick. It reminded me of twilight, driving up to Quebec, on a strange highway. I envied the lights going on in houses. I was going in the wrong direction, away from warmth. I wanted to turn around and could not because the traffic was too heavy and propelled me along with it, beyond my control.

It was snowing the night we met. The snow was so soundless I could hear my own breathing. Pete never looked at me, unnaturally holding the car door open for me, his eyes studying the hood of the car. He kept brushing the snow from his hair as though he did not want it to get wet. Perhaps he had sprayed his hair; it was stiff enough in a pompadour to make me suspect he had.

His cologne permeated the air; like cheap talcum powder, it crowded us. There were small tassels on his shoes, rapidly drooping from the wet snow. His paisley-print ascot, under his turtleneck, reminded me of Adolph Menjou. I expected Pete to speak in a pseudo-English accent any minute.

He felt artificial: a clone who believed the products he was programmed to demonstrate during commercials. Being with him confused and disoriented me. Sitting side by side, even in front of the lawyer's desk, was a natural position for us, but the discussion was unreal. When Pete went to the bathroom and my lawyer said, "Don't argue with him; we'll get everything you want," I did not know to what she was referring. Why should I consider Pete an adversary?

The legal matters were completed quickly. There was very little left for us to decide about. It was difficult to remember what Pete and I had in common after all.

"Let's get a drink!" Pete said when we left the office, so we skidded our way to a deserted bar, uncomfortable and formal.

"Civilization," I said, gulping my gin, "is a big mistake."

"Do you want me to leave?"

"No—yes!—but we have a little talking to do yet."

"What's left?"

"The kids. I think you ought to try to see them more often."

"I don't know if I can, but I'll try."

I asked him what I had been wanting to ask him for months. "Wasn't there ever a time you tried, wanted to tell me."

"Never." So definite.

"It doesn't make sense." My head hurt. Why didn't he move around the table and sit next to me and say, "Why are we sitting in an empty restaurant on such a cold night; why don't we just go home?"

"Why never?"

"I was ashamed. I thought—I'd been convinced by society, by everything I read—my feelings were unhealthy. I spent my time fighting what I thought were sick symptoms."

"But now you don't feel that way?"

"No. It's as natural as a heterosexual's feelings." Pete's smile. Proud.

"And you always had homosexual relations during our marriage?"

"Hundreds."

Was he boasting?

"You needed so many?"

"Yes, because the lack of involvement protected me."

"You mean it didn't interfere with your using us?"

"I mean it didn't disturb the life I'd constructed that I thought was healthy."

"If you make that the life *we* constructed, you might see the problem."

"You might see the problem if you see it wasn't healthy at all. Not for you, not for me."

"Don't speak for me!"

"All right. But I can speak for myself—that is," he added sarcastically, "if it's all right with you. I'm finally living a healthy life and it works. I've never been happier."

His flesh evaporated from his face and his tangled electrode connections emerged before my eyes. I couldn't find a person opposite me.

Nasty, I asked, "Who plays the girl and who plays the boy?"

"Nobody plays at anything. We both do everything. That's a lot of nonsense about roles."

"I never noticed you felt that way when I picked up your socks."

"You loved it. You thought it made you important."

"Did the fact that you're such an authentic son of a bitch also elude me all these years?"

"If you're going to start an argument and begin hashing over the past, I'm getting out of here now."

"And find a quick fuck?"

"We're faithful to each other. That's part of our contract."

"Well, *we* know that never influenced you before."

When he started to leave, though, I asked him to wait.

"I want to try a little more," I said in a normal voice. "I want to try to understand this."

He sat down again, drinking a little, waiting, friendlier. His mouth muscles relaxed. He slouched slightly, ready to listen reasonably. But I held back for a second, not quite ready. I had not anticipated the fury that was thumping around in my chest like a giant trying to find his way out of a miniature house. I waited until the monstrous rage diminished so I could speak naturally about this unnatural situation.

"It isn't quite true, Pete. You did seem to have some feeling about whatever masculinity is. You never bought the kids dolls or play furniture, but you bought them bats and catcher's mitts—and God—all those Little League games we went to."

"Well, of course! That's not a role—that's an interest."

"Doesn't it strike you as strange that all those interests were what people think about as male?"

"Look, I'm the same person I always was. It's only that now I can admit a penis turns me on. See? That's the difference that counts. That's my truth. It's not sick or monstrous or anything but natural—for me. You just didn't have what I wanted."

I studied my nails. They were of uneven lengths, some long and shaped, others broken and irregular. I wished I could go back to those pretty white gauze gloves women used to wear.

I could not put Pete's remarks together with the memory of our sexual experiences, so I did not say anything. We drank silently, separately. Then Pete said,

"Look, can I ask you a favor?"

"No," I said. "I don't think so."

"Let me know how Sol's doing," he asked anyway. Maybe from time to time you can send me a picture . . ."

Against my will, I felt sorry for him.

"I'll try," I said.

But I had no pictures to send, and I did not have any reason to get in touch with Pete. As the months lengthened, somehow I managed to forget the lawyer's conference. My mind skirted the smell of talcum powder and the memory of hair spray. Pete's words became distorted, became sound without meaning. Instead, I felt his presence, remembered his thirty-second birthday. We were dancing in our living room, a large buffet of roast chicken and dumplings, iced champagne and friends and gag presents waiting for us in the next few hours.

Was this an artful arrangement, suggested by my ladies' magazines, my older self criticized?

I shifted his presence to a breakfast we had in the sunny clarity of Antigua, where we were charmed by little yellow birds who shared our sugar bowl. A gift of nature.

We were holding hands, a clutch against terror at Sol's mysterious high temperature. I was phoning Pete with the relief of tears-at-last when my car broke down on the expressway, and the policeman yelled at me, and the tow-truck man said, "Just tell me where to dump this, lady," and I said, "I'll have to ask my husband," and Pete, my husband, said, "Put him on. I'll take care of it."

I was reassuring Pete he could open his own office—buying him a statue of Sysiphus for his desk—hiding bills from him—organizing his telephone file—handing him my salary checks uncashed so he might feel we always had some income, could always manage somehow with it, while he was developing his practice.

I was walking furiously out of our room because he was so goddamn rude when I said I needed the car almost all week, and he was following me, already apologetic, grabbing me, throwing me on the bed and plunging his head down suddenly, uncharacteristically, at my stomach, stroking my buttocks with increasing passion, kissing me wetly, tonguing, until, as we had as kids, we orgasmed without intercourse and I said, weakly, happily, "I must remember to ask for the car more often."

I forgot the present and remembered only the past: I became desperate to see Pete again.

I kept my eyes down as I called him. I did not want the inert figure of myself standing in the bedroom to see what I was doing.

I used Larry's impending twenty-first birthday as an excuse. "Isn't there something we can do as a family?"

Pete didn't think so. "I have a new life now. I just can't get away; I mean, the priorities are different. I can't just take off like that." He could not do anything with me about Larry's birthday. He would send a present or check or something.

"I'd like to see you anyway," I confessed. "Even afterward."

"Why?"

"Well, I could tell you what we did."

I thought he would not answer. He remained silent

so long. But then he said, "OK. It's not a good idea, though."

After we had arranged to meet, I added at the last minute, "So I'll see you then, unless I get a better offer."

I didn't get a better offer, so I went to the airport to meet him. It was August, with a steady, continuing heat—no hint yet of the fall to come—spring too far back to be real—only the heat a reality, burning everything into limp submission.

My own tears surprised me as Pete strolled through the door: his familiar, rhythmic lope and his unfamiliar mustache. I saw him brushing a gray wisp from his forehead.

"Great," he said as I sniveled.

"I'm sorry." I was. "It's a shock to see you older."

I said it without considering the implications: I had insulted him.

"Damn! Let's start again," I suggested. "How are you?"

"Absolutely super. I don't think I've ever been as great."

"I'm sorry to hear that," I said cheerfully. "Maybe next time I'll hear better news."

He grinned. "I'll try."

We decided to drive out to Glen Cove, to the white sands of the island. We stopped at the seawall. The sound moved serenely. Seagulls swooped around the brilliant white posts of the wall. Pete took my hand as we strolled.

"There's no way to go back," he said softly. "We can't sit around the dining-room table naturally. It would feel wrong to everyone and make us feel bad. I feel so rotten about that, you know, because I can't get to the kids now. Can't get to them all together, the way you can."

"Did it feel right to you then?"

"Of course."

"So how did it begin to feel wrong? I mean, I understand you fell in love, but you wouldn't have if you didn't let it happen. You had to set it up so it could happen. Why did you do that? What did you think was going on between us that was so different?"

"Lots of things. You were maturing, growing into your own. You found work to do that made sense not only to you but to all of us. And the rituals. We were going through all the rituals of life—the birthdays, the bar mitzvahs, my father's death. It was all . . . distancing."

"Distancing?" I echoed. "I thought it was connecting."

"I guess that's where we started separating then. Seeing those years so differently."

I wanted to say, "So why the hell didn't you mention it?" but I did not want him to become defensive. So, like a U.N. ambassador, I said, "Couldn't we find some neutral territory, some place, like a resort maybe, where we would do things together but things we hadn't done before, in a new way? We could still, at least, enjoy each other's company."

"When? That's the trouble. I just don't have the time now. And it really isn't fair to—well—getting here today was quite difficult. And I can't see myself having any time for maybe six or seven months."

"Think about it, Pete. You're still at a crossroads with us—me and the kids. If you set up a new way now, while I'm still willing, and at least two of them are still willing, it might work; but if you let it go too long, it'll be all over." Why was I still trying? I wondered. Why didn't I just say the hell with him, and forget him?

"Kids separate now, anyway," I continued against my own thoughts. "Parents can't be part of their daily routine, so if there's no regular something—hell, that's it. Nothing separates like time and distance."

"Yes," Pete said firmly. And I understood that was his decision. He had weighed the factors, maybe even writing them down on one of the yellow legal pads he used in his office. Blocked in time to see Manny and Larry. P.S.'d pictures of Sol from me. And all the rest of the time for his lover and their friends, their vacations, their shopping trips. He said he felt rotten he could not be with all his children. Sometimes I guess he did, but I don't think that was much of the time.

Even if he felt guilty—and I supposed he had to or he would not have met me today—his feelings about us were weaker than his need for his lover.

He needed the time and distance to keep separating from us, to become convinced there was nothing he could do about our feelings. He had to follow his own way, and if his sons couldn't accept it, it was part of the price Pete would have to pay.

He probably saw himself as a tragic figure. Maybe he was.

The rest of the day was surreal, the last moment before the train pulled out and Johnny went to war and Janie watched and knew she would never see him again.

Pete said, "Take care of yourself," as he left, abdicating any responsibility to care for me.

I watched him board the plane. I still felt—even more strongly felt—the destruction of our marriage was willful, deliberate, and unnecessary. Yet above the separation, despite the betrayal, my love for him endured, and my anger was diluted, my desolation thickened.

Seven weeks later, I went to court for the divorce

proceedings. I sat, poised, in the courtroom while waiting to be called. I watched a sixteen year old dissolve her impulsive marriage to a soldier.

"You'll go back to school now, like a good girl?" the judge asked her.

"Oh, yes," she responded.

A young woman asked for a desertion order. "I need child support for the two kids," she said.

"We'll try to find him," the judge said.

A lengthy contract was read on behalf of a tense well-dressed black woman. The plaintiff husband agreed to support the three children through college or until they were twenty-one years of age, whichever came first, with increasing amounts to cover their maturing needs. The woman smiled sweetly when the decree was ordered.

It was my turn. I walked quickly to the enclosure beside the judge, not allowing myself to think I could do anything else. When the clerk asked me to confirm our wedding date, I could not speak through the mucous. He insisted I do more than nod. I transformed everyone into comic strip characters so that a balloon "Yes" could come from my mouth.

"Why do you feel this marriage is irretrievably broken?" the caricature judge asked me.

"Because we married as children and grew apart as adults," the inked balloon said.

The caricature was not satisfied. But that was the only line I knew so I kept repeating it. Finally, he stopped and ordered the decree.

When I left the courthouse, I found the sun had frozen.

The next day, Manny called unexpectedly.

"How about going out to dinner with Betsy and me tonight. Are you busy?"

212

"I'd love it. No, I'm not busy."

I worked on a translation for a couple of hours. Sol called.

"You'll never guess where I am, Ma—right here, in New York. I had to fly in last night to set up an exhibit for an L.A. gallery. How about dinner?"

"Sol! This is so nice. Manny and Betsy are having dinner with me, too."

"Couldn't be better timing. Got to keep moving now. See you later."

I started to take out my clothes for the evening. Larry came in.

"Good night for a free meal," he said.

"My God, Larry—did you know Sol was in?"

"Sure."

I got it then.

"Nice gesture," I told them when we were all together.

"Never mind that," Sol smiled. "Who pays?"

"I knew there was a catch."

"It's really a test to see how woman's lib you are," Manny said.

"It stops at the dinner table."

"Where does it start?" Betsy wanted to know.

"With the person I have to find as a gay divorcee?"

"The singles bars will be blessed."

If it would not have embarrassed them, I would have told them how blessed I felt right then. Instead I told Sol he better quit eating such rich desserts or he'd rot the roots of his teeth before he was thirty-five.

❧ *After part: 1*

DARCY CALLED LAURA. "Patrick has a friend who's a widower. I think he's about your age. Should I invite you both to dinner?"

"Darcy, I'm afraid. I don't think I can act naturally."

"Just make conversation. Anything that happens is up to the both of you. I'm just introducing you."

"What should I wear?"

"Anything but those baggy slacks of yours."

It was a nice party. Darcy's heavy brown stoneware and openweave cloths lent an arty aura to her studio-like living room. Enormous paintings of sombre grandmothers in high ruffled collars looked down on the women in black pajama-loose slacks and sterling-silver earrings.

Laura found Patrick's friend too short and foxy thin. She eyed him warily over Darcy's plates and could not find anything to say to him out of the general conversation. Darcy wanted to play charades. Patrick's friend did not play. Laura thought how Pete would have loved it.

She was very tired the next day and did nothing but watch television.

"What do you do on Saturday night?" Laura asked Larry, as she inspected his musty New York apartment.

"Usually just hang out and wait for the late show to come on."

"Don't you go out on dates?"

"No one *dates* anymore, Mom."

Lilli charged in through Laura's back door, a miniature dynamo ready to generate: "Mr. Right is moving right near you! I've given him your number. His name is Richard Cohen—and this is it!"

"Do you think we have time for a cup of coffee before we go out to buy the wedding dress?" Laura said, dryly. "Who is he?"

"The Cohens lived near us for years and years. They moved to Atlanta maybe three years ago. I understand his wife died—I don't know just when—but he was visiting another neighbor and I met him there and found out he's moving here, so I gave him your number."

Lilli hugged Laura with exuberant delight. "He has the greatest smile!" she said.

"Well, maybe he won't call," Laura cautioned.

But he did. Laura liked the resonance of his loudish voice.

"You don't know me," he said, "but your sister-in-law gave—"

"Richard Cohen," Laura said. "How do you do?"

"Just fine. Do you think we might go out to dinner some night?"

"Terrific," Laura said.

Who told Larry no one dates anymore?

After the first date, they made another; and then another. After that, they did not make dates. They just saw each other regularly. She looked forward to seeing him, although he was an ugly man, his head too deep in his shoulders, his neck not long enough to hold it in proportion. His brown eyes were kind, heavy-bagged. He was jowly, overweight. His weight made him appear shorter than he was.

Laura found his masculinity was pervasive. He spoke loudly, directly, moved solidly, confidently. His car was an old Dodge, with a gear shift. When it stuck, he fussed with the motor and fixed it. His hands were square with tufts of hair above the knuckles. He carried cash in a huge, gold dollar-shaped clip, peeling off tens and twenties when he paid a bill.

Like Laura, Richard came from a poor home and married his childhood sweetheart. He'd been in the Seabees during the war, where he found he liked the work so much he studied construction engineering under the G.I. Bill after the war. He had organized his own company in the late '40s and had been "hustling ever since. Let's face it, no one ever works harder than the boss, not if you want to stay boss."

Laura enjoyed Richard's disregard for convention. He wore heavy work boots all the time. He cooked dinner for her, throwing a frozen liver filet on the frying pan and scattering wheat germ over it as it smoked and burned, until he decided it had cooked long enough. It did not bother him that the middle remained frozen. He ate it with relish, only too pleased to take the center she so carefully left uneaten on her plate.

Richard never revealed the slightest concern with what was proper, what was appropriate. Whatever he felt like doing, however he did it, was right, made it right. Laura, obsessed with the idea her marriage had broken on the shoals of her unconscious rock-like demands for appropriateness, leaned emotionally on Richard for his confidence. She followed his every lead, trying to swallow his strength.

When he said abruptly one night, hitting the arms of his chair, "Let's go to bed," she hesitated only momentarily. She trailed him into her bedroom, watching him take off his clothes immediately, impressed with his lack of shyness, trying to make herself calm, to be a flexible person willing to remodel herself into the image he wanted, the partner he desired.

She sat on the edge of the bed.

"It's better without clothes," he said affectionately. He waited patiently, looking at her. Laura took off her shoes and curled up next to him. She waited, unsure what to do. Richard unbuttoned her blouse and put his hand under her skirt onto her thighs.

"How warm your skin is," he murmured. He kissed her, thrusting his tongue deeply into her throat, then moving it slowly around her teeth. He took off her bra and rubbed her breasts roughly. She wanted him. She lifted up against him, hungrily, quickly removing her skirt and panties, moving her hips around, up, yearning for contact.

"What's the rush?" he said, pushing her hips down, running his hand over her back, buttocks, pressing his finger against her anus; kissing her shoulders, her navel, licking her vagina.

Laura was flooded with feelings; sexually hysterical, she couldn't touch enough of him, couldn't get close enough, couldn't stop finding a spot to kiss.

Richard moved above Laura, positioning her legs on his shoulders. She felt defenseless, frightened. She tried to move her legs down, but he moved quickly in between, his hips holding her legs apart, making her vagina

217

wide, gaping. He put his penis in her, slowly, groaning, thrusting down deep, deep into some place beyond her knowledge. She could not move. He began to thrust rhythmically, rapidly, concentrated on his sensations. She was isolated. She could not reach his peaks. He was too far above her. He orgasmed with pulsating spasm, holding her tightly on the buttocks, fusing her against him.

He rolled over, breathing heavily.

"You're wonderful," he said.

He was right. Laura was full of wonder. She could not think of what she had done to warrant such a remark.

Richard pulled Laura close to him, and began, gently, to stroke her clitoris. "What a beautiful cunt you have," he said. Laura had never heard the word spoken before. "Did you like my prick?" he asked her.

Laura buried her face in his chest, liking the feelings his fingers were giving her.

He lifted her face up. "Did you like my prick?" he demanded.

"Yes," she said reluctantly.

"Say it. Say what you liked."

Laura struggled with her throat. She wanted to do what he wanted her to. She wanted him to stay with her. She did not want his fingers to stop.

"I liked your prick very much," she lied.

"Do you want my prick in your cunt again?"

It was easier now. "Yes."

"Say it."

"I want your prick in my cunt."

"Lick it and get it hard again."

She bent down and put her mouth around his penis, moving her tongue around the tip. "Not like that," he said. "Here, at the base, this spot." She obeyed, proud of herself as his penis started to swell again. Quick learner. A+ student. Total woman.

He moved more slowly, letting Laura keep her legs down, watching her.

"You're so quiet," he said.

"I feel like I'm melting. I liquid run into you."

"Next time, we'll try it another way. My prick will make you yell yet."

She grew to understand that if she made noises, he felt adequate. Only as their intimacy lengthened did she realize his need to feel adequate was connected to his feelings about his dead wife.

He mourned his wife constantly. "I took her for granted. When we moved from Jersey, I was already working in Atlanta. I should have gone back to help her, but I didn't. I kept telephoning orders to her instead. That wasn't right."

"She must have understood, Richard. She must have known how you felt about your business. That's what happens when people are married a long time. Even if they never say it, they understand what's important to the other person."

Oh my God, Pete, Laura suddenly thought, except me. I never saw what was important to you. She clutched Richard because she had never helped Pete.

"When she first complained about her shoulder," Richard grieved, "I didn't even pay attention. She got the heating pad herself. A heating pad for bone cancer—there's an effective cure! And when the pain didn't go away, the doctors gave her Darvon and a sling to rest the muscles. And then exercises. And then radiation. And all they were ever doing was chasing the pain; that's all. They knew all along they couldn't save her."

Richard sat morosely, heavy-faced, deep in the sad

memory of his wife's deteriorating body, her slipping away from him. His panic increased as her strength diminished. He confronted an ultimate impotence which left him forever frightened.

Laura's sympathy welled. She could not soothe him enough, assuage his fear sufficiently. So she made as much noise for him as she could during intercourse and repeated the words he wanted to hear; but when he went home and she was alone again, she would wonder why she did. It seemed so childish and so ugly. There were such beautiful words they might have said to each other.

She denied the shocks she experienced from his taste and his habits, for if she confronted them, she would have to stop seeing him, give up the wonderful sexual release he brought her, return to being alone. She watched Lawrence Welk with him, trying to enjoy his relaxation as he moved his black-vinyl Relaxease chair to reclining position.

"Mollie and I each had one. We'd sit like this, watching TV, and we didn't need anything else. It was paradise, even if she always fell asleep before me. She'd sleep right next to me until I woke her up so we could go to bed together. Always together."

Laura asked him to take her to see an English film but he said no, he couldn't take those accents. Didn't know why, but he never could. But he was happy to take her to a Broadway musical. He sincerely cared about how much she ate. He cut steaks into tidbits for her and fed her in the restaurant, "C'mon sweetheart—another piece. Look how juicy it is. It'll bring roses to your cheeks and stars to my eyes."

Other nights, he was moody and would not speak at all. He sat staring at Laura's fireplace, his hands clenched on the sides of the chair. Once he bought a

220

bottle of Scotch and drank it all; drinking and staring, unspeaking, oblivious to her before drunken oblivion encompassed him. In the morning, he was hearty and brisk. "You're really swell, kid," he told her.

Laura listened for Richard's tone when he called her so she would know if he was up or down. One down afternoon, she left work early and searched in a novelty store until she found a card that said, "Hang in there, baby," and a ceramic heart that said "I care," and a scroll inscribed, "Don't let the bastards get you down." She bought a cake and some green and yellow and red candles and she carefully printed a sign that said, "Happy Blues Day." She strung up balloons and streamers and put on his favorite Welk records.

When he came in, she was very pleased with herself. He smiled slightly and opened the gifts. "This I'll keep," he said as he read the scroll. He went home early, leaving everything else for her to clean up and throw out.

Laura knew she was in a bad relationship, but she did not want to give it up. It was sweet, good to be with someone, to have a regularly scheduled Saturday night and Sunday morning and afternoon.

She became very careful. If she started to quote the poetry she was translating, and saw him move restlessly, she stopped immediately and asked him to tell her about the wiring regulations. She was dismayed by his reports of kickbacks and careless inspections. When he ranted about the shoddy materials, she commiserated with him. When he raved about the damn lazy workers "who don't know what it is to do a fair day's work," she cringed. She avoided hearing his too harsh, "and when that sucker popped up again, I threw him the hell out." She would not visualize his images of a jobber feeding his fat face.

She smiled when he asked her if she had ever tried it

up the ass, hiding her revulsion, afraid to lose his presence. She reminded herself Pete's words were just right, his taste hers, his habits pleasant, but he had shown profound disrespect for her. Richard's coarseness, mediocrity, did not negate his solemn feeling for commitment. He would never break his word of honor.

She somehow could never arrange for them to get together with Fred and his wife, or Janet and her husband.

She did not trust Richard's reactions to Fred's wife's obesity. She did not want Fred to hear Richard say, "Between you and I. . . ." She did not want to see Fred's cool eyes count Richard's drinks.

She could not risk Janet's comprehension that Laura had become a supplicant.

When they met Bobby and Hilda for dinner, however, it was a good evening. Richard and Bobby discussed the comparative value of buying property or gold bars and congratulated each other on their economic acumen.

"The way he looks at you!" Hilda romanticized when they went to the ladies' room. "And he's so pleasant. Laura, I'm so happy for you." Hilda gave Laura a big kiss, leaving a large lipstick mouth of good housekeeping certification on Laura's cheek.

Later, Richard told her Bobby had informed him he had a great girl there and he'd better take good care of her or he'd have to answer to Bobby.

"He's an old friend," Laura said weakly, embarrassed.

"Of course. That's what friends are for."

Richard understood Bobby completely. He'd said the same thing to his own son-in-law.

Darcy and Patrick met them for cocktails. Darcy was

222

upset they couldn't join them for the chamber music. Laura prayed Richard wouldn't mention the music he preferred. They all drank more than they spoke.

"He's not for you." Darcy delivered her fiat flatly, the next day. "He's very pleasant—but he's no Pete."

"How the hell do you know so soon, Darcy? He's a nice man who's lonesome for his wife and wants a decent homelife again. What could be wrong with that?"

"That hearty ha-ha demeanor."

"Don't play cocktail party with my life."

"Don't play beggar with your life."

"Enough," Laura warned.

"OK, enough. Anyway, you won't do it. You'll never compromise like that."

Laura believed she would have, but Richard made any such decision unnecessary. On a business trip, he met another woman he thought he would like to see as well as Laura. "Give me some time," he asked her.

"Anything that will make you happy is OK with me," she told him hypocritically.

When he did not call for a week, Laura experienced intense unhappiness. All color left her world. Each evening was an endless gray. She wandered around the house in the middle of the night, looking out sometimes at the cold, vast sky; too often she found herself sitting, staring at nothing.

When he did call, it was to ask her how she was, not to ask to see her. She felt better for an hour or two and waited for him to call again, dreaming he would, reluctant to go out in case she missed his call. She moped around and started to cry again.

"He isn't for you," Dr. Summers said. "That's all."

"I'm not for anyone. That's the trouble."

"You'll meet someone else. Meanwhile you've had another experience. You have a better idea of what you like and don't like sexually. You're getting to know yourself."

"What I'm getting to know doesn't seem very likeable."

"I find it very likeable."

"You're not enough and I can't find anyone who feels as you do."

"You can."

"What really bothers me most is knowing he wasn't for me—Lawrence Welk for Christ's sake—but not saying so."

Dr. Summers remained silent.

"And dirty words yet!"

No comment from the watchful psychiatrist.

Mucous thickened in Laura's throat.

"What is it?" Dr. Summer's tone was unusually gentle.

"It must have been awful for Pete. Sex must have been a lot of dirty words for him."

"It's possible."

"It's like it's all turned backwards. I mean, I'm the healthy one, super heterosexual; and he's the unhealthy one, nouveau homosexual; and what he used to do was sick in his terms and now it's healthy."

"That's one way to look at it."

"It makes you wonder, doesn't it? I don't think I can ever get it all understandable."

"You can."

Laura's lack of strength to stop the relationship with Richard herself, her adolescent mooning, nagged her. She was ashamed of her doormat personality and couldn't look at herself in the mirror. She avoided looking at the immobile part of herself in the bedroom. She knew it was sneering.

She went for a ride with Darcy, enjoying the whip-

224

ping air as Darcy raced her small red convertible to the Connecticut shore. They walked together along the esplanade at which they stopped. The phosphorous lights played unnatural brightness on their faces and made the water area too dark for them to see beyond. They heard the lap, lapping of small waves on the unseen beach, a constant backsound to their voices. They unconsciously muted their tones.

They sat on a bench looking into the darkness in which they could see nothing.

"I'd like to tell you now about Pete," Laura said. "And about Richard because they both seem to have done something to me I don't like."

"Shelve Richard. He's nothing. Only Pete is worth talking about."

Laura smiled. Darcy could not stop setting up an agenda.

Laura needed to tell Darcy every detail, from day one when Pete first mentioned separation to day last when he left her an unsigned note. Once she started talking, she could not stop. She kept correcting her recital, saying no, he was still there then; that was two months later. Once she became confused about whether it was Pete to whom she had given a Happy Blues Day or Richard. She stopped talking only when she realized Darcy was crying.

"Darcy, honey," Laura crooned. "Oh, c'mon now." She felt guilty because she had forgotten Darcy had known Pete as long as she. She felt Pete was a rock thrown in the water, radiating out hurt in ever-widening waves—first her kids, and now Darcy. Laura felt responsible for the rock being thrown. She should have kept her mouth shut. She hated herself as she stroked Darcy's hair and asked her to please not be so upset. She apologized for telling her.

"But it isn't only Pete, you understand, Darcy. It's

that I can't find a focus that makes sense any more. I can't find a reason to keep going, except that there are too many reasons not to keep going."

"Laura, I feel so bad—all those damn assurances I kept giving you. If only you could have told me sooner. I could have helped you. At least I could have tried. And Pete—that poor guy. That pitiful bastard. How he must have suffered. And all because he was a coward, because he couldn't stand up to his world. God, why do people let themselves be manipulated so long."

Darcy stopped crying and looked at Laura. Darcy's skin was dry under the bright light. Wrinkles had begun to drag her chin down. Dullish gray strands obscured the loveliness of her blond hair. We're getting old, Laura thought, she thought irrelevantly. We can see things from beginning to end and we have the sags to prove it.

"Well, now that I know—though honestly, Laura, I can't take it in. Not really. Not Pete." Darcy started to cry again. "Not Pete and you. It's so unbelievable."

"You're a good friend," Laura said, touched by Darcy's sorrow for her, for them.

"I wish I knew how to help you," Darcy said.

"You help. Just by being my friend."

But Darcy did not think that was enough. She felt the need for directing Laura to some action. Darcy always felt better when she was giving orders. In a few days, she called Laura to inform her they would go to a women's consciousness-raising group.

"Why?" Laura wanted to know.

"You know, all over the country women are trying to help other women, to stop from being pushed around by men."

"I don't feel I was pushed around by men," Laura said quietly. "I don't feel anything of the sort. I explained it to you: I lost someone I loved very much, and I can't seem to find a connection to someone else. What's a women's group got to do with it?"

Darcy said patiently, "It's the same problem—it has to do with reacting all the time instead of acting once in a while, and I think it will help you to find that out. So you'll come with me."

Laura grinned into the phone. Who could argue with Darcy?

The Saturday afternoon they went to women's group was chilly. The trees were just tinged with yellow and red leaves. Most of the foliage was still a dullish green. Laura shivered when she saw how many brown leaves had fallen around the trees during the late summer.

Darcy opened the discussion as soon as the five strangers were settled on the couch and chairs of the prim living room. The lack of books and plants lent the room a sterility that unsettled Laura. A *Horizon* magazine on the coffee table seemed an affectation. Laura was afraid she was wasting her time. It did not seem possible the woman who lived in this house could have much in common with her, much less help her in any way.

"The accident of my hip," Darcy said clearly, "led me away from the natural woman's route. To be crippled when I was a kid was to be a matrimonial leper. So I early learned to do things by myself. I never understood why that was so, you understand—the limp hardly seemed big enough—but I knew it was so."

Darcy unexpectedly blushed. She fondled her earrings, tucked her blouse more securely into her skirt. She presented a picture of confusion and embarrassment.

Laura waited attentively, wondering.

"What the hell," Darcy said. "It's so long ago now. Well—Laura's brother was having a bad time. They'd lost their father. He was suddenly presented with a do-nothing mother, a scared kid sister, and a very small brother. Everything was up to him. But Christ, he was only nineteen or twenty himself. What the hell did he know? He only knew you go out and find a job and get a girl friend and get laid. But you don't get married, be-cause that's the trap.

"So there I was—not marriage material—but clean—and available. We got into it and stayed with it for quite some time. I found having my own apartment made everything much easier. That's why I got one as soon as possible.

"It didn't work out between us. By the time I realized I was as good as everyone else, he'd long since been married. But I knew being a comfort to someone was *my* trap. It was a sob story told by Hollywood. I thought I was so feminine because he needed me, needed a shoulder to cry on, a vagina to fuck, so the cares of his world would evaporate.

"What a crock it really is.

"After that I swore it would never happen again. Being used as a cushion that way. Because I swore that, I found out real femininity is being a real person, reacting back, not just being sunk into or sat on.

"Then later, I couldn't stand anyone handling my money, so I think I was liberated before anyone said anything."

"Weren't you?" Connie, a tall, angular fortyish woman, asked.

"No, I don't really think so, because I knew everyone thought I was a loser. I was still affected by that, even though I didn't believe it."

"You were never a loser," Laura said, still amazed at the idea of Georgie and Darcy . . .

"Still," Margie exclaimed. "It is odd to live alone. I

228

hate it!" Margie's ex-husband, a professor at the university, was living at the time in a graduate dorm with a former student.

"You can always share an apartment," Darcy said reasonably.

"That's not the point at all," Margie said, passionately. "I want someone who'll care for me, take care of me."

"I have that," Evelyn, the last member of the group, said. "Sam always takes care of me. He never wanted me to work, and now, with my daughters gone, I am going crazy. I'm so bored all the time."

"So get a job," Laura advised.

"He won't let me."

"How can he stop you?"

"I can't do it without his permission." Evelyn picked at her manicured nails. Eyes downcast, she looked ashamed.

"I can understand that," Laura said. "I was over forty before I walked into a restaurant alone."

Mulling over the meeting at night, Laura could not share Darcy's conviction a woman's group would help. Laura did not feel her unhappiness had anything to do with playing a woman's role or being without power. She was neither homeless, friendless, nor moneyless because of the situation—which is what the women seemed to think was the real problem. No, the real problem as far as she could tell was she had lost someone she loved.

Fay Bainter flashed through Laura's mind. Sweet, devoted, sexless, old. The perfect wife and mother. And next to her, Lewis Stone. Wise, tolerant, patient, elderly. The perfect husband and father.

She saw Pete drinking a martini, secretly lusting for a young, tanned waiter. He had tried to transform himself into Lewis Stone. Maybe she had tried to transform herself into Fay Bainter. Perhaps they had accepted what they were told was desirable. Perhaps it was time for Laura to question that. She saw how socially desirable marriage to Richard would have seemed. Yet, personally, how disastrous for her. The dirty words alone . . .

So she returned to the woman's group.

Laura tried. She told them about Manny's bar mitzvah, when Pete shone, his hair damp with meticulous combing. Newly shaved, he smelled of the clean yet musky scent he had begun to use. It was a day of crisp new white handkerchiefs; a day each of them, Pete, Laura, Manny, Sol, and Larry dressed in their finest to announce they were one, a family, to acknowledge the fact of them.

Pete said he had seen it as a ritual. Laura saw it as the achievement of a major goal.

The women in the consciousness-raising group gave Laura their total attention during her rather long recital of the bar mitzvah and what it had meant to her. When Laura finished, Katie said Laura was still spending too much of her energy trying to understand Pete. "Do you think he tried to get to know what you were all about? No! He only wanted to know what you could do—or in this case—not do for him. Once he decided you couldn't do enough, goodbye, lady."

Patty, a slim, beautiful young woman with exquisite green eyes, said, "All guys do is fuck you over and leave you to pick up the pieces—especially when their jobs make them too tired to care where their prick goes for the next couple of years."

"Or as long as the household arrangements are organized," Kathy, a subdued Madonna-like young woman, chimed in. Laura thought of them as the Mod Greek chorus. Both women had just been divorced:

230

Patty because her husband wouldn't "communicate" and, it turned out, thought it OK to sock her once in a while; and Kathy, because her husband fell in love with their neighbor's wife. The husband of the original couple still lived next door to Kathy, although he had since remarried. Now, every other weekend, he took Kathy's children to her ex-husband and his ex-wife for a visit, while taking his children back to his home for the weekend. It nauseated Laura.

"What do you do on the weekends when the kids are gone?" she had asked Kathy when Kathy first came into the group.

"Get in bed and read a murder mystery and eat cheese doodles until four o'clock."

"And then?"

"There is no then."

Laura could not accept "There is no then." She went to a singles group with Margie.

"Don't stand together," Margie, the Liberated, said urgently. "No man is going to come up to two women. Sit on the steps alone. Maybe someone will talk to you."

My God, Pete. How could you let this happen to me?

The women milled around the church lounge in which they were "socializing." Fifty, sixty women—all ages. Blue-gray hair, rinsed, set. Blond, shiny lacquered hair. Green-shadowed eyes, white cream base, silver highlights. Red, purple, pink, crimson lips. Ready. Waiting. Aching. Moving below the scanning eyes. "Who's here?" "Who can I talk to here?" "Who will love me here?" "Where is Mr. Right?":

And there he was, seated on the couch. His arm stretched out to encompass the woman on either side. A nice man, anyone's uncle-type. Good natured, dumb, ordinary.

But here—a king.

"No. I won't go there again."

Ultimately, Laura joined another of Darcy's committees, one that lobbied for free child-care centers. Many women joined the executive committee, moving in and out at various times. The younger women spoke of lifestyles and of their right to their own bodies. The older women told of their need to reconstruct their lives, of husbands who abruptly left—either by death or design.

Laura stayed with that group.

"Yes, your groups helped, but at least, before, I didn't know I was such a cliché," Laura commented to Darcy, one day when she had gone over to Darcy's bookstore to help her catalog some German titles. Darcy's file was a hodgepodge of her personal association with books rather than a real subject file. It apparently drove Pat out of the office to discover books about German guns were filed under *Huns–their thing.* But it worked for Darcy, who enjoyed sitting at the large, messy desk, making up her idiosyncratic files.

Laura enjoyed sitting there too. The dusty untidiness of the office reminded her of her mother. Even the fact that all the plants she kept giving Darcy died in the office did not bother her. Laura simply kept buying new ones, sure that someday one would grow.

"Maybe we're all clichés in some way," Darcy said, poring over her files, probably making up a C card for Laura right then and there. "Even Pete, who's supposed to be so odd and queer—he looked like a cliché when I saw him. Even his dungarees were flared."

"You saw him? When was that?"

"After you told me about him. I had called him several times before, but he always said he was busy. This time, I invited him and his boyfriend over for dinner."

"You did!"

"I know I should have told you first, Laura—maybe even asked how you would feel about it. But—I was afraid you might say no—and Pete was always so nice to me, always made me feel so welcome—even important—when I went to your house. I guess I felt I owed it to him."

Darcy's clear eyes waited for Laura's reaction.

"I feel funny about your doing that," Laura said. Then she mumbled, "But not for any good reason. Only for bad reasons. I would rather you were disgusted with him, revolted even, and never wanted anything to do with him again."

"You can see the problem though. You're both my friends—"

"All right! Stop the neutrality already and give me all the dirt. Just tell me he's unhappy."

"Well, in one way, he is. Of course. He feels really bad about Sol, and Larry seems to make him feel like two cents. But in another way, I think he is happy. He was quite relaxed. Very Pete-ish."

"Wonderful. Just wonderful. What kind of a report is that. Why can't you tell me he's got a chronic cold and his nose keeps dripping."

Darcy laughed as she poured coffee for each of them into heavy, hand-painted mugs. Children went sleigh riding around and around the cups with no border to stop them.

"I'm happy to report his boyfriend is a real dope. Pete seems to keep himself pretty busy though. He talked about all sorts of gay rights cases he's involved with. I think he's helping a lot of people."

"His sons will be delighted to hear that—especially if they read it in the newspaper."

"I just don't know who's right and who's wrong on that one," Darcy said. "I kept thinking about the way you've been hurt and then I'd think about some poor guy who's going to lose his job because the boss doesn't like to have a gay around—and I couldn't decide."

Laura scalded the top of her mouth with too hasty a gulp of the hot coffee before she said, "That's what makes it all so terrible. Whatever happened to Jack LaRue villains? It was so much easier when all we had to do was boo."

As their committee's work solidified and enlarged, Laura's room began to be crammed with papers, mailing lists, clippings, drafts of speeches, yellow manila envelopes with minutes, legislative action from various countries, letters from women wanting to start groups, needing information. When the committee decided to build a women's health center, her room burst.

Finally, Laura sorted the material over a two-week burst-of-activity period and stored it all in orderly fashion in Sol's room. His old Phillies pennants now decorated papers that might gain women a center where they could safely leave their kids.

Laura's expertise at translating poetry brought an unexpected promotion to specialist classification. When Fred asked her to translate a four-volume commemorative Portuguese anthology, she found her work extending beyond office time. In addition to her usual notebooks and dictionaries, she needed notecards, reference material, separate folders of lined papers for chronology. Even with the committee's material out of her room, she had insufficient space.

After a night of shuffling through papers to find a note she had written on one corner of a page, she gathered up the material and took it all to Manny's room, where she stacked it efficiently. She gave away his small college desk, bringing in its place a huge rolltop with almost

234

enough pigeonholes for her scraps of reminders and word choices.

The Health Center's executive committee frequently met in her kitchen, the larger group in her living room. When Georgie and Lilli wanted to stay over one night with the children, Laura was surprised to find how little space she had for them.

When a Yugoslav poet came for a visit, Fred thought the poet would be most comfortable with Laura as they both spoke Italian fairly easily. Laura found she had very little time to entertain him. She had to rearrange her schedule of meetings and luncheons and concert tickets.

"You don't have any outside responsibility," Fred said impatiently. "How the hell did you get so busy all the time?"

"Damned if I know," Laura said. "It just seemed to happen."

"How come it never seems to happen that you're busy with me?"

"Maybe that's something that has to be made to happen."

"So?"

"So, maybe." Laura paused. "How busy do you want us to be?"

"Preferably from eight to eleven Friday night."

"And at eleven-o-one?"

"I go home."

"I'll have to think about it."

"Why?"

"Because of eleven-o-two."

❧ *After part: 2*

"I HAVE A BABY!" Hilda enthralled. "A fat little baby girl!"

Hilda had been waiting for this moment from the minute her daughter married, in a wedding that had been an affair of precision. Nothing had been left to chance as Hilda shopped methodically with her daughter for lingerie and dresses, a coat for an unexpected chilly evening, met with florists, liquor dealers, musicians, printers. Bobby had personally checked the steak cuts to be served.

They spent hours deciding the proper point in the music at which the curtains should open to permit Hilda's daughter to begin her walk down the aisle with Bobby. Bobby felt if they waited too long, they would be too nervous. Hilda felt if they started too early, the assembled guests would not have sufficient opportunity to enjoy their daughter's silhouette behind the curtains. Finally they were satisfied with the timing. It was, they agreed, perfect. The only trouble had been that Hilda and Bobby were so tired after the wedding, they had to go away for a weekend to rest up. But there was no question. It had all been worth it.

Saved as memorabilia were samples of the elaborately printed menus, headlined with the gilt-engraved date, announcing A Fruit Compote, Consommé Supreme, Steak à la Maison, Sweets Complete. The menu and monogrammed broad-tipped matches were carefully pasted among the wedding pictures in an enormous white-velvet album.

Hilda and Bobby displayed the album to Laura so they all could relive the details of the evening, from the first arrival of their son-in-law's family to Bobby's paying the bill.

Hilda's image radiated from the pictures. Pink chiffon softened the diamond sparkle at her ears, her neck, her fingers. A red-rose, pink-snapdragon corsage accentuated her aura of happiness.

"You're beautiful," Laura said. "You've never taken a better picture."

"How can you say that? I'm so fat—look how fat I look! All that dieting and for what? My waistline looks like the L.I. Expressway."

"Don't look at your waistline. Look at how happy you look. It makes people feel good to see people looking happy."

Laura remembered trying to look happy at the wedding. Hilda sat her at a "lively" table, away from the center. She'd been surprised not to be seated with Hilda and Bobby, chagrined at being so far from Darcy and Patrick. Hilda seemed unaware Laura conceived of herself as family. It was another reminder Laura would have to accept of the reality of weakening connections, of different connections, if she were to enjoy the present.

She made every effort to befriend the strange couples

with whom she was seated—deliberately chatting, consciously attempting to be interested in the photography salesman who traveled to Japan annually. She wanted to be real toward the salesman and his wife. She wanted to appreciate them for what they were and what they did, without judgment, without criticism; but a snake of impatience slithered through her good intentions. The wife's voice was too shrill. Laura's unattached presence seemed to give her a smugness Laura found intolerable. She fought the feeling, hating Pete, hating the situation, hating herself.

Hilda felt bad that Laura's picture hadn't come out well. She looked nervous and drawn, when really, Hilda said, Laura had looked so pretty in that dress.

It seemed as though the wedding pictures were barely put away before Hilda and Bobby were saying, "You'd think they'd get started already," on the increasingly infrequent evenings Laura saw them. The increasing difficulty about getting together had something to do with their social code. Without malice, their coupled world did not know how to handle a single woman. Restaurants seemed reserved for marrieds only or, at least, going-togethers.

At first, Laura forced the issue, but she found it embarrassing that Bobby felt he had to pay for "his girls." Once she met Hilda alone, for lunch. Hilda assumed she should pay for it. When Laura said that was hardly necessary, Hilda was somewhat taken aback. Single women, apparently, did not have as much money as married women. Hilda was upset Laura insisted on straining her budget when Hilda derived such pleasure from "her treat."

Thereafter, they settled into a more comfortable, if more occasional, visit to Laura. Invariably, at some point, Bobby or Hilda asked if Laura had heard from

Pete. Laura always said no, stopping any further conversation. Eventually, Laura thought this was stupid of herself so, sitting comfortably one lazy Sunday afternoon when Bobby and Hilda stopped by on their way to the Cape, Laura said Pete was very happy. In fact, she understood he was planning to buy a house.

"Around here?"

"No. He's practicing in Detroit now. I imagine he'll find something in one of the suburbs. Or maybe, given the situation, he may want to stay in the city."

"He's living with someone?"

"Yes. A young man. The same one all the time."

Hilda gasped. "I can't believe it." She touched Bobby, "Can you believe it? I can't believe it."

Hilda, very upset, could not accept it. She shook her head, rejecting it. Then, efficiently, "Well, you need someone like that like a hole in the head. I don't want to know anything else about him."

The issue of Pete was settled permanently for Hilda.

"Did you ever suspect anything?" Laura asked Bobby.

"Who would believe it?"

"Not me," Hilda said. "If it were anyone but Laura telling me, I'd never believe it."

"What really gets me," Bobby said, sadly, "after being friends all these years, you'd think a fella would call once in a while."

The reduction of Pete to banality forced Laura to head, mentally, for the nearest door and to scream at the Fates that permitted people to develop lives in which there was no passion, no vivid painted strokes of life; where disorder, chaos, caprice, vistas were constrained into neat boxes of mannered behavior, a structured, sane establishment of marriage, children, grandchildren; an acquiescent, "Well, we're getting older," a smug "What can you expect at our age?" A departure, resignation. "Action is what we're waiting for now all right," no longer Laura's or Bobby's or Hilda's responsibility, but their children's responsibility.

"Fuck it," Laura thought. "I don't like their older generation lessons." She dismissed them as teachers.

So when Hilda was ecstatic about the birth of her granddaughter, when Hilda was proud her daughter had done the right thing, Laura was happy for Hilda. And angry at Hilda. And confused about her own feelings. Why could she begin to accept that Pete had to be what he thought he was, but not Hilda? Grandchildren were a valid, human connection between the past and the future. They continued what had been initiated in a burst of feeling, by repetition. Their presence assured that people felt, acted, related on some level, even for the briefest period of time. For at least a second, isolation ceased and connection intensified.

Laura sensed why Pete fought her rules. He objected to being a father or husband because he viewed it as living a life without élan. Somehow, he had confused homosexuality with life-thrusting energy, mood swings of great transport. Perhaps that's what psychosexual dynamics were all about. The association of beauty, strength, vigor, color—the images fragmentary and clear that float up and through consciousness, intensifying feeling, stimulating feelings to begin with. Perhaps that is why psychologists say sex is all in the head, because that's where the associations are.

Laura did not know how those germinated, what caused the mutation of Pete's sexual direction, the queer displacement as the impact of their lives on him moved them away from, rather than toward, each other. "Distancing," he had said—distinct from her, acts of independence, maturation.

It was true he might have let her know how he felt if
240

he had been courageous enough, but it would have done him no good. In fairness—"Why the hell do I have to be fair!" Laura thought bitterly—in fairness it wouldn't have worked. Laura still would not have understood nor accepted nor helped him. She could have run to his mother or sat in a corner crying or maybe even just laughed it off and gone ahead with whatever Saturday night arrangements they had.

He had shared what he could with her. The women she met in the groups made much about men wanting to own them, but they should have also made much about women wanting to own men. Laura had thought she owned Pete. Even now Hilda continued to believe she owned not only Bobby but her daughter, and her daughter's child. How else could she say, "I'm going to have a baby!" In the end, however, no one owned anyone. Everyone was on voluntary loan to each other.

When Bobby mentioned he had again called Pete, only to find him, once more, very polite and very inaccessible, Laura realized there were some loans Pete canceled. In any case, Laura thought Pete was a fool. Losing the opportunity to hear Bobby complain about his feet was to lose one of life's few certainties.

When she finally mustered the courage to tell Georgie and Lilli about Pete, she told it in that way—that Pete had been blocked by all of them from ever revealing his true feelings, so he loaned only part of his feelings.

"You're sicker than he is," Georgie said. "If someone looks you in the eye and says they're going to a meeting, of course you believe them. The creep lied to you for Christ's sake. And kept on lying.

"If you want to believe he couldn't help it, go ahead and believe it. But so far as I'm concerned, he can rot in his fag beds forever."

Laura found Georgie's reaction easier to take than

Lilli's. When Lilli put her arms around Laura and said, "You must have gone through hell. And introducing you to Richard certainly didn't help," Laura almost broke.

But when Lilli wanted Laura to visit, to give up the house and live near them, Laura knew Lilli did not understand that to be a person, one had to do it alone.

The problem was, being of value, being someone, was a strain. Laura could not just relax and watch television too many nights in a row. She would begin to feel depressed and lonely, think of Pete and Richard, and listen for the phone to ring. She had to call Janet, then, and go shopping for a coat, or work on the *Women's Healthletter*. She joined a group of free-lance editors, who listened to each other read translations for open reactions. She jetted to L.A. for a weekend with Sol and Sarah, and went to a concert with Darcy and Patrick when she returned. Then, exhausted, she was only too happy to put on a housecoat at 6 P.M. and go to sleep at 8 P.M.

She felt she was on a treadmill, running so long in one spot the space beneath it became a morass as her pace became more frantic.

Laura tried not to think at all.

Her days took on the quality of quest, an odyssey for meaning, for signs that she was worthwhile, that what she did affected someone. If she saw Soo the first thing in the morning, it was going to be a lonely day. If she saw Janet the first thing, it was going to be a social day. If it poured on Sunday, that was good. One could relax by oneself. Monday was always OK because on Mondays no one gave a damn if he/she were married or not. All one thought about was one's work.

Despite the conversation with other women, the Health Center work, her children, the circular nature of exhausting activity—to relaxation, to depression, necessitating renewed movement—she needed further validation. As the pain of Pete receded, and the disappointment of Richard evaporated, Laura felt a renewed desire for someone. Somehow, she still believed, he, wherever he might be, could move her away from the fake scenery of her life into a living background.

She found herself studying Fred while she worked. He was only slightly shorter than Pete, his hair somewhat more sparse. She had grown very fond of his oblique glance. Occasionally, he looked at her with a surprised question in his eyes she was almost ready to answer.

For Laura had lied to Fred. It was not 11:02 that worried her. She was ready for the love affair he offered even though it be without love and permanency. What she feared was that the intimate relationship she wanted would reveal a dimension of him she had never known; that although the years they had worked together gave them familiarity and comfortable rapport, much still had to be hidden. Laura was unsure she wanted to uncover whatever aspects of Fred's complexity she would stumble upon in bed with him.

Nonetheless, one Indian summer day when they languished their way to the dining commons, relishing the deep warmth of the day sandwiched between the reminders of frost, Laura said to Fred, "So, how's your extracurricular activity these days?" But when he replied, "Still in the nonchampion stage," she withdrew immediately by insisting they sit with Soo. She bought him an expensive lighter for his birthday, then turned her cheek when he kissed his thanks. When he suggested they go for a drink after work, she sat in the dark, quiet bar and told him how relaxing it was, adding quickly it was too bad she had a seven-thirty meeting.

But, on an icy November night, when Fred said it was definitely time for a drink after a late-hour boring staff conference, Laura said it was too damn cold to go chasing after liquor when she had a cozy bar at home right next to a seductive fireplace.

"Finally?" he beamed at her forehead.

"Finally," she sighed, her resigned air a pose. She was wary, yet saturated with delighted anticipation: she had taken the first step off the treadmill.

As a lover, Fred concentrated on his own sensations. He pounded actively in her during intercourse with a straightforward narrow focus on his orgasm. Laura guessed his years of relationships with passing strange women made him unconcerned about their having a mutual sexual experience. Or maybe he felt, *ipso facto,* the experience was shared.

It did not seem to matter to her. Although his noisy thumping amused her more than it stimulated her, she found his kisses lovingly affectionate and his caresses touches of friendship. There was no sense of haste, no dirty words. When they took a shower together, they fooled around with the soap and water and space between them.

They were kind to each other.

When Fred left, Laura marveled. Without her knowledge, in overlapping time, her relationship with Pete had been disintegrating while her relationship with Fred had been evolving.

She was deeply frightened at what else might happen—even as she settled in to enjoy it as much as possible.

After an initial mild embarrassment, they were natural with each other in their familiar office relationship. Neither Fred nor Laura referred to Friday night. It existed apart from their working roles.

244

Laura glimpsed how it was possible for Pete to have two disparate lives. She was rueful at the realization she could do it as well as Pete had when, on Fridays, she had lunch with Soo and Janet, worked all afternoon with Fred, said *goodnight, have a nice weekend,* and left the office to go home and wait for the man she had indicated she would not see until Monday, whom no one suspected she saw until Monday.

In fact, she loved the secrecy of it. In further fact, she felt great. Fred's enjoyment of her company evoked surprise-party happiness in her.

The dimension she was concerned she would discover was not in Fred, but in herself. She felt she had not only left romantic love behind, she was gleeful to discover she had left Miss Goody Two Shoes behind as well.

She was the cool one when they met Janet on the train to the city one illicit Saturday.

"Hey—I thought the meeting wasn't until Tuesday. How come everyone's showing up so early? First Fred, and now you. Go away, the both of you. I have to get paid to see you." And in the city, smoothly, "Which way are you going, Janet? Uptown? Too bad. And you Fred? Downtown? Swell—let's share a cab, then."

Giggling in the cab, she exuded joyous pride. Fred mused she was a kaleidoscope he wasn't quite certain he wanted to turn so much. She sobered immediately as she felt his fear. Laura felt a mild contempt for Fred's inability to live his life as he wanted. Simultaneously, she sympathized with his pitiful solution. By no stretch of her willing fantasy did she feel his adultery with her was the consequence of a mad passion, worth risking the odd structure he accepted as his marriage.

Their Friday nights assumed a placid routine of

drinks, idle conversation, and Fred's ritualistic "And so to bed" comment. Only after Fred's orgasm, as she cuddled in his arms for the period before he said, "I'd love to stay here—but—have to get moving, sweetheart," only then, in that interval of quiescent bodies and friendship, did Laura know why it made such a difference to her life. She remembered the therapeutic sense of intimacy that gave life a quality of being. In Fred's arms she felt as far from lonely despair as Pete, in reality, was from her.

Needing to share her feelings, she told Darcy and Hilda she was having an affair with a married man.

"Of course," Darcy said blandly.

"Good!" Hilda said, "It's healthy for both of you."

"You're as good as a vitamin pill," Laura chortled to Fred as he lay, his penis straight, heavy-veined, swollen in the air, probably presenting the frankest sexual image Laura had ever seen. She paused, looking. She grinned lewdly at him.

"Get in here," he ordered, "so it can get in there."

Laura took off her clothes, posing naked next to the bed, expressing eager anticipation as her breast pointed directly to Fred's mouth, wanting it that way, finally not worrying if it was the right way.

Her mouth, half opened as she kissed his shoulders, his chest, opened wider as she licked his stomach, hips, penis, staying with his penis, holding it in her mouth, sucking, licking, stopping—then flicking, drawing him nearer, inward, toward.

She was free to enjoy herself and to help Fred enjoy himself. She was almost without pretense. There was no driving love forcing them together. They were not making love because they were going to be married. They were not surmounting daily muted passion, for children, in service to past generations.

246

He was not going to protect her.

They rolled and panted and sweated together because they felt good together. They were greedy, wanting more, wanting feelings for longer periods, stretching themselves: a birthday party, the openness of New Year's Eve drinking. Because they had been disappointed in the Monday morning coffee of their lives.

They lusted. Laura's breasts had strands of hair on them, her hips were calcified bones. Fred had a wart under his scrotum; his breath covering her face in ever-increasing currents smelled faintly of cheese.

They were immoral. He was committing adultery. She was permitting a man to take liberties, to use her, and then to go home at his convenience.

They were two middle-aged naked persons, ludicrous with their pale legs sticking out from under the tumbled sheets, Laura's head pushed accidentally under the pillow, Fred's elbow caught too tightly under Laura's nape.

It did not interfere with their enjoyment of each other.

Laura accepted her sexuality as part of her humanity, as part of her human image—something living, which emerged from her being. She did not have to be pre-designed, as in some commercial to sell soap, into a lithe, young beauty in order to meet qualifications demanded outside herself.

She tried to explain it to Fred. He understood. He told her a story about drinking buddies who helped each other no matter how blind, disgustingly drunk one might become. "It was only human, after all."

Pete hurt Laura because he would not share his human feelings with her. He forced them into a role he envisioned as right, without his body feeling it was right. He solidified them into roles so that Laura could never know what felt right to her. The biblical knowing meant a search for one's mate through sex. Pete spent his passion in an effort to keep himself hidden, unknown.

Laura cried in Fred's arms for Pete's loss; and Fred, without knowing the cause of her sorrow, consoled her. He only asked, "Sad thoughts?"

"Yes," she mumbled against his shoulder.

"It happens sometimes."

They listened to each other's breathing. Everything around them was silent, calm. Laura sensed her immobile self, eyes averted, waiting for the end of their silence. The clock ticked. Fred groaned, deep in his throat, an incomprehensible sound—his signal to himself perhaps, a reminder that soon he had to leave their silence, dress, and go home.

Laura held him more tightly. His belly soft against hers, his leg hard. She touched his shoulder. Cool flesh in silence.

Irrationally disquieted, she moved quickly out of bed, shattering their silence.

"How about some tea?" she asked too cheerfully, putting on a robe, combing her hair. She was already on her way down to the kitchen.

Joining her, Fred sat, waiting to be waited on. Laura gave him bread and butter and cake, offered him a sandwich, an omelet; opened blackberry jam and strawberry jam; thought he might want some fruit, perhaps an orange.

"Nothing, sweetheart, nothing. Just tea. I had a big supper."

"What did you eat?"

"What didn't I eat? Meatloaf, mashed potatoes, cabbage. A tray of hermits. My wife makes wonderful hermits. I ought to bring you some."

"That's a little tacky, don't you think? From wife to mistress. And then do I send something back? How do you handle that?"

248

He smiled; his eyes glazed slightly, fixated just above her hairline.

Laura examined Fred. He drank his tea quickly, pursing his lips slightly at the heat just before he swallowed. His skin gleamed. She told him he looked as though he had jogged eight miles and then taken a shower. Invigorated and relaxed, "Life is good," he said.

"But you don't free yourself to get all of it. You keep yourself—unfree."

Fred looked beyond her forehead.

"That's the way it is," he said.

"How? How is it?"

He picked up a spoon and studied it. "You want to know everything about me. You don't have to know so much. I've already told you too much."

"I don't want to know to use it against you," she said evenly. "I just want to know to understand you better."

"There's not much to know. I'm a shallow man."

"In the women's movement, this is the pits, you know. Being mixed up with a married man."

"Why? Seems liberated enough to me."

"Oh, c'mon. You decide when we'll meet—how—for how long."

"Not totally. You decide if you'll be there, if I can come."

"I guess that's so—but a person could start waiting by the phone like a good mistress should. I think a person could do that very easily."

"Well, don't. If you want to go out, go out. Don't wait for me. I can't promise you anything—but this." He pointed his finger in the air and slowly turned it toward her.

"Not even an aura of romance occasionally?"

"Of course." Fred was impatient. "You know I like you, but I'm not free. I can't take you to dinner or to the theatre. The best I could offer is a conference."

"That's OK. Really. I don't think I want more than that. In fact, I doubt it would work very long if it were more than that. I mean, you like sailing and bars, and too much of either one has me green and vomiting—but—still, that—but—why do you keep yourself locked in like that?"

"It starts too early," Fred said. "You don't know what you are when you're young. Later, you want to reach for the stars but your wife doesn't even know there are stars. Well, she's straight—so you compromise. You don't break straight arrows. You gave your word."

"So you keep your word and find fun, too?"

"Right. You'll get the hang of it."

Laura did not know if she would have wanted Pete to compromise like that all his life. She did not tell that to Fred.

"As long as it's fun then—" she said.

"Exactly."

She kissed him goodbye warmly, nicely, because he was a nice man and he had breathed with her in silence. But she wondered how "It's fun" had become her moral standard; and later she told Darcy, "It's like the eleventh commandment these days."

"There's nothing wrong with having fun, is there, Laura?"

"No—but I can see it could get to be a terrible strain in a very short time."

"Well, then it isn't fun and there's no problem. You just stop seeing him."

"Just like that—on-off—no emotion."

"Sadness, you can have sadness if you're so insistent. As long as you understand it can't be what you want it to be."

Laura understood. She continued to see Fred privately.

✤ *After part: 3*

LARRY BREATHLESSLY ANNOUNCED he was getting married. He continued breathless as he told Laura the plans for the wedding and her role in it.

He was marrying Tena because he went to college with her and worked in the chem lab with her and never had to worry about a contaminated vial when he was with her. Laura thought that was as good a reason as anyone could ask for.

Tena was a little older than he, so she did not want to waste too much time just living together. If they were going to have a family—and they were—they had to hurry just a little.

"Old age seems to show up in different numerals," Laura commented, pleased with them.

Tena liked family. She wanted everyone at her wedding—everyone she knew and everyone to whom she was related, and everyone Larry knew and everyone to whom he was related.

"So, you're planning to ask your father."

"Definitely. Whether I like it or not—the involvement is there."

"What will you do about your father and Sol?"

"We'll take care of it, Ma. That's our problem."

"God, I can't stand the idea your father is 'a problem.'"

"Well, that's one of the truths of our lives. The faster Sol sees that, the happier he'll be. You just can't run away from something that's there. It's part of our scene, and every once in a while—like every time I get married to little miss 'but I want them all!'—every time that happens, Dad is part of the all. You wouldn't expect Tena not to invite someone in the family if the person had bad breath, would you?"

"You liken your father to bad breath?"

"The analogy is close enough."

"Your cool is becoming a little cold, there, son."

"I had a great teacher."

Laura chose not to ask whether he meant her or Pete.

The wedding was planned at Tena's friend's house, an old dark-brown shingled two-story on the Long Island Sound. Wraparound porches on the first and second floor stood, waiting for rockers, above a grassy patch that ended on a rocky slope. The slope formed the coastline of a still cove, from which the water stretched to a misty horizon. Scrub pine trees grew next to larger, more venerable trees, just before the rocky line. Under these trees, Tena planned the ceremony.

She and Larry set out wicker tables and chairs on the grass. Laura decorated the tables with purple wild flowers. Lilli made enough pot roast for three weddings, and Hilda baked a white sheet cake in four sections so it stretched right across two tables.

Tena asked Darcy to find a book with a really nice cover, which she planned to give the justice of the peace. It would give him something to hold, and something into which they could tuck the ceremony she and Larry planned to write themselves.

252

They asked everyone to pray for a sunny day.

The day, however, was neither sunny nor rainy. It was mild and it was cloudy. The breezes were sweet, inoffensive, off the water, bending the trees only slightly.

The water, the rocks, the trees, the furniture, the flowers, the porch buffet made a pretty scene. Everyone said it was such a pretty scene as they came.

Tena's father, a boisterous insurance salesman, stereotypically loud, said it was as pretty as a fifty-cent postcard. His very young, very thin wife said nothing. She smiled vacantly at the water.

Tena's mother and stepfather sat on chairs they had moved under one of the trees. They each drank Scotch and water, steadily, soberly, all afternoon. From time to time, Tena stopped next to her mother, to hug her or caress her shoulder. Her mother kissed Tena's hand every time in an odd, humble gesture of gratitude.

Pete appeared, his hair ruffled in the soft breeze. He stood motionless, expressionless, at the edge of the grass. Watching him, aware that all his connections were around him, Laura thought his immobility might be a defensive stance. Uncertain, but wanting to help him if he had to pass his own Falcaro dog, Laura went over to him and took his hand.

"How pretty you look," he said.

"You look pretty, too," she teased so she could see him smile. He wore a blue-streaked Madras jacket and white linen-like slacks. He had a heavy gold ring on his pinky, a ring that appeared to be shaped like a serpent with a ruby eye. Gold chains glinted at his neckline, beneath his open-necked cream shirt. His eyes were the blue the sky should have been.

Darcy came over and gave him a big kiss. "Cool hand Luke," she murmured affectionately.

He hugged her. "Where's Pat?"

"His kid's having a hernia operation. So . . ."

Sol turned away when he saw his father, moving to the far side of the lawn. Manny said hello and busied himself thereafter at the bar on the downstairs porch.

Georgie and Bobby nodded at Pete, but did not speak to him as they sat down at a table nearby.

"So how's it been?" Hilda said conversationally, plunking herself down in one of the chairs so she sat equidistant between Pete and Bobby.

"Did you see," she continued, "cutoff jeans yet. These kids are really classy, let me tell you. At least Tena had the sense to dress. At least, I think it's a dress."

They looked at Tena's wispy brown sack-like dress. Barefooted, she was in the process of putting some flowers in her hair, stretching on tiptoe to reach the back of her hair.

"They live in the garden of Lady Chatterley's lover," Laura said. "It's probably not a bad place to live."

"So, Pete," Hilda said, turning her attention to him. "How are you?"

"Good. Wonderful." Pete said. "Very busy." He moved away to get a drink.

"I can't look at him," Hilda confided, as soon as Pete was out of earshot.

"So don't. Look at the kids. They're something, aren't they?"

"But so nutty—"

"Yes—that too"—watching one of Larry's friends prepare to go swimming before the ceremony.

"Who's he?" Pete asked, returning with a drink for Laura.

"Probably the best man . . . the best man, what does that mean anyway? Why isn't the groom the best man? And does that mean the ushers are not as good men?"

"Ushers? What ushers?" Hilda asked, confused.

"She's just fussing about some words," Pete said.

254

"Don't explain me," Laura said, quickly angry. "You don't have to explain me to Hilda."

"Now, now," Hilda lifted her hand toward Laura. "Don't fight now. Don't spoil Larry's wedding. Be nice."

Sol slipped behind a tree, carefully away from them, carrying the book for the justice of the peace.

Tena and Larry positioned themselves on a rock, looking out to the water. Georgie took Lilli's hand as the justice of the peace informed everyone these two young people had promised to respect each other's personhood.

Laura touched Pete's arm, but he did not move. She clasped her hands behind her back, resisting an impulse to hold them, akimbo, tightly against her chest.

Manny and Sol stood together. Laura kept glancing at them, trying to catch their eyes, but neither looked toward her.

Pete's presence was increasingly a dead weight in the buoyant afternoon. After the ceremony, the kissing and the movement stopped in a kind of five-inch circumference everyone seemed to recognize around him.

Tena's father's wife filled a plate from the buffet for Tena's father. She carried it silently across the crowded grass.

"What's the matter? Isn't he old enough to get his own food yet?" one of Larry's friends said. A twig was caught in his long, dirty-blond hair. One of the girls removed it and sat down, yoga-fashion, to study the twig.

"Don't knock it until you try it," Tena's father said jovially to Larry's critical friend.

Tena's mother kissed Tena's new wedding ring. Larry brought his new mother-in-law another Scotch. She began to blink sleepily in the lengthening afternoon shadows.

Tena threw her dress off, her small breasts wrinkling

255

in the cooler air. "Let's all go swimming before it's too late. All together now!"

"A family that swims together," someone said.

"Is all wet together."

"Drowns together."

"Finds hidden treasure together."

"My God," Georgie said. "They're crazy. They're really insane."

"I'd go swimming too," Pete said, "if I didn't think it would drive half of them out of the water."

Georgie did not answer him.

Laura looked at the kids—some splashing, some swimming strongly, some floating, some standing knee deep talking. Some were naked, some had shorts on, some bathing suits, some the clothes they had worn all afternoon.

She looked at Larry and Tena, wrestling just then on a float. They had greeted a gay father; two sets of parents; women, like Hilda and Lilli, quite dressed up; men like Bobby and Georgie, who forged new feuds in their icy silence toward Pete; men like Sol and Manny, who stood together against the pain of their father. And then the newlyweds, having accepted all these people, went on to enjoy themselves.

"They probably think we're crazy too," she told Georgie. "We think they're crazy, and they think we're crazy. Did you ever think Ma was crazy? Or Dad?"

"No. Actually, they always did just what I expected them to."

"Well, maybe that was crazy, having everything just as anticipated."

"He died at forty-two, for Christ's sake. Was that anticipated?"

"Well, there you are. They did the unexpected too."

"I don't know what you're talking about," Georgie grumbled.

256

"I'm talking about noticing that things aren't the way you thought they were—or should be. You seem to see it after the fact, so to speak. I mean, if I asked you to describe a bride you'd talk about a white gown and a rabbi. You'd never see her swimming (naked yet), would you? Yet, there she is and I like her."

"Why shouldn't you like her? She's such a sweet kid."

"But crazy?"

"I'm afraid so."

"But not really crazy. Just different."

"Different, OK. But not *other*, like—" Georgie nodded in Pete's direction.

"I could never say for sure, now, could I?"

She joined Pete and Darcy, watching the kids come in from their swim. Wet towels grew on the trees. Plates dotted every part of the lawn. The smell of pot wafted from the water's edge.

Sarah approached Laura hesitantly. "Sol wants to talk to you a little before he leaves. Can you come to the porch?"

"Maybe I ought to go," Pete said, his face expressionless again. "Maybe if I go, everyone can relax."

"Yes," Laura said, "maybe that would be best now."

Larry and Tena were on the porch with Manny and Sol. Pete looked over toward it. Then he went away.

❧ After part: 4

A CONVERGENCE OCCURRED—a slate-gray twilight, chilly, promising winter and continuing cold, merged in an early-lighted room into a Sabbath eve atmosphere. The early evening felt as though it were summer to me, as though I were on vacation during the sun-drenched days when anxiety abated and there was no need to remember anything.

I looked around the living room, wandered into the kitchen, sighed myself happily into an easy chair in the den. I felt wrapped in a blanket of serenity, woven slowly, but apparently surely, during the six years since Pete had gone.

Quieted, I dreamed into the lengthening evening, half listening to the fluid melody of a piano concerto coming from the radio, reading with intermittent concentration.

I ambled through a field of dusky-rose will-o'-the-wisps. I blew them and watched the specks turn to taupes and aquas, drifting across the field to my im-

mobile self upstairs in the bedroom; and as each speck
touched the body, the image shrank imperceptibly.
Lazy, almost lethargic, I sank in the taupe and aqua
field, next to Larry's baby, as Tena answered the unin-
hibited demands of the quivering, ravenous, baby-son
mouth. And the baby, sated, laughed with delight and
reached out for a motionless figure standing at the edge
of a dark grove. But the figure remained unresponsive.

I moved from the downy taupe, to hold the baby, to
feel the wonderful, soft nestling of his pleasure into my
welcoming arms. As I carried him away from the dark
grove, I looked back and saw the figure was Pete, except
his eyes were devoid of pupils, emptied of all the blue I
had found so particular. Blind, he could not see me nor
Larry's son.

"No," Larry had said to me when his baby had been
born, "no, I won't call Dad."

"But you invited him to your wedding," I had said.

"No, I won't call him," Larry said again. And that was
that.

I admitted now, as I awoke visualizing Pete's unsee-
ing eyes in the lovely field that Pete was dead to us.

With him, once, there had been a radiant spectrum of
life forces, a rainbow of feeling and strivings and desires,
flecked with pinpoints of rights and wrongs, and
sheathed in the mist called love.

But Pete never could get it together. He jumped from
one part of the spectrum to another, without getting the
flow. If he stayed with the generations, if he acted the
husband and father, he lost himself. And he could not
find a way to be himself without severing himself from
the spectrum.

He damaged us. He left ugly scars behind instead of
the hazy, deep fibers connecting us. He knocked them

259

away in a gesture of terrible need, and left me adrift, out of the spectrum, unsure I knew anyone, a disconnected plug, currentless. I had to wander around through the nightmares and the minutes, void of sound, without stars, until I found again some of the hazy fibers through my family, and my friends, and Fred, and the strangers I met.

The serenity I felt before I dreamed off was gone. I walked aimlessly from room to room, unsettled, uneasy, until finally, forced by a restlessness which seemed without source, I left the house, to drive some-place where life was new, where people were truly strangers, where I had no history but one I would create tomorrow.

First, I drove up to Connecticut, to the unexpected rural roads of the eastern shore, following the winding lanes until the road abruptly ended at marinas crowded with docked boats, whose owners waited for the clear days of sailing.

I did not know what their lives were like, how it felt to search for fat worms for a day's fishing, to want to awaken before dawn to do that, to enjoy doing that. I sat on the dock, studying the boats I knew nothing about, discouraged because there does come a time when it is too late, when new things—even those promising delight—can not become part of one's self without dis-comfort.

I drove the rest of the night away, looking now for my old neighborhood, wanting to relieve my restlessness, to leave the idea of a living Pete behind somewhere in that geographic past.

When I found the neighborhood, the houses were all there—ours, the Falcaros', Hilda's—but there was a subtle difference in the blocks, an oddness having something to do with my memory-sense of distances. Hilda's house seemed closer; the streets leading toward the spice factory and high school longer.

Our house had been recovered with aluminum siding. Practical people lived in what I now saw as a nice house in a shabby area. Hydrangea bushes still grew next to the front stoop, but the backyard had been transformed into a patio, on which green tarpaulin-covered chairs and tables stood together with what appeared to be a child's pool. There were no trees at all back there.

In the quiet morning light, I visualized the floor plan inside the house, recognizing, after all these years, how little privacy any of us could have had in a walk-through arrangement of living room, kitchen, bedroom. That I had considered Pete's family rich seemed incredible now.

I resumed driving, headed toward the library. I lost my way in a maze of one-way streets, elevated apartments, stores, and parked cars. I turned a corner to find a thoroughfare, and there was our high school, still distinct and recognizable, dominating one square block.

I parked across from it, watching students begin to enter. I had no reason to do that. The truth was I knew no one who lived there any more. Maybe some of the customers who ate in Pete's Dad's store had stayed, and I was looking at their children now, maybe even their grandchildren—but I would never know the old connection.

It saddened me to be confronted with the knowledge that time passes, to understand that no matter how important it all might have been, it cannot all be remembered, and so much is never seen at all, forever missed.

I buried Pete then, crying, because I seemed the only one left who wanted to remember him.

An old man passed, shuffling along the sidewalk, exercising painful, cramped muscles. He stopped next to the car window, looking at me curiously.

"I'm mourning," I told him.

He resumed shuffling. I would never know if he heard me or understood me, or merely labeled me crazy and, satisfied with the label, moved on. An echo of my ignorance about Pete, who, withal, would maintain a subterranean presence in my memory. For one thing I could not do. I could not learn to unlove him.